Gisela got th...
still mourned some great loss.

...with feverish confusion. Was it the king's pain or her own that filled her heart with sorrow?

Already strained by the gash on her head, Gisela whimpered softly as tears formed.

"Whoa." The king pulled his mount to a halt. He shifted, and a moment later Gisela felt his hand on her face. "Are you getting worse?"

The touch of his hand imparted comfort, and when he drew it away, she missed it.

"Rest if you can," he murmured, slowly urging the horse up to speed. "We have a long way to travel yet."

The king's words were a reminder she sorely needed. Yes. She had a mission to fulfill. She couldn't die.

The people they'd left back at the dock were depending on her. If she didn't make it, there would likely be war, not only for her father's people, but for King John's, too. She owed it to them to survive.

More than that, she owed it to King John himself.

Books by Rachelle McCalla

Love Inspired Historical

*A Royal Marriage

Love Inspired Suspense

Survival Instinct
Troubled Waters
Out on a Limb
Danger on Her Doorstep
Dead Reckoning
†*Princess in Peril*
†*Protecting the Princess*
The Detective's Secret Daughter
†*Prince Incognito*
†*The Missing Monarch*

*Protecting the Crown
†Reclaiming the Crown

RACHELLE McCALLA

is a mild-mannered housewife, and the toughest she ever has to get is when she's trying to keep her four kids quiet in church. Though she often gets in over her head, as her characters do, and has to find a way out, her adventures have more to do with sorting out the carpool and providing food for the potluck. She's never been arrested, gotten in a fistfight or been shot at. And she'd like to keep it that way! For recipes, fun background notes on the places and characters in this book and more information on forthcoming titles, visit www.rachellemccalla.com.

RACHELLE McCALLA

A Royal Marriage

Love Inspired

Recycling programs
for this product may
not exist in your area.

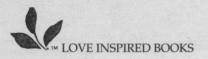

™ LOVE INSPIRED BOOKS

ISBN-13: 978-0-373-82944-6

A ROYAL MARRIAGE

Copyright © 2012 by Rachelle McCalla

www.LoveInspiredBooks.com

Printed in U.S.A.

To everything there is a season, and a time to every purpose under the heaven… A time to love, and a time to hate; a time of war, and a time of peace.
—*Ecclesiastes* 3:1, 8

To Gisela, daughter of Charlemagne, and all her sisters throughout history whose stories have been lost to us. While we don't know precisely how you spent your days, this book shows how I imagine you to be based on those few details we do know. Most importantly, we know you were a woman of faith. I hope my words have been faithful, if not to the facts long lost to time, then at least to your spirit.

Chapter One

Castlehead, Lydia, A.D. 801

"A ship approaches, Your Majesty. Her sail is spread with the Carolingian cross." Renwick, chief messenger among the Lydian guard, bowed low before the king.

"Charlemagne." His Royal Highness, King John of Lydia, lowered the sword with which he'd been sparring with his younger brother, Prince Luke. Why would the Holy Roman Emperor send a ship to Lydia unannounced? Charlemagne's realm had expanded vastly under his leadership, but John had assumed the renowned ruler would have no interest in the tiny kingdom of Lydia. Was he wrong?

King John turned to face the messenger. "She approaches directly?"

"Making for the wharf at high speed, sire," Renwick panted as though he, too, had run to reach the king quickly.

"Then we shall make haste, as well." Sheathing his sword, John headed for the courtyard gate, the fastest route to the Mediterranean shore.

"To the lookout tower, Your Majesty?" Renwick appeared confused by the king's choice of direction.

"No, Renwick." John led the way. "To the wharf."

Prince Luke ran beside him. "Why would Charlemagne visit Lydia? We are not his vassals."

"I doubt it is Charlemagne himself," King John acknowledged. "The emperor regularly sends emissaries throughout his empire to report back to him." He prayed that was true this time, irregular though it might seem.

"But Lydia is not part of his empire." Luke chafed visibly at the idea.

"We are part of Christendom. As such, we ought to ally ourselves closely with the Holy Roman Empire. Such a position could prove to be advantageous." John reached the end of the wharf and shielded his eyes from the sun, examining the quickly approaching vessel, her sails emblazoned with the distinctive Carolingian cross, four triquetras joined at the center to form the distinctive symbol of Emperor Charlemagne's reign.

"Three masts!" The sight filled John with awe. Lydia had no ship to match it. And yet, "She looks to be wounded."

"Aye, brother." Luke clapped one hand on John's shoulder and pointed with the other. "Her foresail has been rent and hastily mended. Do you think she has weathered a storm?"

"Or an attack." John met his brother's eyes.

"Saracens?" Prince Luke spoke the word softly, as though saying it aloud might draw the vicious pirates closer.

"They raid the Mediterranean waters regularly."

"Never so close to Lydia."

"We don't know how far this ship has come," King

John acknowledged. "Or whether the Saracens may have taken her."

"Taken her?" Fear sparked in his brother's blue eyes as he looked out to the ship and back at the ramparts of their castle. If the pirates had taken the ship, they could approach under Charlemagne's cross and dock before the Lydians realized trouble had reached their shores. The castle's defenses might be breached before they could even prepare for battle. "Why would Saracens approach so boldly?"

"For no good reason." John shook his head. He didn't want to believe that Saracen pirates had taken the emperor's ship, but given her condition, it was a distinct possibility. "Let us pray for Lydia's safety."

While the brothers murmured hasty yet heartfelt prayers, King John heard the rumble of boot steps on the wharf. He turned to find Eliab and Urias, two courtiers who'd been his father's close advisors, panting as they trotted down the wharf.

"Your Majesty," Urias called out. "You should not be out here!"

"This does not look good." Eliab gestured to the ship as he bent to catch his breath.

"His Majesty should hide until we've determined the motives of the approaching vessel."

John dismissed their concerns. The pair often treated him as though he was still a child, though he'd weathered twenty-eight winters and had ruled Lydia capably since his father's death four years before. "I may determine their motives much faster if I stay here."

"They've put down a boat!" Renwick had hardly taken his eyes from the ship.

"They're worthy seamen, then." John approved of the ship's rapid loss of speed. They'd obviously put down an anchor. It was wise. He'd never docked such a large vessel alongside the wharf, and though he couldn't be sure the depth of the ship's rudder, he doubted they'd have made it to the dock without scraping against the submerged rocks that hid not so far below the water at low tide.

"What are they loading?" Luke studied the men as they carried a large fabric-draped bundle onto the boat. From the care they took in handling it, the cargo must have been delicate. The dark green cloth glistened in the sunlight like silk. Whatever was wrapped inside must be quite valuable.

A plump, wimpled figure was loaded next, with no shortage of howling admonitions. Then six burly men boarded and took to the oars with vigor, slicing through the water as though Charlemagne himself was watching.

"I believe that bundle is a person." John observed the way they'd propped the bundle in the stern with the wimpled woman fussing over it. "A slender figure, perhaps a youth or a child."

"Or a woman," Prince Luke offered.

"On a ship?" Urias scoffed.

"It *is* possible," Luke pointed out as the boat drew nearer and its contents easier to see. "The cut of the silk clothing is certainly suggestive of a female. And it would explain the lady in waiting."

"Bah. A nurse to the child," Urias insisted.

"Whatever it is, I hardly think myself to be in immediate danger from it." John felt glad that he hadn't run and hidden as his father's advisors had suggested. Granted, he had an obligation to protect the throne. Urias and Eliab were understandably skittish about the issue of safety, having been with his father, King Theodoric, when he'd died defending one of Lydia's villages on the Illyrian border.

But King John had two younger brothers and a much younger sister, as well. Prince Luke was a worthy leader, and Prince Mark would be, too, if he ever returned from his long journey by sea. God would provide a leader for Lydia. When his wife had died in childbirth three years before, John had resolved that his line would end with his death. He would not ask another woman to risk her life trying to bear an heir for him.

"You don't suppose it's a ruse?" Eliab watched the fast-approaching boat with skepticism. "To lull us into thinking we've nothing to fear and take us while our guard is down."

"Eliab, you are far too suspicious," John chided him. As the boat moved closer, the shrieks and groans of the white-faced woman in the wimple grew louder. If she was part of a ruse, she was overplaying her role. Rather than pay the woman much heed, John examined the faces of the other men in the boat. To his relief, none of them had the stature or features of Charlemagne.

John had met the emperor once, before Charlemagne had been crowned Holy Roman Emperor of all Europe. Then King of the Franks, Charlemagne was an impressive bull of a man who ruled with an iron fist. Despite the power and gusto with which he governed, the man was also an intellectual and a devout Christian of renowned faith. John not only respected and admired him, he also feared him.

And he feared, too, the reason for this unannounced visit under Charlemagne's sails. Protocol would have had them send greetings well in advance of their visit so that John would have an opportunity to make preparations to host them. Obviously, there had to be some reason the men hadn't wanted him to meet them well prepared.

The wimpled woman howled. She swayed on her feet

but refused to sit. Her cries carried ahead of the rowboat through the warm August air. "*Must* you lurch so? Oh, I fear I shall faint before we make it to the shore!"

The rowing men grimaced, and John suspected they'd have liked for the woman to faint, if only to still her cries. As the boat drew nearer, the man closest to the prow, the only man without an oar in his hand, called out, "Greetings in the name of Charlemagne, Emperor of all Rome." The man spoke in impeccable Latin. "What lands are these?"

John could only hope his own linguistic training was up to the imperial standard. "Friends, this is the Christian Kingdom of Lydia."

A relieved smile spread across the man's face, and John realized his expression had been quite anxious up to that moment. The man tossed a rope. "We seek King John, the healer."

"You have found him." The symbol of cross and crown that decorated John's habergeon signified his position. He caught the rope and pulled the boat toward the dock with a mighty heave. Behind him, Luke and Renwick grabbed the line, while Eliab and Urias stumbled over themselves.

The man's smile grew broader. "Then God has surely been with us. I am sorry to arrive unannounced, but we had no alternative." As the boat was pulled alongside the length of the dock, the man bounded onto the wharf and bowed low. "I am Boden, a servant of Charlemagne and acting captain of the emperor's ship."

"*Acting* captain?" John looked the man over. Clearly the youth was a strong and strapping lad, but he hardly seemed old enough to be a captain. Indeed, he was certainly younger than John or Luke.

"Alas, my beloved father was commissioned captain by Charlemagne himself and vested with a mission of the utmost importance—to carry the emperor's most precious cargo. But we were attacked at sea by Saracens, and my father died defending his ship." Boden's face blanched as he spoke.

"You have done well to continue on his mission." John hoped his words would provide some comfort to the youth.

But Boden only shook his head. "I implore thee, Your Majesty John the healer. You are our only remaining hope that this mission might succeed." He raised his hand toward the boat.

The wimpled woman had quit her moaning and now peeled back the silk veil that covered the face of the bundled figure the men had so carefully loaded onto the boat.

John saw a flushed jawline and rosy lips that could only belong to a woman. So Luke had been right. This was no boy but a female of about twenty years of age. In fact, whoever she was, her features were beautiful, her complexion pale, save for a flush John recognized all too well.

Fever.

Her drawn lips confirmed it. The woman was suffering. No wonder Boden had twice referred to him as John, *the healer*. It was a title he was loath to use, but one which desperate men rushed to give him, especially when they had need of a man to stand between their loved ones and the advancing scythe of death. Yes, he'd been trained by his mother as a healer—a practice her family had observed for generations. When he'd taken to his studies with far greater success than his brothers, some had said he had a gift.

Now he considered it a curse. He hardly considered himself worthy of the title *healer*. Not when he'd failed to save his own wife or the mother who'd trained him.

Boden nodded to the lady in waiting, who peeled back more of the cloth.

"Ah!" Urias and Eliab recoiled at the sight of the infected gash above the woman's right eye, which followed the curve of her eyebrow. The angry wound had swollen her eyelid shut, festering across her face in fever-reddened waves.

John understood immediately. He'd seen injuries that had deteriorated to a similar state before. Rarely had the sufferer survived. Rather than ask the men to lift the young woman, John lowered himself into the boat and approached her. He could smell the rancid scent of the infection and recognized with dismay the golden yellow crust that seeped from the gash.

The sight and smell carried as clear a message as any tolling death bell.

The lovely woman had less than a day to live.

And the herb that could save her grew half a day's journey into the mountains, in the borderlands Lydia shared with the Illyrians. John's father, King Theodoric, had died defending those borderlands. And yet, as John observed the woman's fever-flushed features, he realized she'd have to have crushed hare's tongue leaves applied to her injury by nightfall. Even then, it might be too late to save her.

He turned to Boden. "Was she injured two or three days ago?"

"Three days," Boden answered. "How did you know?"

Relieved that the Saracens hadn't attacked closer to the Lydian coast, John nonetheless felt the weight of the young woman's grim prognosis. She'd already gone too long without treatment. "Infections of this nature always run the same course. Once the secretions turn yellow, the sufferer has less than a day to live."

Boden's face blanched, and his men at the oars hung their heads.

John didn't doubt the sailors had been at the oars to bring the ship to Lydia—with her sails rent and patched, they'd have rowed in desperate hope of saving the woman's life. Obviously the woman must have meant a great deal to them for the men to take on such a strenuous task. John wished he could tell them their efforts hadn't been in vain. "You mentioned the emperor's precious cargo." He began the question slowly and found his throat had gone dry.

As he'd feared, Boden pointed to the woman. "*She* is the precious cargo—Princess Gisela, one of Charlemagne's daughters. She has been pledged to marry an Illyrian prince. We were to have her delivered by Christmastide."

"You were running ahead of schedule."

"That we were," Boden acknowledged with a bittersweet smile, "until the Saracens found us. If she dies, there will likely be war."

"War!" Urias exclaimed.

"And you've gotten us involved in it?" Eliab added.

John raised a hand to quiet the courtiers. "Boden made the right choice." He looked at the flushed face of the princess and felt sorrow rise inside him. Such a beautiful young woman. It would be tragic for her to die so young. His heart beat out a desperate prayer that somehow, in spite of his failures as a healer, God would see fit to spare the princess from death.

Princess Gisela felt the boat rock as someone stepped out from it. The sun burned hot against her face, even hotter than when the stifling veil of silk had covered her. Or perhaps her fever had grown that much worse.

"Can you save her?" Hope sprang to Boden's voice.

"I *could.*" The voice of King John, the healer, followed him as he climbed back onto the dock. "Hare's tongue leaves have proven an effective cure against this type of yellow secretion. But the leaves must be freshly picked, and the nearest plants grow in the mountains on the Illyrian borderlands. A swift rider could reach them by nightfall."

"Then send your swiftest rider," Boden insisted. "We will pay the expense—"

"It is not the expense that worries me. The rider must know what he is looking for." King John's tone grew pessimistic. "*And* have daylight enough to find it. Besides that, if the hare's tongue leaves are not applied today, there won't be time to stop the spreading infection. She'll be dead by morning."

"She is a vigorous one," Boden insisted. "There is fight in her."

"I can see that. Otherwise she would be dead already."

"Oh!" Hilda, her maid, who'd been simpering through the conversation, sounded as though she might faint.

Another voice, similar to the king's, spoke with challenge. "*You* could find it, John."

Gisela noted that the man hadn't addressed the king with his title. A peer of some sort? Perhaps a brother or uncle.

The king didn't chastise the man for his familiarity but answered his question. "If God is with me, yes, I could likely find the hare's tongue by nightfall. There is, however, the matter of bringing it back in time to save the emperor's daughter."

"It would be dark out by then, Your Majesty," one of the earlier naysayers cautioned. "A dangerous time to ride through the mountains."

"And it would be too late," another naysayer noted. "You said she has to have the hare's tongue by nightfall. You'd have to ride through the night to bring it back by dawn."

Princess Gisela thought quickly. She hadn't faced a long journey and Saracen pirates just to be defeated by a horse ride. If she could have opened her eyes, she'd have taken a good look at the naysayers and had them chastised after she recovered. She had no intention of dying—not this day, nor any other soon to come.

How could she make them understand she would do whatever was necessary? Already the hot fingers of fever clawed their way across her face. If the king's herb could stop the pain, she'd make the journey herself. As for the expense, her father was a generous man. The Emperor Charlemagne would see that King John was handsomely rewarded.

Princess Gisela licked her lips and tried to find her voice.

Young Boden spoke first and sounded as though he might cry. "Then it has all been for nothing. My father has died, and we will lose the princess, too."

"You shall not lose me." Gisela resented the weakness in her voice. She cleared her throat to muster enough volume to be heard. "I shall ride with the king. If I am with him, the hare's tongue may be applied as soon as it is located—before dark, in time to stop the infection."

John studied the face of the princess who spoke with apt appreciation of the situation. Her eyes were still closed—the one being swelled certainly shut, the other swollen as well and lidded out of sympathy. Even slumped in a bundle, Princess Gisela had an air of dignity and the shrewd intellect of her father.

He found himself *wanting* to save her—not just for Boden's sake, or her sake, or even to prevent war with the Illyrians, but to save this sensible, strong-willed woman. He wanted to *heal* her.

But he'd felt that impulse before and still failed. He'd buried his skills since then. What was the use of trying to help someone, of offering them hope, only to have them linger a bit longer and die in pain?

To his relief, the wimpled woman began discounting the idea immediately. "Your Highness, you can't even open your eyes. How could you ride?"

"It would be a grueling journey," Urias added. "Surely in your present condition—"

"She *is* a capable rider," Boden offered. "But given her injuries…"

Gisela raised her chin with a stubborn tilt. "I could share the king's horse."

Her assertion brought a roar of disapproval from the courtiers, and even Boden's men, who'd silently manned their oars all this time, appeared to have some difficulty maintaining their impassive expressions.

Boden, especially, looked vexed. As Charlemagne's acting captain, no doubt the man was expected to grant any request Gisela made. As the emperor's daughter, she was of higher rank than anyone there, except for John himself, and that was only because they were in Lydia and not her father's holdings. Had they been standing on the soil of the Roman Empire, he'd have bowed to her.

Boden brushed the sweat from his brow. "Perhaps, Your Highness, you could be carried in a litter after the king. Your maid could accompany you."

"Litters travel slowly. There isn't time. My maid can follow on another horse." Princess Gisela spoke in a commanding voice and clearly expected her father's servants to obey. "Now help me up. We must make haste. Already the day grows long."

The men laid down their oars and helped the maid from the boat first. Then they gingerly hoisted the princess toward the dock. She stood, half leaning on her maid, her injuries once again covered by the veil.

John felt a sense of relief that the woman was able to stand. Perhaps she *could* stay on a horse. A litter, as she'd aptly noted, would be much too slow. Nor could he afford to have her ride another horse behind his. If he became separated from her party, especially as darkness fell, they would waste precious time finding one another again in the thick woods.

And one horse had a greater chance of slipping unseen through the Illyrian borderlands. The larger their party, the greater the risk of being spotted. Relations with the Illyrians were fragile enough. He had no desire to strain them further.

"What do you think?" Luke leaned close and spoke in a hushed tone. "She might be able to make the ride. Will you be able to find the herb?"

"The summer draws to a close. Hare's tongue isn't so abundant now, but yes, I should be able to find some."

"Is there any chance you could bring it back in time to save her if she stayed at the castle?"

"None." John wished he could tell his brother otherwise. It was foolish enough to get involved in the emperor's dealings, situated as they were between the Roman Empire to the west, and the Illyrian holdings of the Byzantine Empire to the east. If the Illyrians and the Romans decided to play tug of war with Lydia, his tiny nation would never know peace.

But if he let the emperor's daughter die without even

trying to help, the empires would obliterate Lydia for revenge.

He didn't like it—not at all. But neither did he see any way around it. And there wasn't time to waste fretting. There was more than one woman's life at stake—there was the safety of all Lydia. If the Illyrians went to war with the Roman Empire, Lydia would be trampled between them—especially if Lydia was blamed for bringing war upon them.

King John raised his voice and addressed those gathered on the dock—including half a dozen soldiers who'd been dispatched from the castle and now stood at attention near the head of the wharf. "Ready my horse and falcon and prepare a horse and party for the maid." He looked to the wimpled woman. "I'm sorry, I haven't been told your name."

"Hilda, Your Highness."

"Prepare a litter for Hilda." He lowered his voice and explained to those standing nearby, "The retinue can follow as best they can."

"But, Your Majesty," Urias sputtered, "you're not really thinking of taking a riding party to the Illyrian border?"

"Certainly not," John assured the courtier. "The riding party won't be able to travel nearly as quickly as my horse. Once I've applied the hare's tongue to her injury, the princess and I will double back and meet up with her maid. If we must encamp on the road, she'll have a proper attendant."

"Your Majesty," Eliab simpered, "who will be in charge of the castle while you're away?"

Only respect for his father and the trust he'd placed in the courtiers kept John from uttering a prickly retort. But even the trust of his late father wouldn't earn either man a custodial role in his absence. "Prince Luke is more than capable of overseeing matters while I'm away. With your prayers for my safe passage, I should be back by sundown tomorrow."

"And if you're not, what then?" Eliab pressed. "Shall we send a regiment to look for you?"

"No." John gave them a hard look and made sure Luke heard him clearly. "If I am delayed beyond next evening, it may be a sign of trouble with the Illyrians. Dispatching soldiers would be the worst possible response. I'll have my falcon. If Fledge returns without me, then you may be concerned. Whatever happens, you must trust Luke's judgment. He is a prudent and capable leader."

Luke gave him a firm smile in return for his compliment. "God be with you, brother."

John met his brother's eyes and was glad to see that Luke understood. They hadn't asked for this, but it wasn't a challenge they could walk away from. As rulers of Lydia, they had an obligation to protect their people—as their father had done—and to die protecting their people, if the situation called for it. Despite the political entanglements, this mission was no more difficult than others they had undertaken in the past. But there was a great deal more riding on the outcome.

Chapter Two

Gisela leaned on Hilda and tried to catch her breath. Really, standing upright should not require such exertion.

Nor should thinking.

But the blearying effects of the throbbing wound above her right eye made her head swim as though their ship hadn't escaped the Saracens at all. If they'd been sunk in the Mediterranean, surely even then her thoughts would not swim so. The constant roar of the sea echoed through her head as though she held a great seashell to her ears to listen.

But there was no seashell, only these unending waves of fever that gripped her with their relentless thrashing.

She could hear the rattle and clank of gear and smell the scent of a horse over the brine of the sea, which lapped gently at the wharf beneath them. At least King John had been sensible enough to accept her plan. There really wasn't any way around it. If she'd had use of her eyes and known what she was looking for, she'd have gone after the hare's tongue herself.

"Your Highness, the ride will be difficult." That was King John's voice, much nearer to her now. If she reached out, she could touch him.

She remained still. "I'm quite sure the alternative is worse." She wished she could open her eyes and look at the man, but even her left eye, though uninjured, was swollen shut by the spreading infection. Every time she'd tried to raise the lid, she'd felt such a horrific spasm of pain that she'd stopped trying.

"I thought I should extend a word of caution. I'll do my best to make the trip a smooth one, but we'll be riding over uneven ground—"

"Your attention should be on the terrain, not on me." She quieted his apologies. "And I expect you'll need to be looking for this hare's tongue. Don't let my presence distract you, King John."

"We should be going then, Your Highness. The sun reverses its course for no one, not even kings and emperors' daughters." His voice betrayed a melancholy sadness. Gisela couldn't help wondering what had caused it. At the very least, she hoped he didn't terribly mind the inconvenience she'd caused him—or if he *did* mind, he could blame the Saracens, since they'd started the trouble.

For her own part, though her injury concerned her, Gisela felt a mixture of dread and relief that her trip to Illyria had been interrupted. Thrilled as she'd been to get out from under her father's overprotective hand to see the world, she hadn't been particularly looking forward to being tied down by marriage, least of all to an Illyrian prince. Like a diver holding his breath for just a few minutes before coming up for air, Gisela felt the pressures of her impending marriage and the loss of freedom that would accompany it. This was an opportunity, however brief, for her to gasp a breath before going down again.

Her marriage was politically necessary and couldn't be avoided. All too soon, she'd become the bride of a prince she'd met only twice before. She didn't welcome her injury any more than she'd welcomed the Saracens' attack on their ship. But she couldn't be unhappy for the excuse it gave her to extend her freedom, if only by another day or two. Perhaps she could see a bit of Lydia—assuming she survived and retained her vision. She'd heard of the tiny Christian kingdom and always been curious about the place.

Rather than allow herself to be consumed by worry, she tried to find the good in the midst of her dire situation. King John was willing to help her and did not seem to be overly upset about being suddenly burdened. And they'd be leaving Hilda's anxious fawning behind.

That alone would be worth the rigors of the journey.

"Are there any preparations you need to make before we leave? Do you have everything you need?" King John sounded as though he was ready to be off.

"I'll need my sword."

"Oh, my lady, no," Hilda protested.

"We brought it with us from the ship." Gisela turned back as though she might fetch it herself. "I never ride without it."

"You should have no need of a sword." King John's voice sounded close, indicating he was nearby. "I'll have mine." A protective note sounded through his words.

"You mentioned possible trouble with the Illyrians. I won't allow myself to knowingly enter a potentially dangerous situation without the means of protecting myself."

"You can't even see, Your Highness," King John protested.

"Then stay back from me if I have to use it, Your Majesty."

Thankfully, Boden spoke up in her defense. "She is quite skilled with the sword, King John. She saved our ship. Had she stayed below, as instructed, the Saracens would have taken us. As it was, she surprised them and tipped the battle back in our favor."

As he spoke, Gisela felt the familiar weight of her sword belt pressed into her hands. She quickly linked the scabbard around her waist. "I'm ready. Shall we depart, Your Majesty?" Not only was she eager to begin the journey, but she feared she wouldn't be able to stand upright much longer, and she didn't want to do anything that might give away how very weak she felt. King John might realize she wasn't up to the journey after all. He might change his mind.

She couldn't risk that.

With a fair amount of shuffling and no shortage of exclamations from Hilda, Gisela was lifted onto the horse. She found they'd situated her in front of King John, who wrapped his arms around her to hold her steady while he guided his mount.

The gentleness of his touch surprised her. She could tell from his stature that he was of good size, possibly even as tall as her father, who stood taller than nearly every man in his empire. Yet King John's arms wrapped around her as though she was some precious, delicate thing and he was afraid she might break.

His consideration penetrated her haze of fever, and she took note. Yes, she'd have to be certain her father compensated the king generously. "Hilda?" She pulled the lady in waiting to her side the moment the woman offered her hand. "Whatever happens," Gisela whispered, "make sure my father knows that King John is to be rewarded for his efforts."

"Oh, Your Highness." Hilda started sobbing again, as though the very likelihood of Gisela not living to deliver the message herself was more than the servant could bear.

Gisela feared King John would notice the maid's blubbering, but his attentions seemed to be on his men. The king gave instructions to those who'd be traveling with Hilda. As long as they kept to their intended path, they'd meet back up with Hilda's party shortly after nightfall, and could stay together at the wayside inn he appointed as a rendezvous point.

Assuming everything went according to plan.

"And if you don't arrive?" Hilda recovered from her crying enough to anxiously ask.

"Then wait."

The prancing horse moved forward, and Gisela felt King John nudge the animal on.

"You have our prayers!" a voice called out from behind them, followed by a chorus of voices assuring them of the same thing and giving their blessing on their journey.

Gisela tried to sit upright, but the motion of horse beneath her taxed her reserves of strength. The spinning sensation in her head had picked up considerably when they'd placed her on the horse, and instead of easing now that she sat, it grew steadily worse.

The sun felt hot on her face in spite of the veil that covered her. Or did the heat radiate from inside her? Whether it came from the sky or the wound on her forehead, the searing fire grew uncomfortably warm. She wished she could crawl away from it. But if it originated from her injury, there would be no crawling away, only increasing discomfort from this wilting heat that made her feel as though she was about to shrivel up and blow away with the slightest breeze.

An exhausted moan escaped her lips.

"Are you well?" King John's voice held concern, though he did nothing to slow his horse.

"I'm as well—" she pinched back another moan and

tried to straighten her back "—as the circumstances— Oh!" The horse beneath her lurched back as it leaped over something, and she found herself falling, against her will, back toward the king.

"Rest now. Rest as much as you can." King John's gloved hand brushed her shoulder, steadying her against his chest. "You can lean on me."

"It doesn't seem proper." She realized her protest was simply an excuse. She'd shared horses dozens of times with members of her father's household—relatives and servants alike. Rather, she didn't like giving up any measure of her independence, including her ability to sit up on her own. And she'd heard the warm tone in Hilda's voice when King John had addressed her. Gisela knew her maid well enough to recognize that Hilda had blushed at the king's attention.

Why? Because he was royalty? No, Hilda regularly interacted with Gisela's father and brothers without that note entering her voice. The maid only spoke with such resonance when she interacted with a man she found particularly handsome.

So, King John must be comely, then. If Gisela could have mustered the strength, she might have been curious to see him. In spite of his gentleness, the muscles that supported her felt strong. Gisela tried to recall if she'd ever heard anything about the distant Mediterranean ruler, but precious little news from Lydia traveled as far as her home in Aachen.

With no prior knowledge of him, without even the use of her eyes, Gisela couldn't explain precisely why the man made her feel protected—cherished, even. Perhaps the sensation arose from the disorienting influence of her fever. She tried again to force her left eye open, hoping to get a glimpse of him. Her efforts were rewarded with a shot of pain that lanced through her with alarming speed and ferocity.

"Careful," King John soothed, having obviously felt her fighting the pain. "You won't make it unless you rest. It's a long ride to the borderlands, and your condition will only be getting worse. Shall we turn back now and tell them it's no use?"

The horse slowed slightly, as if anticipating instructions to reverse course.

Gisela relaxed backward and let herself droop into a slightly reclined position, resting more of her weight against him, comforted by the feel of his strong arms that held her so securely, yet at the same time, so tenderly. She exhaled a painful breath. The darkness over her eyes grew heavier, and the roar in her ears clamored in counterpoint with the horse's stride and the unruly beat of her heart.

The dizziness that had threatened to topple her on the wharf now returned with stomach-lurching spite. The site of her injury throbbed, producing flashes of colorful light that swooped and swirled across her field of vision. And through it all, the relentless fever threatened to bake her like grapes laid out to dry in the sun. She heard a plaintive moaning sound and realized it came from her own throat.

"Don't worry about staying on the horse. I won't let you fall."

Gisela clung to the promise in his words. King John's voice was pleasantly deep, his accent alluring but not so foreign that she couldn't readily understand his words. Indeed, she found the sound of his voice soothing. Gisela wanted something to think about that would distract her from her pain—preferably something more intellectually engaging than mere curiosity about the handsomeness of her benefactor.

Was he young or old? Married? Betrothed? It shouldn't matter, but as she drank in his masculine scent, she couldn't help wondering. If she could learn more about the king who'd set aside his plans on a moment's notice to help her, perhaps he would distract her from her pain. She found her voice. "Your reputation as a healer must be widely known. Have you been practicing for many years?"

The king seemed to appreciate her need to talk, and answered readily, as though hoping to distract her from her ailment. "My mother began teaching me about herbs and injuries when I was young. Her family has had a gift for healing for many generations."

"I wondered—" Gisela had to struggle to speak past the pain "—why a king would also be a healer. Most men settle on one or the other."

"Actually, the healing lessons were originally intended for my brother Luke. My mother named us after the New Testament gospels, and she hoped my brother would become a great healer like the physician, Luke."

"Didn't he?" Gisela would have finished the question, but the aching in her head caught up to her, and the bone-rattling pace of the horse didn't help.

John answered quickly, as if he didn't want her to strain herself by trying to speak. "Luke tried to learn. So did my youngest brother, Mark. But for whatever reason, I'm the only one who ever caught on. The other two had no success or interest and quickly gave up trying."

"You have to have a gift for it," Gisela agreed, understanding. "I wanted to play the lyre, but no amount of practicing would make me half as good as my sister, and she didn't even care for the instrument."

"That's precisely how it was. I took to it readily. For many years, I thought I had a gift." A melancholy note infused his words.

"Had?" Gisela repeated.

She felt the man behind her tense. Was there something that had caught his attention, which she couldn't see due to her injured eye? Or was his sudden change in demeanor due to her question?

Finally, the king murmured. "The results of my efforts haven't always been successful in recent years."

A melancholy silence followed his statement. Gisela got the sense that he still mourned some great loss. Was it the loss of his gift? But then, surely his knowledge of herbs and how to use them had not been taken from him. He wouldn't have tried to help her if his skills for healing were completely gone.

She couldn't sort it out. The more she tried to think, the more her injury throbbed, distorting her thoughts with feverish confusion. Was it the king's pain or her own that filled her heart with sorrow? It couldn't be her own—she'd earned it honorably defending the ship from Saracens. If she hadn't been injured she'd have likely been killed.

So then, it must have been King John's past hurts that prodded her heart to the verge of mourning. Already strained by the gash on her head, Gisela whimpered softly as tears formed under her eyelids, adding pressure to her already-swollen eyes.

"Whoa." The king pulled his mount to a halt. He shifted, and a moment later Gisela felt his hand on her face. "Are you getting worse?"

His touch imparted comfort, and when he drew his hand away, she missed it.

"Are you thirsty? Can you drink?"

Gisela mustered her voice. "Please."

Moments later a flask touched her lips, and cool water flowed into her mouth. It tasted so much better than what they'd had on the ship, which had begun to carry the flavor of the wood barrels in which it was stored. The water John gave her was slightly sweet and blessedly refreshing to her fever-parched tongue.

"Now rest if you can," he murmured, slowly urging the horse up to speed. "We have a long way to travel yet."

Rest. If only she could—if only the pain would fade away and allow her a measure of peace. The cacophony of sound and light roared inside her head, thundering with each rise and fall of the horse's stride. Would this infection be the end of her?

"You need to rest if you're going to keep your strength."

The king's words were a reminder she sorely needed. Yes. She had a mission to fulfill. She couldn't die. She had to keep up her strength. To rest.

The people they'd left back at the dock were depending on her. If she didn't make it, there would likely be war, not only for her father's people, but for King John's, too. She owed it to them to survive.

More than that, she owed it to King John himself. His willingness to help her, politically motivated as it may have been, was nonetheless an act of charity. It would be ungrateful of her to die when he'd gone out of his way to procure for her the means of life. Besides, she had to recover if she was ever going to see if King John was half as handsome as she imagined him to be.

John kept to the main road that led southeast down the Lydian peninsula. When the woman in front of him finally slumped into a fitful sleep, he prodded his horse to greater speeds. He hadn't wanted to upset Gisela too much, but they needed to hurry. He'd wasted precious time arguing with his courtiers.

Fortunately Moses, his favorite stallion, had been bred for speed. The animal hadn't been out for a hard run in weeks and was eager to stretch his legs. "Good boy, Moses." John reached past the Frankish princess and patted the stallion on the neck, encouraging him. If he had to take the emperor's daughter to the Illyrian borderlands, there was no animal he'd rather ride.

And Fledge, his falcon, perched upon his shoulder with her beak pointed forward, the wind produced by the horse's speed hardly ruffling the raptor's feathers. Fledge was used to diving on her prey from blustery mountain updrafts. Their pace didn't bother her in the slightest.

The only one John worried about was the Frankish princess, who moaned and twitched as she fought her rising fever. The late-summer day was warm, but her flushed face felt warmer still. John had seen this type of infection far too many times, and he knew its usual pattern. Without the hare's tongue to stop it, the fever would continue to rise until the woman was dead.

It was just such a fever that had killed his own mother when he was a boy of twelve years. Tragically, she'd fallen sick during winter when there was no hare's tongue to cure her. Nonetheless, John had set out with a search party in hopes of finding some tucked away under the snow.

He'd returned in the night half frozen from his search, with nothing to show for his efforts.

His mother had died the next morning.

The memory spurred him forward. It had been his last failure for many years. Some had said that with his mother's passing he'd inherited her healing gift full force. For a while he'd almost believed them.

Then his own wife had taken ill during childbirth three years ago, after years of battling recurring illness and a miscarrying womb. In spite of all his efforts, he'd lost her and the child she carried. From then on, failure haunted his every effort at healing. Even simple maladies had spiraled out of his control, as though the touch of his hands carried death instead of healing.

His conscience tugged at him. What if his efforts at helping Princess Gisela only led her more quickly down the road to death? The Emperor Charlemagne would blame him and rightly so. Illyria, too. He'd bring war upon his people. Gisela's death would bring more death until Lydia itself was conquered by foreign empires, dying to rise no more.

The thought of losing the princess prodded at a tender spot in his heart, and he pulled her closer against him, almost as though he could hold her back from death by the strength of his arms. Over the distressing smell of her infection he caught the delicate scent of rose perfume. He fought the temptation to bury his nose in her silk veil and breathe in deeply.

What would Charlemagne say? And yet, John found the impulse surprisingly difficult to resist. The woman's obvious charms fascinated him. He would do well to find the herbs quickly so she could be on her way.

They passed vineyards and orchards and olive groves. Moses slowed as they came to a stream. John supposed the animal would have liked a drink, but he knew the water here was salty. The sea had cut a ravine through the slender bend in the finger of the peninsula. Every tide washed it wider.

John led the horse upstream to where the locals had

improvised a bridge of beams. The site, John realized, could use some attention. Someday the sea might divide the peninsula into its own island. Even now, the beams barely stretched the width of the ravine, and John eyed the waters ten feet below with a wary eye as Moses's hooves clattered across the sturdy planks. The princess shifted restlessly.

John peeled back the veil that covered her face from the sun and felt her forehead.

She was burning up.

He held his relatively cool hand against her skin as though it could absorb her heat and relieve her discomfort. But the touch imbued more than mere heat. Emotions that had lain dormant deep in his heart roused as though warmed by the sun after a long winter. But John had no intention of letting his feelings blossom to full flower.

"On, Moses," he encouraged his horse. They still had a ways to go before they reached the point where the peninsula joined with the mainland. From there, they would turn northeast, toward the mountains. The ride lay long ahead of them.

The sea breeze faded behind them as they entered a more heavily wooded stretch of road. Here on the peninsula, travel was quite safe. Seaside villages clung to the rocky coastlines on either side of them. The road connected them to the mainland with its agricultural produce and access to the lands beyond.

But once they entered the dense woods at the foot of the mountains, John knew he'd have to be alert for trouble. Though Lydia's borders had once followed the ridge of the mountains, the Illyrians had been encroaching on their land for generations. John's father had died defending a village there. He'd lost his life and the village.

John's younger brothers, Mark and Luke, sometimes talked about trying to take back those lands, but they hadn't been with their father that day. They hadn't seen him die or felt the sharp tang of fear as death dogged their heels. Had it been up to John, he would have died there next to his father. But he'd been injured as well, and Urias, his father's one-time right-hand man, had pulled him away and fled toward home. They'd lost two dozen men that day in a skirmish that should never have happened. They could have let the Illyrians take the village without a fight.

He couldn't change what had transpired that day, but John wasn't about to invite death and trouble into his kingdom by trying to get those lands back. His brothers feared that the Illyrians would one day take over the entire kingdom. Luke had thoroughly scouted throughout the area and had even asked to be dispatched with a team to recover the closest villages.

John wasn't sure how to handle the situation. He wouldn't risk his brother's life if it wasn't necessary.

As the woman who shared the horse with him moaned and twitched, John's thoughts turned to her father, Charlemagne, who'd famously united the various tribes on his continent into one Holy Roman Empire. The man didn't seem the least bit intimidated by a fight.

How would Charlemagne handle the situation with the Illyrians?

Charlemagne wanted to marry Gisela off to an Illyrian prince. From what John understood of the emperor, Charlemagne preferred to keep his family close. What had prompted him to seek a marriage agreement with Illyria? What did he hope to gain? John wished he could discuss the issue with the emperor. Perhaps, if he saved

Gisela's life, he could meet Charlemagne and learn about his political strategies.

But he'd have to save her life first. Could he do it? Uncertainties raged inside him. He'd failed so many times before. He prayed that God would be merciful and grant him success, not for his sake, but for the lovely princess who suffered so.

The road bent northward as they cleared the end of the peninsula. Moses shook his mane as John pointed him toward the mountains instead of riding into the city of Sardis. Of course, the animal wasn't used to traveling away from the city. He hadn't been born yet when John had last traveled there seeking herbs. Moses hadn't known John during his years as a healer. He wouldn't understand.

"Yes, Moses, we're going toward the mountains." John bent his head past the woman to speak to the horse, encouraging him on the right path, prompting him to gallop faster. They needed to move quickly. Gisela's suffering was a constant reminder that every minute was precious.

Gisela fought against the pain that threatened to keep her from sleep. She'd been told to rest. Why? By whom? She had to rest to get better. But what was wrong with her?

Pounding sounds and flashing lights filled her mind. She couldn't see. She could hardly think. She was too warm, and yet, she shivered. Words pattered against her ears like gently falling rain, making no sense. She wasn't near any mountains. She'd been at sea. Yes, her ship had been at sea when the Saracens had attacked them. They'd told her to stay below—Hilda had nearly strangled her trying to keep her below deck—and yet, Gisela had heard enough of the battle to know they needed her.

They *had* needed her.

Perhaps, if she'd gone to help sooner, their captain would not have died.

And if she'd been a bit quicker with her blade, perhaps she wouldn't have been injured herself.

Injured. That's right. *That* was the source of the throbbing pain in her head. The pirate had sliced her just above her right eye, catching her off guard while she battled with another man. She'd forced them both overboard before she'd had a chance to staunch the flow of blood. First she'd thought she'd bleed to death. Then she'd thought Hilda might smother her with her sobbing.

But they'd brought her to a healer. Some king who was supposed to be a healer. And...what was it he'd said?

She'd be dead by morning.

How soon was that? And where were they going?

The man's voice spoke again. "Faster, Moses. We've got to help the princess. We can't lose her." His arms tightened around her, pulling her close against his muscle-hardened chest as the horse charged on at greater speeds. "I can't lose another one."

Determination and sadness laced through his words, and Gisela felt her heart lifting up a prayer, that this kind man wouldn't lose... Who was he afraid of losing?

She tried to remember, but her thoughts were blurred. So instead, Gisela snuggled into his embrace, grateful for the solid arms that kept her on the horse, since she was certain she would otherwise fall.

Moses wouldn't go any faster, and they'd finally entered the wooded region where John had some hope of finding the hare's tongue at any time, so he let the animal slow his steps. Fledge had been sleeping on his shoulder, her head tucked in the crook of her wing, but now she looked about as though the scent of the woods sparked in her a hunger for wild game. She pranced impatiently. Her sharp talons prickled him through his leather shirt.

"You want to find a hare, Fledge?"

She cocked her head and trained her bright eyes on him.

"Fly, then. Find a hare. Perhaps it will lead me to the hare's tongue."

The bird flew to a branch not far ahead and looked back at him impatiently. John kept his eyes down, scanning the underbrush for a sign of the distinctive leaf pattern he sought. Hare's tongue tended to grow in shady areas, often in loamy soils, in earth enriched by a long-fallen tree, or among the pebbled manure of the rabbit warrens, as the name of the herb suggested.

The soil was too rocky here, with too much hard yellow clay. John looked past Fledge to the forest beyond. If he traveled farther north, he'd only skirt the rich soil. The chance of him finding the necessary herb wouldn't be good there.

And yet, if he turned east and plunged into the cool darkness of the woods, he'd quickly enter Illyrian territory. Yes, hare's tongue might await him there.

But so might his enemies.

For an instant, John recalled the distinctive crooked beak of a nose and the sneering face of the man who'd killed his father. A bandit of sorts, powerful in his own right, Rab the Raider lived by the sword, took what he wanted and didn't seem to care what destruction he left behind. As John understood it, Rab had come from the north years before. He thrived on war and had moved south to conquer more villages, leaving the once-Lydian village of Bern in Illyrian hands.

Luke kept John updated on the Illyrians' movements,

always with the unspoken implied request to go to war with them. But the situation was stable, if undesirable. John wasn't about to invite bloodshed on his people—and on his own brother—just to satisfy a desire for revenge. A thirst for revenge could never be satisfied. Even if he killed Rab to avenge his father's death, one of Rab's men would then come after him in return. To meet death with death was only to create a cycle of death with no end.

It simply wasn't worth it.

If he'd had his way, John would have kept to the tip of his peaceful peninsula. But Gisela's fever grew, and John's concern for her grew with it. He couldn't let this precious woman die. She meant more to him than continued peace, more to him than proof that his skills had not dissolved completely. The warm bundle in his arms provoked a sense of protectiveness and allegiance he didn't fully understand. But there was no time to examine those feelings now. He had to act quickly to save her life. He turned Moses toward the east, to the cool shadows of the mountains. He prayed the shadows held only hare's tongue and not Illyrian war scouts, watching him.

Chapter Three

The deeper they traveled into the forest, the greater John's sense of anxiety grew. He recognized these woods. They were transformed from the snow-covered lands that had hidden the herb that might have saved his mother, but they looked all too much as they had the day his father had died here.

Woods of death, that's what they were. And he'd been foolish enough to travel here in search of healing.

"Almighty God in heaven, have mercy," John prayed in a low voice as Gisela's moans became less frequent and her fever grew. But hadn't he prayed for God's mercy when his mother had died?

He scanned the underbrush, spotting bladderbark, motherwort, hyssop, wormwood and devil's nettle—enough herbs to cure a host of other ailments, but none that would take care of the infected injury above Gisela's right eye. The shadows lengthened, threatening to cloak the tiny leaves of hare's tongue in darkness.

There was nothing for it but to give up or continue deeper into the territory the Illyrians had stolen from Lydia over the past several generations. If Lydia hadn't lost those lands, the hare's tongue would have been easy enough to get. The loss tugged at him. Perhaps there was something to be said for taking back these lands.

But there was no point thinking about that now. Gisela lay deathly still, with only the fiery warmth of her fever to reassure him that he hadn't lost her yet.

Fledge had flown back to him and now pranced in place on his shoulder, straining forward, pointing her beak toward potential prey. John recognized her dance and followed the aim of her gaze to where a plump bunny sat among the underbrush, a long leafy stem drooping from its mouth, half-eaten, dangling like a green tongue.

Hare's tongue.

The animal had sensed their approach and stood frozen like a furry statue.

Fledge's wings beat thrice as she lifted off from John's shoulder. As she sped toward the hare the animal took off, the falcon in hot pursuit.

John didn't waste any time watching to see if his falcon caught her prey. Noting the place where the rabbit had been munching on the precious herb, he scooped Gisela up in his arms and slid from Moses's back, settling her in a soft bed of leaves.

"Lie here. I'll be right back," he promised the princess, though he doubted she was in any condition to hear him. He darted to the spot where the rabbit had been munching the herb, and found, to his relief, several plants nearly as high as his ankle—a good size for the reclusive vegetation and an indication that these late-season specimens were mature enough to contain the fever-reducing oils. Grabbing them up roots and all from the loose soil, he stuffed all but one into the bag he wore strapped crossways over his chest.

He tore leaves from the last plant, crushing them between the gloved fingers of his left hand as he hurried back to the princess.

The underbrush beyond him rustled with movement. His attention on the herb and the suffering princess, John paid the sound no heed until a flash of activity ahead of him caught his attention.

Fledge had her hare to the north beyond him.

So what was that sound coming from the south, behind him?

John had his right hand on his sword hilt as he spun around. Branches shifted in a stand of bushes.

Something was there.

It could be a bear or a fox or possibly a slighted falcon that had lost his lunch to Fledge. Or it could be an Illyrian war scout. Whatever it was, it wasn't attacking, at least not yet.

But the Frankish princess needed the herbs, and the sun was sinking fast, taking with it any hope for her recovery. Even if that was an Illyrian in the bushes, it would take a flurry of arrows to kill the princess any faster than the fever that already had her in its grip, dragging her relentlessly through death's door.

Crouching at her side, John hastily applied the crushed herbs to the festering injury, ignoring its ugliness. He'd seen worse.

Of course, most of those had killed the men who'd borne them.

The pungent scent of freshly crushed herbs teased her nostrils. Gisela tried to think past the pain. Herbs were important somehow, vitally important, but she couldn't think how.

Suddenly jabbing spears prodded at her eye and light

exploded across her field of vision. She tried to cry out, but all she managed was a whimper.

"It's all right. I've found the hare's tongue. You'll be fine," a deep voice soothed. The spears stopped jabbing, and coolness ebbed through her fever, with every feverish pulse of her heart drawing relief out of the mass that had been crammed against her eyelid.

A gentle hand cupped her cheek for just a moment, then slid under her head, lifting her, tying something around her eyes, binding the cooling herbs against the point of pain. "There now." Fingers brushed her face again, tenderly, almost reverently. She heard a whisper of words, realizing only after a moment that the speaker wasn't addressing her directly. It was a prayer.

With the crushed herbs packed over and around the open wound, John peeled off Princess Gisela's silk veil to use as a bandage to hold the healing compress in place. A long, thick braid of golden hair brushed his hand, freed from the veil that had hidden it. The silken strands were scented like roses, and for an instant John pictured her with the lovely locks cascading about her shoulders, and imagined what her flowing mane might feel like if he ran his hands through it.

John immediately chastised himself for being distracted by her beauty. She was the emperor's daughter. It wasn't proper for him to feel these swirling emotions that cracked the crust of his hardened heart. His job was to save her life. He hastened to fulfill that obligation.

In spite of his chastisements, John couldn't help picturing how the lovely princess would look without the injury above her eye. If she was fortunate enough to survive, the wound would likely blend in with the fold of her eyelid. She would be a picture of royal beauty.

His work done, there was nothing more he could do but pray.

The bushes rustled again, nearer this time, and John looked up.

Three red feathers stood stiffly like a plume from the helmet of the man in the bushes. An Illyrian—the distinctive feathers indicated his status as an infantryman. He'd obviously been watching John.

For an instant, John considered speaking to the man, explaining his situation and excusing himself.

But the man had obviously realized he'd been spotted. He raised an arrow and fitted it in his bow.

John scooped up the princess. "Still, Moses," he insisted, grateful when the horse stopped his nervous prancing long enough for John to toss the princess over his withers before leaping on after her. It wasn't graceful, but the whiz of an arrow's flight just past his ear told him there wasn't time to attempt a more genteel position.

Nor was there time to find Fledge. The bird would have to find him.

"Fly, Moses, fly!"

The stallion pranced backward a few steps before he spun around and took off to the south, more than eager to return the way they'd come. After wrapping one hand tightly around the reins and looping his other arm around Gisela's waist so she wouldn't slide off the speeding horse, John risked a glance behind him.

The plumed man had turned and headed north on foot, leaping over logs and underbrush in a mad dash.

Back to his village? John had posed no threat to him. He obviously wasn't running for safety. No, there was only one explanation for the man's mad-dash flight through the woods.

He was going to get reinforcements.

Rather than risk injuring the princess any more, John paused just long enough to hoist her upward, so that she was resting on her rump instead of her ribs. They'd make faster time, and she'd handle the trip better.

Her head slumped back against his shoulder almost lifelessly, but the sound of her sigh told him she still had the breath of life in her. For now, at least.

"Fledge?" John called out and whistled for the falcon, but saw no sign of his bird. When she was hunting for herself and not for him, she liked to carry off her prey to an isolated spot where she didn't have to share. He didn't usually begrudge her the indulgence, but today he did not have time to linger. "Fledge!"

No sign of the bird, and John couldn't wait. If his estimations were correct, the Illyrian would reach the nearest village in a matter of minutes. If he returned on horseback, single-mounted riders on fresh horses might easily overtake Moses, encumbered as he was after a long journey.

"Fly, Moses, fly." John gave the horse his head. The animal knew how to find footing in the woods better than John could guide him. Darkness fell as they dashed through the trees. John could only hope the lengthening shadows would camouflage his position from the Illyrians who were sure to be close behind him.

"This way." As they came to a path, John nudged Moses in the direction of the wayside inn where he'd agreed to meet Renwick and the riding party traveling with Gisela's maid. It was out of the way of the route they'd taken earlier and far off the meandering path they'd picked out while looking for the hare's tongue, but the inn at Millbridge still lay much closer than his castle or the walled city of Sardis. Nonetheless, there was little chance they'd reach it before the Illyrians caught up to them.

John regretted that he hadn't had an opportunity to change from his cross-emblazoned habergeon before departing. Though its metalwork would protect him from the direct hit of an arrow, the symbol nonetheless clearly identified him.

Assuming the Illyrian recognized the Lydian crown, or could describe what he'd seen well enough for another to identify it, the Illyrians would know who'd trespassed on the land they'd taken. Luke always had his scouting men ride in the unassuming leather garb of huntsmen. The Illyrian's bright red plumage told John that the Illyrians hadn't caught on to Luke's disguises, since they'd failed to adopt the technique themselves.

Nonetheless, *he* was bound to be recognized by the inlaid mother-of-pearl disks that formed the design splashed across his front and back. So in spite of his determination to be a man of peace, he'd end up bringing trouble to Lydia after all.

Something thwacked at the leaves near him. John glanced back.

The Illyrians were gaining on him quickly, even as they fitted arrows to their bows.

Suddenly Moses reared! John spotted the spot where an arrow had grazed his haunch. Moses took off at a fierce speed while John struggled to keep Gisela upright. He couldn't lose her now. The very thought tore at his heart, and he pulled her tighter against him.

Trees barred their way. In his frightened state, Moses had left the path and now dipped and darted between the trees in a frenzy.

John let the horse find his own way. He had his hands

full holding on to Gisela, keeping them both on the rocking back of the pain-crazed stallion.

With a twang, an arrow lodged itself deep in a tree just ahead of him.

The Illyrians were gaining on them.

Splashing sounds below told him Moses had found a stream. The horse took advantage of the creek's clear path, charging through the shallow waters. John tried to think of all the streams he knew of in the area. If he had the right stream, this one met the river up ahead, just before the place where the miller's wheel churned the waters beside the wayside inn.

Splashing sounds behind told him the Illyrians had found the stream, as well. John scanned the steep banks, looking for a place where they might leave the open streambed. They made too clear a shot here. Once the stream joined the river, the water would be too deep for Moses to run through it.

But there wasn't a low spot on the banks. Their steep muddy sides rose up higher than John's head, and it was all he could do to keep Gisela on the lurching horse's back while he ducked low over her, shielding her from the flying arrows with the chain mail on his back.

Roaring water up ahead told him the river was near—and surging with water from the summer rains that had fallen in the snow-capped mountains. The water would be frigid.

John tried to pull Moses to the side, but the banks grew steeper as the water plunged over the falls.

John had forgotten about the falls.

They weren't high—no more than half his height—but Moses leaped over them as though he were leaping from the earth itself. John gathered Gisela in his arms, dropping the reins and allowing Moses free use of his head. The animal would need it if he was to find his feet.

As they came down in the deep swirling pool at the foot of the falls, the water scooped him up like a hand, sweeping him off Moses's back. John cried out as the cold water swept through his clothes, chilling his skin with its overpowering grip, carrying him downstream. John held tight to the princess and struggled to right himself. The water swirled halfway up John's chest, and he recalled another disadvantage of wearing chain mail.

It was heavy.

So was the princess, with her draping robes now sodden with water. He struggled to lift her above the level of the churning waters, to keep her safe from the hungry river. His leather boots slid against the smooth rocks of the riverbed. Beyond him, shining pale in the moonlight, the miller's wheel turned steadily in the surging current.

Gisela's prayers for relief from the unrelenting fever had stilled on her silent lips, yet her heart still pounded with the plea. Numb as she felt, she couldn't be sure what was happening, but it seemed the mount they rode had bolted in fright.

Should she be frightened? No. She trusted the arms that held her, wrapping around her more protectively as the horse galloped frantically. With trembling fingers she grasped the strong arms, holding on. Whatever was happening, she felt instinctively that she could trust these strong arms. She could trust the man who held her.

The sound of splashing water teased her thirst. She'd give anything for a taste of cool water to soothe her parched tongue and throat.

Suddenly cold water enveloped her, dousing the flames of fever and rushing into her open mouth. She drank deeply, grateful for the relief, more grateful still for the strong arms that held her securely and refused to let her go.

John lunged for the banks. The waters tugged at Gisela's robes, threatening to tear her from his arms. He tried to hoist her higher, fighting against the current and the slippery rocks, nearly falling twice before movement on the bank caught his eye.

Illyrians stood above him on the shore. They fit their arrows to their bow strings and took aim.

There was nowhere to go. Moses swam far beyond him, his nose pointed to the narrow path that led down to the water from the miller's house.

John gulped a breath, covered the princess as best he could, and bent his knees, plunging them both beneath the surface of the chilly stream. He let his feet leave the rocks, and the greedy current took them both, sweeping them swiftly toward the turning paddles of the miller's wheel.

At least, in the darkness, the Illyrians would have trouble finding the swirl of water that marked where they swam. And the swift current would deflect the arrows.

John kept his head down until smooth rocks knocked against his knees. He realized that, as the stream widened to meet the miller's wheel, it also became shallower, and its water flowed less swiftly.

Raising his head and gulping a breath, John stood and found the water reached only to his hips. He could walk, and made for the path by which Moses had already clambered free of the cold waters. Glancing back, he saw the Illyrians in retreat and caught enough of a glimpse of the activity in the moonlight to guess that Renwick and the guards of the riding party had heard the commotion and rushed to his aid.

"Your Majesty?" a voice called from the bank just beyond him.

"Yes. Here! Lend me your hand!"

In a moment two pairs of feet splashed through the shallower waters, and Gisela's sodden frame was lifted from John's arms. His hands and fingers trembled after the aching ordeal, yet he still felt a strange sense of loss now that he was no longer holding her. Renwick's shoulder propped him under one arm and he stumbled toward the bank.

"The Illyrians?"

"We ran them off," Renwick assured him. "We'd been watching for you anxiously. We heard the commotion and saw them shooting. We knew they had no right to be here."

"Good man." John stood straighter as he stepped up the dry path. "You did well."

"Oh, my lady!" Hilda squealed as she ran from the inn toward them.

"Let's get her inside," John instructed the men, who carried in the princess.

They hastily brought her in and laid her on a bed while the innkeeper's wife fussed about the soaking mess she was making on the freshly ticked mattress.

"I thought you were going to pack her eye!" Hilda cried as sputtering oil lamps were brought near enough to see.

With disgust, John saw that Gisela's eye pack had come off completely and was likely torn apart by the miller's wheel or swept far downstream. He pulled his pouch from over his shoulder, disheartened to see that the plants inside had been soaked through.

"I'll make another eye pack." John tried to be calm, but Gisela's potential to recover wasn't good—especially not after the dunking she'd suffered in the chilly waters of the stream. At least she was breathing evenly after her impromptu immersion.

"I need to get her out of her wet clothes. All the men should leave the room." Hilda began to shoo them out.

"They can leave now." John got to work quickly crushing the leaves of the best-looking plant. "But I've got to get this on her eye. Then I'll leave and you can undress her." He hurried to apply the crushed leaves, wishing the light would allow him to inspect her injury more closely.

Instead he ran one hand down her silken cheek, but his hands bore the chill of the river, and he couldn't gauge how hot her fever burned. Quickly, while Hilda's back was turned, John pressed his lips to Princess Gisela's forehead, trying to discern how fiercely her fever raged.

Heat speared through his lips, imparting a far stronger message than the one he'd sought. He recoiled, but not before the memory seared itself into his mind like a firebrand. It was more than mere fever. His lips hadn't touched a woman since the day his wife had died.

Shoving aside the temptation to press his lips to her again, John focused on her medical condition. Though her fever was down slightly following her unintentional dousing, she would likely suffer chills. How much water had she breathed in? It could kill her even if the hare's tongue worked.

With a heavy heart he finished and closed the door to her room behind him and prayed silently that his efforts would not have been in vain.

Renwick met him at the door with an anxious expression.

John was soaking wet, cold, hungry—and bone tired.

"The men looked after Moses, Your Lordship," Renwick offered, using a loftier title than usual.

It made John suspicious. "Moses was nicked by an arrow."

"We saw, Your Highness. The bleeding has stopped on its own."

"Good." John wondered what vexed the man.

Renwick didn't leave him curious for long. "The men gave chase to the band of Illyrians. They wanted to make sure they were out of the area. They sent a volley of arrows after them." He gulped a breath. "One of the Illyrians was struck, sire."

"So was my horse." John headed for the single flight of stairs that led from the inn rooms above to the common dining hall where a warm fire and roasted meat awaited. He hoped the innkeeper would let him pay for a set of dry clothes.

"He fell and didn't rise."

John froze and squinted at Renwick in the darkness of the hallway. "Did he die?"

If they'd killed a man, the Illyrians could use it as an excuse to attack. Death begat death. If his men had killed a man, the Illyrians would kill one of his men—or likely more than one.

"The rest of his band plucked him up and carried him off, but…" Renwick sucked in a breath. Though technically a messenger, Renwick had seen his fair share of battle. He'd ridden with John the day his father died. "It didn't look good."

John clapped his hands over Renwick's forearms and addressed him with greater severity than he'd intended. "Pray that man doesn't die."

Renwick winced. "What should I tell the men, sire?"

"Give them my thanks. They did as they were told. They saved my life."

"And the Frankish princess?"

John shook his head morosely, guilt from his confused feelings swirling with his prayers for her recovery. "Pray for her, as well. If we lose her, we won't just have the Illyrians to worry about, but the Holy Roman Empire." He continued to the stairs, the war he'd tried so hard to avoid dogging his every step.

His men looked up at the sound of his boots, their faces drawn with concern.

John offered them a forced smile and held up his hand. "The Frankish princess lives, for now at least—with many thanks to all of you."

"Sire," one man spoke up, "we wounded an Illyrian."

"So I've heard. We'll post a double guard around the inn tonight and dispatch riders to Castlehead to explain the situation to Luke. He'll need to increase his guard, as well."

"But, sire," one of the guards protested, "there are only five of us. If you send two men, there will only be three left to split the guard. One man will have to stand guard all night."

John sat on a bench as he began the work of prying his water-swollen leather boots from his feet. When he got one off, he addressed his men. "I can take a shift at guard. The Frankish princess lies on the brink of death. It's not as though I could sleep, given the circumstances."

As he set about prying the other boot free, John felt a ripple of tension flow through the men. He hadn't meant to disquiet them, but given the situation, perhaps it was best that they appreciate the potential danger. After all, if Lydia went to war, they'd be on the front lines fighting alongside him.

Chapter Four

His arms no longer held her. Gisela shivered, so much colder now that his strong arms were gone. She heard a voice, but it wasn't the deep, comforting voice of the man who'd protected her. It was Hilda's voice. The woman's scent was far more like boiled cabbage than the woodsy, manly scent she'd grown so fond of.

"Where?" She found her voice after a surprising struggle. "Where has he gone?"

"Who, my lady? King John?"

At the sound of his name, Gisela felt her tension ease. Memories returned and chased away the empty darkness. That's right. King John had kept her safe. His arms had held her so tenderly and so securely. She shivered, missing his warmth. "Yes—King John. Where?" The strain of speaking silenced her question before she could articulate every word.

"Easy now, Your Highness." Hilda patted her hand. "The king must see to his men. They've posted a watch. I don't know if he can spare a moment for you. Would you like me to ask him?"

Gisela struggled to consider the question. Would she like Hilda to ask King John to see her? She imagined she must look awful. Likely she was in no condition to receive a visitor. And yet, she wanted so much to hear his voice and to feel his strong arms again. Her shivering continued uncontrollably. Could King John ease her fever? They'd called him a healer.

"Yes, please. Ask for him."

"Patrol the entire perimeter," John advised his men. "Don't neglect the far bank of the river. The Illyrians could easily cross the bridge past the mill or ford the creek upstream and catch us by surprise. We can't risk that. If they attack with more men…" He shook his head, letting the threat linger unspoken. He could see in the eyes of his men that they understood how outnumbered they were.

In any other situation, he'd have fallen back, emptying the settlement of Millbridge of its inhabitants and fleeing under the cover of darkness to the walled protection of the city of Sardis.

But Sardis was too far away. They didn't have the luxury of falling back tonight. Princess Gisela had already suffered far more than she should have. He couldn't risk trying to move her, not after all she'd been through, not even if they tried to keep her comfortable on the litter.

Besides, litters traveled slowly. If they were overtaken on the road without even the walls of the inn to protect them, the Illyrians would finish them off swiftly. Prince Luke would have the war he'd wanted, but it would be on two fronts: with Illyria by land and the entire Roman Empire by sea.

Lydia would be obliterated.

"Do nothing to provoke them," John cautioned the men. "Even if they attack, don't fight back unless they threaten the inn itself. Do you understand?"

The men nodded solemnly, and the two appointed for the first shift headed out to patrol. John turned to consult with Renwick but was surprised by a female voice behind him.

"Your Majesty? The princess is asking for you."

Warm feelings flooded him. Their suddenness and intensity only increased the guilt he felt after kissing Gisela's forehead, but he couldn't stay away if she needed him. He'd hoped to survey the area now that he'd changed into dry clothes borrowed from the innkeeper, but the emperor's daughter would have to come first. She might not be awake for long.

John hurried after the maid, dismissing Renwick. "Try to get some sleep. You and I will have the next watch."

He entered the private room where the princess lay resting in fresh, dry clothing her maid had brought. Hilda had pulled Gisela's long hair from its braid. He could see the comb she'd been using to untangle its vast matted wetness. The golden color glowed in the flickering lamplight.

So did her feverish skin. Everything around her eye was still swollen, but at least the herbs were still packed in place where they could do their work.

"Your Highness?"

Princess Gisela turned at the sound of his voice. Relief erased the tension from her features just before a convulsive shiver ran through her.

"Are you feeling worse?" He rushed to her side and felt her face. It was burning hot. Had he imagined it, or was her fever slightly less intense than it had been on the road? Surely the cold river waters had diminished it somewhat, but he couldn't risk pressing his lips to her again just to be certain. "What can I do for you?"

"I—I'm—" even her voice shuddered as chills quaked through her "—so cold." Her jaw quivered.

John addressed the maid. "We need more blankets. Tell Renwick to peel the curtains from the litter, if necessary. We've got to keep her warm. She'll waste all her strength shivering otherwise."

Her fingers felt icy cold as she found his hand, clinging to it as though for dear life.

"S-so c-c-c-old."

John scooped her up in the crook of his arm until she sat beside him. He pulled her against him and tried to still her shivers. Hilda headed for the open door, her efforts focused more on fretting than carrying out his instructions.

"Ask the innkeeper's wife to bring hot water. We'll have to soak Her Highness's feet. If they're half as cold as her hands, they must be like ice."

"Yes, Your Majesty." Hilda lingered in the doorway wringing her hands.

"Hurry!"

The woman startled and leaped through the door.

It was only after she'd gone that John realized he should have run the errands himself. But he couldn't leave the princess now. She'd burrowed against his shoulder. Her violent tremors stilled until she merely trembled against him, her feverish breaths even against his neck.

With the pack of herbs still tied tight against her eyelid, there was little he could do but hold her and try to keep her shivering to a minimum. "Is there anything you'd like me to do for you, Your Highness?"

The princess had grown so still in his arms, her shivering reduced to mere quivering, that John wondered for a moment if she hadn't lapsed out of consciousness again. But then she clenched his hand more tightly and whispered, "Don't leave me."

The sincerity of her plea, voiced in such a faint whisper, doused him with an overwhelming desire to see her safely through this ordeal. She was more than just a political pawn, an inconvenience whose arrival might bring war upon his peaceful kingdom.

She was also a woman whose rare bravery had saved her ship. She didn't deserve to die in return for the good she'd done. An unfamiliar fascination pulled at him. If he could do so without awakening further the emotions buried inside him, he'd like to learn more about the remarkable daughter of the emperor. But in order for that to happen, she'd have to survive the night.

Gisela clutched at the coarse fabric of King John's tunic. This wasn't the same chain mail habergeon he'd worn over leather garments when she'd ridden with him earlier.

But he was still the same man, his woodsy scent already chasing away the boiled cabbage odor that had trailed through the open door after Hilda. His deep accent lilted pleasantly as he promised to stay by her side, to see her through her injuries until she'd recovered.

A sense of peace seeped past her fever as he held her securely, promising to do all he could to ease her pain. She'd have to be certain her father compensated King John for his selfless assistance.

As her chills subsided, she managed to find her voice. "I can't see."

"Your injury has swollen your eyes shut. When the infection subsides we'll be able to assess the damage, but from what I've seen, the blade missed your eye. You should retain your vision."

Relief eased the last of her shivers. She relaxed as her fear of living as a blind woman subsided with the king's assurances. After all, Warrick, the Illyrian prince she'd been betrothed to marry, would likely frown on the idea of taking a blind woman for a wife—not when he could have his pick of unblemished women.

Again, she found herself wondering what King John looked like. Was he as handsome as Hilda's inflection had led her to believe? He certainly had a beautiful spirit and a kind disposition. She could only imagine his physical features would match his generous soul.

But what did he think of her? Concern over the festering wound forced words to her trembling lips. "Will I be ugly?"

The question came out bluntly, but to her relief King John took no offense. "The natural fold of your eyelid should disguise the scar. I may be able to suture the gash as it heals to minimize its appearance."

Gratitude welled inside her, but in her feverish state, she couldn't find the words to express her thankfulness. Silence stretched between them. Warmed by his presence, her shivers abated and she felt a measure of her strength return.

The king continued in a musing voice, as though almost to himself, "Not that such a little thing could diminish your remarkable beauty."

"You're already in my good graces, King John. Don't trouble yourself flattering me."

He straightened at her suggestion. "I didn't realize you were still awake. You had relaxed so." He sighed. "That wasn't empty flattery, Princess. You are as lovely a woman as I have ever seen. Your Illyrian prince is a fortunate man. And I will consider myself equally fortunate if your fever erases all memory of this conversation."

"I think my fever is easing, Your Majesty."

He touched her face. "Perhaps it is. And I hear Hilda approaching with your blankets, so I'll give you my leave before I embarrass myself further." Gently, as though he feared she might break, King John eased himself away from her, tucking blankets up as far as her chin and instructing her maid about soaking her feet.

Warmth spread up Gisela's legs as Hilda dipped first her toes, then, by stages, her whole feet into the heated water.

And yet, as she heard John's footsteps retreating down the hall, Gisela couldn't suppress a cold shiver, missing him.

John rubbed his temples as he fled from Princess Gisela's bedside. He was tired. He'd been through a great deal and still had a long night ahead of him.

Still, that was no excuse for the way he'd let down his guard, speaking aloud words better left only in his thoughts. The princess must think he was full of empty flattery!

He tried to tell himself it didn't matter. He might have been caught muttering far worse, especially with the threat of war foisted upon them. But he knew his lapse rankled him precisely because it was the worst possible thing the royal woman could have heard him utter. Ever since his wife's death three years before, he had taken great pains to make it perfectly clear to everyone in his kingdom that he had no interest in taking another wife.

Even after so long, the eligible maidens and their eager parents were only now beginning to believe him. If it became known that he'd heaped flattering words upon the emperor's daughter, people might think he'd changed his mind about not wanting a woman. And with the princess obviously unavailable, he'd be back to discouraging eager females again.

But Princess Gisela was the only one who'd heard him. Was there any way he could beg her not to repeat what he'd said?

Not without revisiting it. And if there was any hope that she might not remember his words, he wasn't about to remind her of them.

Unless she gave him the impression that she remembered, after all.

John rubbed his temples again as he fled outdoors, grateful for the relative cool after the distressing warmth of the feverish princess.

He'd passed Renwick's sleeping form in the main hall of the inn, and so sought out his men patrolling the perimeter. He could only pray the Illyrians would think better of launching an assault. At the very least, they might postpone their attack until the Frankish princess was safely ensconced in the queen's tower, the most securely buttressed point of the fortress at Castlehead.

The thought of further harm coming to her filled him with cold dread. Obviously his reaction was due to their political entanglements. She was under his protection now and would remain so until he could hand her off to her betrothed or until her father sent a more substantial escort than the wounded ship with its inexperienced captain.

Assuming, of course, she survived long enough for that to happen.

As the warm blankets and heated water chased her chills away and the cool herbs above her eye purged the poison of infection, Gisela's thoughts began to make more sense, except for one thing.

She missed the king's presence.

It was odd. She'd never been one to rely on any specific person to make her feel better. Her mother had died when she was a toddler, her father was a busy man and she had enough siblings, half siblings and servants that for most of her life she hadn't concerned herself much about who was around. It had been enough to know that there were plenty of people nearby and that they all cared for her with more or less equal devotion.

It was a strange sensation, wanting a particular person present, even though between Hilda and the innkeeper's wife bustling about offering her blankets and hot tea, she might have preferred to be left alone.

She told herself she simply wanted King John near so he could monitor her injury. And of course, she felt she could trust him.

But it wasn't as though she *dis*trusted her middle-age maid or the innkeeper's wife.

Still, the inexplicable longing wouldn't go away.

"Is he coming back?"

"Is *who* coming back, Your Grace?" Hilda's voice sounded haggard, and Gisela realized the woman would have normally been snoring for hours by this time of night.

"King John."

"He just left not so long ago. I imagine he has matters to attend to."

"I see. Of course." Gisela resolved to rest and forget about the king. "Don't bother about the heated water, Hilda. You need your sleep."

"Thank you, Your Highness."

As Hilda settled onto the other mattress, it occurred to Gisela that, really, someone ought to fetch the king to look at her injury again *before* her maid went to sleep.

Otherwise, assuming the innkeeper's wife didn't return (and she'd been gone long enough, Gisela supposed she'd retired for the night), there wouldn't be anyone to fetch the king, if she needed him.

"Hilda? Could you please ask the king to check my injury one last time?"

"Yes, Your Highness." The maid heaved herself to her feet and shuffled past.

Gisela listened to the sounds of the night and wished she could see, but the swath of fabric that secured the herbs to her eyelid stretched across both of her eyes. Whether she'd be able to open even the left one without it, she wasn't certain.

The minutes crawled by slowly. Gisela had tried so hard to ignore her fears, but in the dark silence they taunted her with every unfamiliar noise. Without her sight she was particularly vulnerable, especially alone. Had she been unwise to send Hilda to fetch the king? Worse yet, what if the king and his guards were in the middle of some vital operation and Hilda stumbled into it?

Gisela wasn't entirely clear on the events that had preceded her arrival at the inn, but she'd caught enough of the discussion through her fever to deduce that they were in danger from enemy war scouts in the area. Was King John needed outside more urgently than she needed him inside?

Had she exposed them to danger through her selfish request? And why did she feel so strongly about seeing the king again?

"Your Majesty?"

John turned at the sound of Hilda's voice, instantly concerned. The maid should be at Princess Gisela's bedside, not out here by the river, looking for him. He darted downstream, speaking softly before she called out for him again. "Yes, Hilda?"

"She's asking for you again."

A wave of relief hit him with force, followed by an almost euphoric joy he attributed to happiness that the princess was well enough to speak. Certainly it had nothing to do with her request to see him. She only needed his medical knowledge—not anything more personal than that.

Still, he hurried after the maid, fearful that she'd already left the princess unguarded for long minutes while she'd been out searching for him. John had traveled upstream, expanding the search perimeter looking for signs that the Illyrians might have forded the creek.

The darkness had yielded no sign of them. He passed the other two guards on his way to the inn and was relieved to see them patrolling attentively.

Hilda panted as she held her oil lamp aloft and led him into the low-beamed private room.

"Did you find him?" Gisela asked.

Realizing the princess had heard her maid but was unable to see him, John hastened forward and scooped up her hand. "I'm here."

A smile spread across her lips and the anxiety fled from her features.

John found the expression contagious and couldn't help grinning back. Certainly his relief stemmed from finding her responsive—from finding her alive at all. He'd not stopped praying for her since he'd left her bedside.

He pressed his hand to her forehead. To his immense relief, her fever had already begun to abate, even from its reduced state when he'd left her last.

"Hilda? Where are the herbs I brought in my pack?"

"I gave them to the innkeeper's wife, Your Majesty. She was going to put them in a pot."

Instantly alarmed, John snapped, "She can't cook with them! The princess is still in a precarious state. I need those herbs—they must be fresh!"

"I'm sorry, Your Majesty. I didn't mean a cooking pot. She was going to plant them in soil to keep them alive, sire. That's all. Shall I fetch some?"

Mollified by her reassurances, John softened his tone. "Please, if you can find them, bring me the whole pot. I'll pick what I need."

"Yes, sire." Hilda shuffled past him, taking her oil lamp with her, leaving him only one sputtering flame to see by.

"I'm sorry if she interrupted your patrol." The princess looked repentant.

"It's fine. You don't need to apologize. I've seen no sign of the Illyrians, and my guards are actively patrolling. In any case, your condition is of paramount importance. I'm glad you asked for me before your maid retired for the night. I was hoping to change your bandages again and refresh the herbs. They seem to be helping."

"Yes. I'm feeling more alert and less feverish already."

"Good," John said, though he felt a prickle of distress that she might remember the words he'd spoken earlier when he hadn't expected her to hear. His mouth dry, he posed a tentative question. "Have you been awake since..." His words dropped off as he tried to think of the best way to pose his question.

"Since you heaped flattering words upon me?" Princess Gisela's slight grin told him she was teasing him.

His heart stuttered at being caught, then an unfamiliar thrill of relief rippled through him. The princess wasn't upset. In spite of her continued fever, she was playing with him.

King John wasn't used to lighthearted repartee. Few were the men in his kingdom who would dare to jibe with him. His brother Luke was far too serious in demeanor, and his brother Mark was away on a journey. That left only his little sister, Elisabette, and though she'd once enjoyed nothing more than goading him to laughter, the girl was growing into a woman and leaving her playful ways behind.

Gisela's smile spread across pearly teeth. "I haven't forgotten, Your Majesty, though I struggle to understand your embarrassment. Your compliments were quite kind, considering my condition."

"I hadn't meant to be heard. I would appreciate it if you keep those comments to yourself. I can't have anyone thinking that I…" John tried to think of an appropriate way to express what he meant without making the situation worse.

"That you revere the emperor's daughter for her beauty?" Gisela finished his statement for him. "It is well-known that Lydia is a Christian nation. My father's empire is Christian, as well. We do not worship our leaders as some nations do. That fact is well-known. I doubt anyone would misinterpret your words, but since you've requested that I not repeat them, I shall refrain from doing so."

Relieved as he was by her promise, John didn't bother to correct her interpretation. Everything she'd said was quite true, other than her guess at his reason for making the request. And he wasn't about to correct her on that, since it would require him to explain feelings he neither wanted nor understood.

John hastened to change the subject. "Assuming Hilda

is able to find my herbs, I'd like to change your compress. Do you mind if I remove the bandages?"

"Please do. I feel as though the swelling has gone down, and I'm curious to discover whether I can open my left eye."

"I'm not sure that's wise." John began tugging at the knot that bound the herbs in place. "You ought not strain yourself too soon."

"But how will I know…" The princess began hesitantly as a coy smile graced her lips.

"How will you know *what?*" The knot came free at last, and John eased the bandage away from her eyes. The crust of infection that sealed her lids shut had trapped even her left eyelashes. "Don't try to open your eyes just yet," he cautioned her. "Let me use a warm compress to soften the film."

The pot of steaming water had cooled somewhat, but John found it still warm enough for his purposes. He dipped a soft rag into the boiled water and pressed it gently against her left eye.

"Does that hurt?"

"It's soothing." Her demeanor had grown more serious.

John found himself longing for her to toy with him again. It was a silly thing to fancy, but it made his heart feel far lighter than he could recall it feeling in recent memory. "If you can see," he adopted a serious tone, "what is it you want to know?"

The smile returned to her face, this time with an impish dimple that winked at him from high on her cheek. He hadn't noticed it before because the bandage had obscured it. Now he instantly wished to see it again.

"I would like to see—" the dimple flashed at him, then disappeared as the princess matched his tone in mock-seriousness "—if the king who heaps such flattery upon me has a face that begs for accolades as well."

"I cannot answer that, but you may find out for yourself in a moment."

Gisela's heart beat as rapidly as it had at any time during the height of her fever. She wasn't usually so bold in her chatter, certainly not with near strangers, although in feasting season her father's household was filled to the rafters with joking and jesting, and several of her brothers prided themselves in their skill at exchanging jibes.

She was no match for them, but there was something about King John's otherwise melancholy spirit that challenged her to make him smile. And after her long journey holed up in a ship's cabin to keep her away from improprietous sailors, she was ready to accept that challenge with gusto. Uncertain as she was about his physical appearance, she had nonetheless long believed that a smile improved the features of any person.

Besides, when she heard the sadness in his voice, all she could think about was easing his sorrow, if only for a moment.

"There." John dabbed gently at her left eye. "The light is not well, but if you can open just your left eye, we'll see what you can see."

Cautiously, taking care not to disturb her injured right eyelid, Gisela lifted her left eyelid until she could just make out the yellow glow of the oil lamp. She let out a relieved breath, grateful that she still retained the ability to see. Then she lifted the lid a little farther and turned her head to the place where John's voice had last sounded.

It took a moment for her vision to focus. Then she saw him dipping the rag he'd used in the pot of warm water and wringing it out carefully before turning to face her.

Dark hair revealed that he was young for a king—young enough that no gray hairs discolored his ebony locks.

And he was handsome. As he bent over her, she was able to get a better look and felt a smile spread across her lips in spite of her best efforts to stop it. Had she ever seen a more handsome man? Not with only one eye, that was for certain. She could only imagine he'd look even better when she saw him with both eyes.

King John's serious expression lightened. "Why are you grinning?"

"I can see you." She felt herself blushing and wished she could think of a lighthearted jab to cover her reaction at seeing him for the first time. But all she could think of was the way his arms had felt around her earlier. Her blush deepened.

His expression sobered again. "I wonder what's become of Hilda."

The giddy delight she felt while looking at him was quickly replaced by fear for her maid's safety. How long had Hilda been gone? Gisela realized she'd been so distracted by her conversation with the king that she'd lost all track of time.

John set aside the bandages. "I'll go look for her."

"Is it safe?"

"For me to leave or for you to be left alone?"

"Either."

"Safe enough. Try to rest. I should be back soon to redress that eye." He darted away quickly, almost as though he was in a hurry to be gone from her side.

Chapter Five

❧

John rushed outside looking frantically for Hilda or either of the guards. Were they safe? He could only pray they were. As for his safety, he'd quickly realized he'd be far safer outside than he was in Princess Gisela's room. Even if the Illyrians had them surrounded, that was preferable to the dangers of getting close to the emperor's daughter.

At what point had their discussion turned so coy? He reviewed their course of conversation as he trotted around the inn in search of Hilda or the plants she'd gone to find.

With chagrin, he realized he'd been afflicted the moment he'd entered her room and a thousand times more so when he'd taken her hand.

By the time he'd seen the dimples on her cheeks, he'd been utterly smitten.

Was he a fool? Her father was the greatest leader the Holy Roman Empire had ever known. Everyone knew Charlemagne was a zealous family man who adhered strongly to the tenets of the Christian faith.

John embraced those same tenets himself. So how had he let himself get so close to a woman who was promised to another? If they suspected him of any impropriety, he'd have the wrath of both Charlemagne and the Illyrians on his head—and on his kingdom.

"Hilda!" He spotted her making her way up from the river, huffing along carrying a burden he couldn't identify in the darkness, though she acted as though it was much heavier than his herbs should have been.

"Sire," the maid wheezed as she made her way up the bank. Her words came out in spurts between gasping breaths. "She took it down to the river to water it."

John could only assume Hilda was referring to the innkeeper's wife, and her plan to pot his herbs like some sort of domesticated houseplant. He rushed forward and helped Hilda carry the heavy pot.

It wasn't a bad idea to attempt to grow the plants in a portable container, although the pot the innkeeper's wife had chosen wasn't particularly portable. And he couldn't imagine why the woman had decided to carry his precious herbs to the riverside instead of fetching water and bringing it up to the inn.

But as they stepped into a patch of moonlight, John was able to get a better look at his plants and realized they'd survived. Was there any way he could get a fresh bunch of crushed leaves on Princess Gisela's eyelid without talking with her?

"Hilda, could you pack the herbs—"

"Oh, no, sire. I haven't got a healing bone in my body."

"But it's really just a matter of placing the herbs—"

Hilda waved her hands in refusal as she panted back toward the inn. "I'm no healer, sire."

John stared after the maid for a moment.

"Lord, what does it mean?" he asked, looking up at the sky, where the stars winked down at him, reminding him of Gisela's dimple.

He sighed. He wasn't going to find the answer tonight. The princess needed another compress of crushed hare's tongue, and according to Hilda, he was the only one who could do it—though the placement of the herbs was simple enough.

No, keeping his heart safe from the emperor's daughter—that would be the real challenge.

Gisela recognized Hilda's huffing as the woman approached down the hall. The smell of boiled cabbages preceded her, and the maid slumped onto her mattress without taking off her shoes.

"Did you find him?"

"Aye," Hilda panted.

"Is he coming? Does he have the herbs?"

"Yes," the maid answered, and the sound of approaching footsteps confirmed her words.

Suddenly nervous, Gisela wondered what she should say to the king. Somehow, when she hadn't been able to see him, he'd seemed…safe. Tame.

But when she'd seen his face for the first time and the silhouette of his broad shoulders in the flickering lamplight, she'd realized he was dangerously handsome. Strong. Regal. Not someone she'd have chosen to spend time with, given that she was promised to another. At least this time she had Hilda in the room.

"Your Highness?" John asked quietly from the doorway.

As Gisela was about to answer, a loud snore rose from Hilda's mattress.

Gisela giggled, and an instant later the king knelt beside her.

Hilda snored again.

King John smirked. "I knew that wasn't you." He carried a few plucked sprigs of herb in his hand. As he crushed the leaves between his fingers, their pungent scent filled the room.

"You don't sound so sure. Who's to say I don't snore?"

"You're far too lovely." His words dropped to near silence, almost as though he was ashamed of having spoken them.

Gisela wasn't sure how to respond. She lay still as he bent over her and pressed the leaves into place over her injury. To her relief, the application didn't pain her one fraction as much as the first dose had. "How does the gash look?"

"It's on the mend. And so are you. You won't need me for the ride to Castlehead tomorrow."

"You're leaving?" She felt shocked by the intensity of the pang that struck her at the thought of their separation. "Why?"

"I need to secure this region against the Illyrians. You need to rest in safety."

"What if my condition grows worse?"

"You're on the mend," he repeated as he tied the binding that secured the herbs in place over her eyelid.

Gisela understood. She knew her intended was the only man with whom she should spend any time. And yet, the thought of John's leaving shook her with surprising force.

"You should rest now." King John stood and took a step toward the door.

"Your Majesty?"

"Yes?"

For long breathless seconds Gisela tried frantically to think of some way of keeping him at her side. But just as when her father headed off on his missions, there was nothing she could say to keep him near her. Not then. Not now. Her life was not her own.

"Thank you for all you've done for me. I owe you my life. My father will see that you are generously rewarded."

He lingered a moment and cleared his throat, as though grasping at the proper words that fit their circumstances. Royal positions were all about etiquette and formalities.

But she knew of no formality that covered a king saving the life of the emperor's daughter. Perhaps she could salvage a bit of her dignity yet. "I'm sorry if I said anything unbecoming. The fever went to my head."

"You have nothing to apologize for," John answered finally. "And you don't owe me anything. I am honored to have been of service to the empire and to you."

Gisela opened her mouth to respond, but he was already gone, his footsteps retreating rapidly down the hall.

Gisela groaned softly, regretting her words, regretting that she and the king were so soon to part ways. Was he really not going to be traveling back with her? What if she didn't see him again before her party struck out for the Illyrian kingdom where her prince awaited?

The thought of her coming marriage burned more deeply against the pain in her heart. Why had she agreed to marry Warrick the Illyrian? Granted, the political situation required that one of Charlemagne's daughters enter into such a union. The Illyrians had requested her specifically. She'd wanted to experience life outside of her father's household, and given her father's overprotective nature, nothing short of a marriage agreement would suffice to accomplish that. But now she was set to be wed to a man she'd met only twice. There was no way around it, so there was no sense wishing otherwise.

"In the past two days we've seen no sign of Illyrian scouts." Prince Luke pulled his horse's head even with that of the king's mount. "They've made no move to attack. I've never known them to be so quiet."

"They're surely biding their time, plotting their strategy for the perfect assault." John heard the morose tone of his words, but he did nothing to hide his attitude from his brother. Luke already knew perfectly well how much he detested war.

"Is that what's put you in such a bad mood? The thought of war?"

"Fledge is still missing."

"I know you love your falcon, but I can't believe your attitude is due to her absence. She's been missing far longer before and always returned."

John looked at his brother and tried to judge where the younger prince was headed with his line of questions.

The way Luke pursed his lips, John could tell he was forming his next question.

"You were in perfectly good spirits while we were fencing before the Frankish princess arrived."

"Yes," John acknowledged. "That was before all the trouble began."

"And yet," Luke continued as their horses picked a path along a deer trail that led up from the river to the mountains, "I don't believe your doldrums set in until we parted ways with Her Highness."

John wasn't about to let his brother lead him into a discussion about Princess Gisela. Luke knew him far too well and would pick up on his divided loyalties.

"You don't suppose the Illyrians have circled around us to attack Sardis, do you?"

"They couldn't organize an assault so quickly." Luke dismissed the suggestion. "Are you worried for the safety of Her Highness? She'll soon reach Castlehead, even accounting for slow travel by litter."

"Knowing her, she had the men roll up the litter and she's taken a horse."

"You know her that well, do you, brother?"

Unsure how Luke had so quickly trapped him, John evaded his brother's jab. "She's easy enough to read. Stubborn. Spirited. Impossible to reason with once she's set her mind on something."

"You paint her in a negative light." Luke drew his horse nearer and spoke in a musing tone. "Why are you so eager to heap insults upon a woman you ought, for the sake of international peace, to hold in high esteem?"

"I esteem her well enough. But let's not let ourselves be distracted from our plight with the Illyrians."

"I've seen no sign of any Illyrians," Luke refuted. "But I can't help wondering why you're so dismissive of Her Highness. I got the impression she was *quite* fond of you."

John could think of no words his brother couldn't twist, so he remained silent.

"You've gone rather red in the face, dear brother."

"It's a warm day."

"We should stop and rest, then."

And face his brother? John was loath to risk it. "We should keep going."

Luke began to laugh.

"Quiet. You'll give away our position."

Luke laughed harder.

"There could be Illyrian war scouts hiding behind any bush. Pray tell me, brother, what you find so humorous that you're willing to risk giving away our presence because of it?"

"You fancy her."

"What? Who?" John sputtered, recovering from the question more slowly than he would have liked, the mad thumping of his heart making it difficult for him to form coherent thoughts. "My missing falcon? Fledge is one of the finest birds I've ever owned. Of course I fancy her."

"Stop your horse." Luke held his mount and studied his brother's face.

John dropped his voice to a whisper. "Illyrians?"

"Emotions." Luke let his horse proceed again. "Yours."

"I have none. I gave them up when Dorcas died." John spoke of his late wife's passing, knowing his brother respected his loss. Perhaps Luke would leave off his questioning after that reminder.

"She died. You didn't. You're still here and still capable of feeling."

"Don't speak so brazenly of my loss. I shall mourn her passing every day of my life."

"I mean no disrespect, John." Luke's voice grew serious. "You loved your wife with your whole heart, with every fiber of your being. I find it difficult to believe that someone who loved so well and so fully could live out his days without loving again."

"It's not a matter of loving again. My heart still belongs to Dorcas."

"But she is gone, and you are here. If you never take another wife then I will be your heir." Luke gave him a long look.

John remained silent. He was certain Luke understood full well his resolution not to remarry, just as he understood Luke's disdain for his position in line for the throne.

Finally Luke sighed. "I have never loved as you loved, so I cannot judge. But I saw the look Princess Gisela gave you as you were parted. If a woman ever looked at me that way, I don't think I could turn my back and ride off as you did."

"What look? She only had use of one eye."

"You know the look I mean. And I am correct in thinking you have feelings for her. Your distress betrays that."

"She is promised to another man—and not just any man! A prince among our enemies. Do you want to be destroyed by the Illyrians for revenge? Or are you so eager for war that you would use her as bait on your hook?"

Luke's face flashed with anger. "I am not eager for *war,* brother. I'm eager to have our land united again. As king, you have a duty to protect your people. I cannot fathom why you choose to turn your back on that duty."

"I protect my people—from warmongers like you."

"Is that what I am?" Luke turned his horse and pranced the steed backward, away from his brother. "Go back to Castlehead and check on your princess, but think on what I've said. I'll be here, protecting the borderlands."

"I can protect my kingdom," John shouted as his brother rode away.

"Can you?" Luke's voice faded with the distance between them.

Gisela lay back on the litter and tried her best to rest, though her strength had returned in the three days since King John had helped her. She'd have gladly taken a horse instead of resting, except that she'd only find herself en route to her intended that much sooner that way. "Do you think we should stop again?" she asked Hilda.

"We've only just got going again from the last break we took," the maid chided her. "Are you that reluctant to return to your ship?"

"I don't believe it's safe to continue on," Gisela asserted. "Our vessel is wounded, and our crew is shorthanded."

"But we're nearly to our destination. With a brisk

wind, we could make it up the coast in three days and deliver you to your prince."

"Hilda—" Gisela felt her distress increasing at the mere thought of the Illyrian who awaited her "—don't you think it rude to take leave before King John returns? He must be compensated for saving my life. At the very least, I owe him a debt of thanks."

"Your father will send payment. King John left on some expedition—"

"Made necessary by my injury," Gisela finished for her. "You do realize that his quest for the hare's tongue herb created the situation on the borderlands."

"There was trouble brewing long before you arrived, my lady."

"Yes, but I was the spark that lit the fire. My conscience plagues me. What if war breaks out on my account?"

"I trust King John can put out any fire you light. You've got an Illyrian prince waiting to wed you. Let's not keep him waiting."

"I'm not due until Christmastide."

"No, but I expect he'd welcome your arrival sooner." Hilda chuckled.

Gisela squirmed, disturbed by the tone of Hilda's chuckle. The maid seemed all too eager to see her married off.

Her uneasiness was brief enough. The litter slowed to a stop.

She stuck her head out to inquire of the reason.

"A rider approaches swiftly," Renwick informed her.

"Is that a bad sign?"

"Your curtains are spread with the royal crest. All riders give way to the crown."

Gisela's fear spiked. "Perhaps it's a messenger with

important news." She squinted with her lone good eye toward the approaching horseman. "Isn't he wearing the same royal crest?" Sunlight glinted off the mother-of-pearl inlay on his habergeon.

Renwick's stiff posture relaxed as he let out a breath. "Your Highness is correct. I do believe—" he eyed the horseman as the figure drew nearer "—it is King John himself."

"Help me down." Gisela shot her hand out before Hilda could stop her. With Renwick's assistance she was standing on her own two feet as King John's horse came to a stop in front of them.

"Is everything all right, Your Majesty?" Renwick asked.

"As right as it can be with one Illyrian war scout dead at our hands." He dismounted, holding tight to his stallion's reins. "There's no sign of Illyrian activity along the borderlands." He nodded to Gisela. "I thought you'd be relieved to hear that, Your Highness."

"Quite relieved, Your Majesty, and honored that you took the time to deliver the message personally."

John nodded, but his eyes roved the road instead of meeting hers. "After finding the border in such a peaceful state, my concern immediately arose for the safety of those in Sardis and Castlehead. I wouldn't put it past the Illyrians to circle around and mount an attack."

"Are they able to organize themselves so quickly?" Gisela had spent her youth discussing military strategy over meals, while traveling—any time she was around her father. Her interest was immediately piqued, especially since any attack had essentially been provoked by her intrusion.

"The possibility exists, although I believe their prime window for attack is only now beginning to open."

Gisela appreciated King John's astute appraisal. Since he had yet to cast more than the briefest glance her way, she took a step toward him. "I fear my imposition has brought trouble on your peaceful kingdom."

"Trouble has been brewing for many years, Your Highness."

"And my arrival has brought it to a full boil. I can't, in good conscience, allow your people to be endangered for helping me." She reached for his hand.

He drew back and placed his hands on his horse's neck.

His action jabbed at her heart, stinging like a tiny spear, but she didn't allow the pain to show on her face. The guards were watching and listening. She couldn't show any weakness in front of them.

"You're injured," John stated flatly while fussing with his horse's mane. "The best thing you can do now is be on your way. If trouble comes, I don't want you to have to meet it."

Gisela felt as though the tiny spear that had snagged her heart had begun to tear it open. Had John made the journey to meet her, only to send her away?

"Please, Your Majesty. I owe you a debt of gratitude. My father has immense resources at his disposal. Allow me to do whatever I can to assist Lydia's defense."

King John felt the eyes of his men upon him. He was trying to push the princess away, but he couldn't be rude to her.

And he heard the double-edged warning in her words.

My father has immense resources at his disposal. Allow me to do whatever I can to assist Lydia's defense.

She was offering to help, true enough, but he didn't miss the implied threat if he failed to accept her help. *My father has immense resources at his disposal.*

The last thing he needed was for the emperor to turn those resources on Lydia to avenge a slight against his daughter. But at the same time, he knew it wasn't wise to spend time with the lovely princess. Even Luke, who was far more adept at spotting signs of war than signs of love, had picked up on the attraction he felt for her.

"Your Highness." He risked looking at her, and felt his heart lurch inside him as he caught her one good eye. Even injured, she held herself with dignity. "The situation with the Illyrians is quite complicated."

"Then explain it to me." She placed her hand over his. "Please?"

He couldn't risk insulting her. And something deep inside him cried out for her presence as his lungs cried out for air. How could he deny her request? It wasn't in him.

"Are you able to ride a horse?"

Relief filled her face. "Yes."

John called for his men to bring a spare horse. "Ride with me, Your Highness, and I shall tell you the ugly story of the relations between Lydia and her Illyrian neighbors."

With the other riders spread over the road before and behind them, John felt slightly more at ease in the princess's presence than he had at the inn three nights before. Any of his men or her maid could vouch for his propriety.

They were simply talking. She was well guarded.

He would just have to keep his heart guarded against her as well, and prove to himself and his brother that whatever strange emotions she'd evoked in him were not permanent, and would soon be squashed.

"Tell me more about your kingdom," the princess prompted as they got underway. "How long has Lydia been a Christian nation?"

"Lydia has always been Christian—the Kingdom of Lydia dates back to the days of the New Testament."

"In the Bible?"

"The very same."

"I have read the New Testament several times. I don't recall reading of any Lydia other than the woman who was a dealer in purple cloth."

John couldn't suppress a smile. Princess Gisela was well schooled and astute. "In the book of Acts, Paul met a woman named Lydia, who became one of the first converts to Christianity in this region. She set up a church in her house. It grew to encompass many households, until this entire peninsula was filled with faithful Christians."

"But didn't the Roman Empire consider Christianity a crime? Weren't they persecuted?"

"Very much so. The Christians went into hiding and retreated to Castlehead, where they built the fortress that is now my home. The mountains where we found the hare's tongue provided a natural boundary for the fledgling nation. The Lydians considered themselves a separate people."

"I find it difficult to believe they weren't overpowered or overrun."

"For several centuries we were left largely alone. Few have bothered to peek past the ridge of mountains to learn about the small kingdom of Christians who cling to the coastline. We have been safe because we are small and not worth the effort and expense of sending an army through the mountains."

"But aren't you vulnerable by the sea, as well?"

"Ah, you were consumed by fever when your ship approached, or you would have noted the rocky shore."

"Our ship put down anchor at some distance to avoid the rocks."

"And you came in at our most passable point. Castle-head provides a watchtower over the only possible point of approach by sea. The rest of our shoreline is completely impassable, except by small fishing vessels. And I must add—" he leaned a little closer as their horses trotted side by side "—the fishing off the Lydian coast is excellent."

Gisela beamed at him. "Then I must be sure to sample the fish while I am here."

Her sunny expression highlighted her beauty, in spite of the bandage slung across her face at an angle to cover only her right eye.

John returned his attention to the road. He didn't need to be reminded of the woman's loveliness or the power she held to sway his heart with only a smile.

She, too, seemed to feel the need to keep their conversation on the approved topic. "Now I understand how Lydia has survived since New Testament times. But how is it that the Illyrians threaten you now?"

"The Illyrians have been a source of irritation for the past few centuries. As their population has grown, they've sought to expand their boundaries."

"They do seem to involve themselves in constant warfare." Gisela sounded thoughtful.

Her response intrigued him. How did she feel about marrying into a battle-hungry empire? Would she be able to influence the Illyrians toward more peaceful relations with their neighbors? If she could, her friendship would be worth any strain on his emotional state.

Encouraged, he finished his story. "They have made several attacks on our borderlands over the years. The most recent was four years ago." John felt his throat swell at the memory of that battle.

"Were you King of Lydia then?"

John let out a slow breath. "Not when the battle began. My father died defending a village called Bcrn. I was at his side."

"I'm sorry."

"We were outnumbered, vastly outnumbered. We never had a chance. Their attack was unprovoked. We weren't expecting them. My father had brought me there as part of his annual tour. The Illyrians heard about our visit and struck just as we reached the village. We should have fallen back when the first wave of attackers hit. If we had, my father would still be alive."

Chapter Six

The sun had begun to set, its red-tinged glow lighting on the distant towers of Castlehead, painting the fortress in shimmering gold.

Beautiful though the image was, Gisela's heart felt heavy. Sorrow carried through King John's account of the loss of his father. She hated to see the strong king's head bent in grief. More than that, she felt her anger rising against the enemies who had taken the Lydian village out of sheer greed.

"Who were these men who attacked you? I understand they are Illyrians, but many tribes go by that name, and not all war parties operate under the consent of their regional king."

"The war band moved northward again after the attack. The village was incorporated into the holdings of the nearest Illyrian king."

"The Illyrians have many kings, but they all must ultimately answer to the Empress Irene of Constantinople, who has an explicit agreement with my father to keep these lands where our two empires meet in a state of peace, with stable borders. Irene has granted my father leave to enforce that peace as needed, even if it means taking action on her side of the border. An unprovoked attack on a neutral kingdom like Lydia should not be tolerated. Who commissioned the attack?"

"To my understanding, the war party wasn't commissioned by any king. They were led by a rogue leader named Rab the Raider."

"Rab the Raider," Gisela repeated the name with a scowl. "He has a crooked nose?"

"Yes. They say his nose was broken in battle."

"His nose was broken by my father," Gisela seethed, "as an ever-present reminder that the kingdoms of the Roman Empire are to live at peace with one another and their neighbors. Rab's mother was Frankish, and he was raised under my father's rule. But rumors say his father is a man of some rank among the Illyrians, and that is why Rab roves these borders. Whatever the reason for Rab's actions, my father made it perfectly clear that acts of war would not be tolerated—not within the Holy Roman Empire, nor along her borders, nor against her neutral neighbors such as yourself."

"When was this?"

"It was the first year I was old enough to travel with my father on his imperial tour. I was fourteen. That would make it six years ago. And your father died when?"

"Four years ago this winter," John answered.

Gisela felt her fury mounting as they drew closer to the king's fortress. "Rab the Raider was supposed to be under the supervision of a local tribal king."

"Do you know which king?"

King John's question was innocent enough, considering that he didn't already know the answer. He didn't know the name of Gisela's future husband. He didn't know that her future in-laws had benefited from his father's death—that the family of the man she was supposed to marry should have prevented the battle that killed John's father.

Castlehead lay before them, and Gisela spurred her mount forward, launching into a gallop. She could see Boden, the acting captain, on a boat nearing the shore. He'd likely been making provisions to head out again.

King John cried out behind her, asking what had caused her to sprint away, but she kept her good eye focused on the road and encouraged her horse to run faster. She couldn't face King John. How could she admit to him that she was pledged to be married into the family that sheltered his enemies and held the town that had been stolen from him?

Instead she met Boden on the wharf. He'd spotted her rapid approach and ran up the dock to meet her.

"Your Highness? Whatever is wrong?"

She slid from her horse and found herself panting from the exertion of the swift ride. Her health had not yet returned completely. She glanced back to see King John riding at a full gallop toward the wharf.

Her message would have to be delivered quickly. "Is the ship provisioned to sail?"

"Yes. Everything is loaded but your personal items, which have been placed in a suite at the castle."

"Good. Have repairs been made to the ship?"

"All of them. Are you eager to sail? We can have your trunk returned."

"No. I need you to deliver a message to my father." Though young, she knew the captain was both honest and clever. He'd have no trouble accurately relaying her words. "My life has been saved by King John, the Healer of Lydia. I owe him a debt of gratitude. For that reason, I cannot in good conscience marry Warrick until a certain murderer has been disciplined. The man who killed King John's father is under the protection of Warrick's family."

Anger flashed in Boden's eyes, as well. "While we've been in port I have heard about this man—the one who killed the Lydian king, Theodoric. It was Rab the Raider, the notorious warmonger. Didn't your father break his nose?"

"Yes." Gisela smiled, feeling confident now that Boden would have no trouble remembering the names of those involved. Still, she asked him to repeat back the message so she could be sure he'd gotten it right. Her smile grew as he accurately recounted everything she'd said.

"Good man." She clapped him on the shoulders. "Tell my father that Warrick's household must chasten Rab the Raider and make compensation to Lydia. Can you carry the message to Rome?"

"The men are all on board, Your Highness. We can sail straightaway. Are you sure you'll be safe if I leave you here?" Boden looked up the road to where John rode toward them, his pace slowed only slightly as he studied them, as though wondering if he ought to interrupt.

"Far safer than I would be in Illyria. You'll be sure to carry the message to my father?"

"Swiftly and accurately, Your Highness."

"Good. Godspeed to you."

"Should I wait for the king—"

"Please, no. Leave before he reaches us."

"Give him my thanks. His household has provisioned us well." Boden broke away and clambered back into the rowboat. Seconds later the oarsmen had pushed off, and they were headed back to the ship at a steady clip, each dip of their oars rippling through waters painted red by the dying light of the sun.

John's boots echoed against the planks of the dock as he approached her.

Gisela prayed silently that God would help her to explain what she'd done—and that King John wouldn't blame her for her association with the men who'd killed his father.

"Your Highness?" John's deep voice sent a shiver of awareness up her spine. His words carried concern along with a hinting suspicion of betrayal.

She chided herself for her reaction. She was promised to Prince Warrick. Depending on the political maneuvering her father might have to engage in to convince Warrick's family to discipline Rab the Raider, she'd likely be bound more strongly to her contract, with an increase in dowry and other contingencies tacked on for their trouble.

But it would be worth it, knowing that the man who'd killed John's father would be held accountable for his crimes. She owed King John for her life. She'd already very nearly started a war by forcing him to the Illyrian border. How could she sleep at night knowing her future family was in allegiance with the rogue who'd killed King Theodoric?

"Are you all right?" King John stepped closer while Gisela gathered her thoughts.

She turned to face him with a meek smile, fearing she'd insulted him by riding off so swiftly. And yet, if he'd known what she was doing, he might have tried to prevent her. "I'm better now."

"Why have you sent Boden back to the ship? He and his men may sup with us tonight. Shall I call him back?"

"Please, no." She took hold of his outstretched arm. "I've dispatched him to carry a message to my father."

Distress shot through John's concerned expression. "He's leaving you here?"

"It's the safest place for me while I recuperate. If you don't wish to have me as your guest, I can find lodging in Sardis."

"Of course you are more than welcome to be my guest, but, Your Highness—"

"Thank you. My father will compensate you for your trouble." She dropped his arm and started to step past him up the dock. Hilda had broken away from the riding party as well and advanced upon them at her fastest lumbering speed. If Gisela waited for the maid to arrive, she'd waste many long minutes, so she set off to greet her.

"I am not in need of compensation." King John cupped her elbow and turned her back to face him.

She looked down at his hand.

"I'm sorry." He withdrew his hand quickly. His accent grew stronger—an indication, she'd noticed, that his passions were rising. "I must understand why you've sent your ship back to your father. Isn't your prince expecting you?"

"By Christmastide," she admitted, praying the date wouldn't be moved forward as part of the negotiation process. "But that is still three months away. Boden can reach my father and be back in plenty of time." She tried to keep her tone cool, but John's concern, as well as her guilt at what she had yet to confess, softened her words until they sounded nearly like an apology.

King John shook his head, obviously trying to understand. "Have I offended you?"

Guilt speared through her. Perhaps she ought to have discussed the message before she ran off toward the wharf. But she got the distinct sense that John would have protested her intentions. And she was determined to have the message delivered. Powerful men were always trying to "advise" her. They hated giving heed to a woman.

But perhaps she hadn't been fair to assume John would have done the same. From all she knew of him, he was caring and attentive. But he was, still, a man. The two thoughts warred inside her as her thumping heart pounded with guilt.

When she didn't answer, he prompted her, "Your Highness?"

"If anyone should be offended—" she looked up at him with her one good eye and wished she could see him better "—*you* should be offended by my behavior. It was rude of me to run off without warning, but I needed to reach Boden."

"He was coming to shore. You wouldn't have missed him."

"I wanted to speak with him before you arrived."

"If you'd asked me to, I would have lingered behind. As it was, I hastened to learn if you were in distress." He dipped his head and looked into her face more closely, blinking in the absence of light since the sun had set and the stars had not yet appeared. "Are you in distress?"

"Perhaps somewhat," she admitted reluctantly.

"I apologize for any alarm my story may have caused you—"

"No, please, I am the one who needs to apologize."

"Why should—"

Gisela cut him off before he could ask another question. "Your father's death. His unconscionable loss." She let her good eye settle closed for a moment, blocking out the sight of the pain that filled his face at the mention of his beloved late father. Searching for words, she asked him, "Have I ever told you the name of my betrothed?"

"An Illyrian prince. There are many."

"I am pledged to be married to Prince Warrick, eldest son of Garren, King of the Dometian tribe."

Angry realization flashed in his eyes, but Gisela pressed on before he could react to her confession. "The very house that pledged six years ago to restrain Rab the Raider and prevent him from further warmongering."

"They count the village of Bern among their holdings."

"I can only pray that is through some oversight, but whatever the cause, I've dispatched Boden to explain the situation to my father, and compel the king to discipline Rab for your father's murder."

John studied her face as the first stars began to appear in the eastern sky. Gisela wished she was brave enough to return his gaze, but she felt far too ashamed for her association with those who had committed such grave crimes against his kingdom and his family.

Hilda approached, stopping at the head of the wharf with her hands at her hips. "Your Highness," she gasped for breath.

"It's all right, Hilda. Everything is all right."

"The ship," Hilda wheezed frightfully. "It's leaving."

"I know. I sent it away."

A series of groans and whines carried up the dock as the maid slumped to sit on one of the many boulders that lined the shore. "They've abandoned us here?"

"Lydia is a very pleasant place." Gisela picked her way up the dock, holding on to the arm King John had offered her as she made her way to shore, and then up the road toward the Castlehead fortress.

"I'm glad you find it so," John murmured softly. "I imagine dinner has already been served for the night, but I suppose you'd prefer to take a light supper in your room. Tomorrow, if it pleases you, we'll have a noontime feast celebrating your arrival. I'd be honored if you'd agree to attend."

"Thank you for the kind invitation." Though normally not particularly fond of formalities, for the moment she was glad to retreat to the safety offered by speaking the expected words. It was certainly preferable to not speaking at all.

"I'll have a room made up for you and your attendant." He paused and studied her face until she was forced to meet his eyes. "Please promise me you won't run off without telling me where you're going? The Illyrians aren't to be trusted, and they may have sympathizers among us. I wouldn't presume to limit your freedoms, Your Highness, but it is for your own safety."

Gisela smiled meekly, knowing her sudden flight had caused him undue vexation. "I shall do my best not to bring any further trouble upon your household. That includes taking care not to endanger myself and risk international war."

A smirk bent his lips, letting her know he appreciated her appraisal of their predicament.

"And I'm sorry to have been so much trouble," she added.

He squeezed her hand briefly before letting it go. "You have been no more trouble than you are worth."

Attendants hurried out toward them, bowing as they approached, and within seconds Gisela found herself pulled away, off to find some promised tub of steaming water large enough to soak in, where the trunk that held her clothes had been taken, and supper—she'd overheard John telling a courtier that she'd expressed interest in sampling the fish.

It wasn't until the tub soaked away her worries and her stomach was calmed of its clamoring for food, that she had a moment to consider the words King John had spoken.

You have been no more trouble than you are worth.

Warmth flooded her on a deeper level than the tub waters could ever reach. The good king, she'd realized already, had a gift for speaking deliberate, well-measured words. He'd certainly known what he was saying when he'd paid her such a compliment.

She'd caused a great deal of trouble.

In spite of his exhaustion, King John lay awake, disquieted by doubts raging inside him. By rights, he should have checked Gisela's injury before retiring for the evening. He'd promised to suture the gash to minimize the appearance of the scar—and should have performed the procedure already.

But the thought of being sufficiently close to the princess to study her eyelid was enough to send him running to the far end of the castle, or even to the far end of his kingdom.

He tossed and turned on his bed trying to sort out why she had such an effect on him.

It wasn't just her beauty. The festering wound on her face had done enough to minimize that, though it could in no way diminish her stately bearing or the alluring curve of her lips.

John beat his pillow and tried not to think about her lips.

What would Princess Gisela say if she knew his thoughts? What would her *father* say? The good princess had done nothing unbecoming, save for the way she'd clung to him while on the brink of death, and he couldn't blame her for that, given the circumstances. Her behavior had been nothing but honest and pure. She was a godly, Christian woman who'd read the New Testament and knew the scriptures well. She was faultless, above reproach.

No, the fault was all his. He'd sworn never to look at another woman after his queen had died. He couldn't bring himself to consider another woman, even at his courtiers' urging. Why, then, did Gisela fill his thoughts? Why was he drawn to her like a bee to a flower?

John pushed aside his pillow and tried not to think about bees or flowers.

How long would it take for Boden to return, for Gisela to leave his household? At least a fortnight or two, and that was assuming favorable winds and avoiding the Saracens. How would he ever make it that long without pulling her into his arms and confessing the feelings she provoked in him?

How would he hide his feelings, which Luke had already begun to suspect, which were surely as visible as the glow of a candle in darkness? He couldn't avoid the woman. *That* wouldn't be proper at all. She was a guest in his house, and given her father's influence in the area, John knew he ought to do everything he could to foster friendship between them.

Friendship. Purely platonic, practically emotionless friendship. His relationship with Gisela should mimic his relationship with his little sister.

His little sister. Yes, Elisabette! *She* could help him. Bette was eighteen, only a couple of years younger than Princess Gisela. And ever since the loss of their mother when John was twelve and little Bette only two, there had been a void of royal womanly leadership in their household.

John thanked God for providing him with a solution to so many problems all at once. Gisela could mentor Bette.

The two would become fast friends, Elisabette would learn the ways of a royal woman and John wouldn't have to torture himself by pretending to feel nothing in Gisela's presence, because *he* wouldn't be the one spending time with her—his sister would.

He could ride off to the borderlands and monitor his brother, and all would be well.

As well as they could be, anyway, given that he fell asleep with his thoughts dancing with visions of the golden-haired beauty.

"King John to see you, Your Highness."

Gisela's heart rate quickened at Hilda's announcement. She checked her reflection in the large mirror of polished silver that hung on one wall of the suite she'd been appointed.

She looked as well as she had in a week. Even her right eye was now capable of opening, though she'd replaced the bandage to hide the ugly gash. "See him in."

Gisela rose to greet the king. In the full daylight that streamed through the large open windows with the lush ocean breeze, the king looked even better than he had the day before. Hilda bowed low before retreating through the curtained doorway to the bedroom, leaving Gisela and John more or less alone in the open receiving room.

Birdsong and the laughter of men in the courtyard below reminded her that she had nothing to fear, even if the king hadn't already proven himself to be honorable. No, her fear stemmed from the growing sense of attraction she felt toward the king and the knowledge that she must somehow stifle her inappropriate affections. Warrick would expect her heart to be his alone.

So she couldn't possibly let King John capture any more of it.

"Your Majesty." She was tempted to mimic Hilda's bow but settled for dipping her head slightly his way. She was the emperor's daughter, after all. There was no reason for her to bow to King John, just because everyone else did.

"Your Highness." He dipped his head in return. "Did you find your accommodations acceptable?"

"More than acceptable. I adore this ocean air—the scent is fresh, the temperature perfect and there are no insects."

"Then perhaps I shall have some ocean air bottled up and delivered as a wedding gift. Prince Warrick lives many leagues inland, past the mountains."

Gisela appreciated the reminder of her approaching wedding. It was nearly enough to keep her heart from fluttering at John's witty response. Still, she couldn't help giggling, whether from nerves or his words or the way her heart shivered happily when he smiled at her.

Fortunately, King John moved on. "I hope I'm not intruding, but I do recall having promised to suture that gash for you. The procedure probably should have taken place yesterday, but this morning will have to do."

"Thank you for remembering. I examined my eye in the mirror this morning and was hoping you'd take a look at it." Gisela saw that the king carried a small wooden box, which he placed on a side table next to a vase of fresh-cut flowers. "Should I sit?"

"Sit or stand, however you're most comfortable. The biggest issue will be the pain. I must warn you, the eye is a particularly sensitive area. I've brought along an herbal numbing solution—" he opened his box and drew out a small bottle "—but it will only decrease the sensation, not limit it entirely."

"I see." The procedure didn't sound very pleasant,

though Gisela was certain it needed to be done. She wanted to look her best for her marriage and that meant dealing with the scar above her eye before it was too late to do anything about it.

"There's a fine beam of sunshine coming in through the window." John picked up the table and set it closer to the sunbeam. "This will be the best spot for me to see what I'm doing."

Gisela followed him and stood in the bright beam of light. "I suppose I should stand," she noted as he reached toward her with a small brush, which he'd dipped in the bottle of numbing solution. She held herself still as he peeled back the bandage that covered her eye. "How does it look?"

"It's healing nicely." He daubed the tender spot with the numbing solution. "I believe I should be able to close up the scar with two or three stitches. I've brought my finest needle, and a slender thread of silk." He held it up for her inspection.

"Thank you for your consideration." The silk thread was so fine she could hardly see it at all. And she knew from her earlier examination of the wound that it needed attention. Still, she found herself growing tense at the thought of being stitched up so close to her eye.

John must have sensed her nervous state. "Breathe slowly and deeply. The most important thing will be for you to hold completely still. Don't get nervous or you might twitch at the wrong moment."

Panic nipped at her. "I might twitch," she confessed.

"No." He held her head steady with one hand and met her eyes. "Breathe with me. In—" He paused. "Hold it until you feel your lungs asking for air. Now out, slowly. And breathe in again."

She gazed back at him and felt a sense of heady calm

envelop her. "I've never paid so much attention to breathing." She followed his lead as he led her through the pattern again.

"Feeling calmer now?"

"Yes, thank you." She'd breathed in the woodsy scent of him. It evoked memories of the way he'd made her feel protected and cared for on their flight through the woods. How luxurious would it feel to rest against him again? And yet, that was the very indulgence she must try to avoid.

"Good. All right now, keep breathing. In, hold it." The tip of his needle touched her eyelid.

Gisela froze. The numbing solution dulled the pain, but she could still feel the movement of the needle as it passed through her skin. She wanted to cry out, but she knew the men in the courtyard would hear, and the last thing she needed was for an audience to come running and witness the rest of the procedure.

"You're doing very well. Don't forget to breathe out." His fingers caressed her skin lightly as he held her face steady. "Stay calm," the king whispered. "You're doing just fine."

Reassured by his words, she focused on breathing in again as he leaned closer, intent on his work, his brow knit with focus, his lips slightly pursed. Gisela had closed her right eye while he worked on it, but in the brilliant illumination the sunbeam provided, she was able to study his face at close range as she hadn't before.

He'd shaved off the stubbly beard that had grown over the course of their travels. While her father and many of the other kings she knew preferred to wear a well-trimmed beard, John's strong jawline was most favorably displayed without any obscuring facial hair.

"Remember to breathe," John whispered, all his attention on his work.

Gisela realized she needed the reminder. She exhaled slowly, still captivated by watching his face as he worked. The man had a fine, high forehead and deep blue eyes. His nose was well shaped and not as prominent as her father's and his skin, in its freshly shorn condition, begged to be touched.

A hum escaped her lips as she exhaled again and tried to disregard the sensation of the thread passing through her skin. Her fingers itched. She needed to hold on to something to distract her from what the king was doing, but there was nothing to hold on to.

Her arms rose of their own accord.

"Breathe in," John reminded her.

She inhaled as instructed and grabbed his tunic at the waist, bunching the fabric between her fingers to ease the tension she felt.

John paused and glanced down.

"Sorry." Gisela bit her lip.

"You're fine. I should have thought to give you something to hold on to. We're almost done. One more stitch. Can you make it, or shall I pause?"

"I'm fine. Finish quickly if you can." She didn't let go of his tunic. The needle speared through her skin and she breathed out slowly, twisting his tunic in her hands as she waited for the moment to pass. "Are you done, then?"

"That was the first half of the stitch."

"They come in halves?" Her tense hum raised in pitch. Gisela fought to keep her volume down. She still didn't want to attract any attention, even if he was almost done.

John finished the stitch and nipped off the remaining thread with scissors.

Gisela slumped against him, still tightly gripping his

tunic. "You're done now?" Her question came out almost as a moan.

"I'm done. You did very well." He settled his arms lightly against her back.

Trembling with relief, Gisela knew she ought to peel herself away from him, but she'd used up all her reserves of fortitude holding still for so long. He didn't push her away, and she didn't move. She breathed in his calming scent and wished she had an excuse to hold him without letting go.

Chapter Seven

John was pleased with how the sutures had turned out. Perhaps that was why, when Gisela embraced him, he didn't immediately step out of her arms. That, and standing near enough to her to stitch up her wound had stirred up a longing to be far closer still, and she settled against him like a bird to its nest, clinging tenaciously to his tunic as though she feared he might try to wrest her away.

"Your Highness?" He settled his arms against her back, unsure what foreign custom she might be invoking, or what the prescribed reaction on his part might be. Perhaps all Frankish royalty embraced after minor medical procedures.

"Thank you," she sniffled as she burrowed her face against his shoulder.

"Are you weeping?" he whispered a moment later, as she clung to him still, and he fought the urge to plant a kiss on the face that nuzzled just under his chin. The soft scent of rose water wafted up from her, further muddling his thoughts.

"My tears were provoked by the needle, I think." She pulled back from him and took a step away.

Though he could see her face clearly now at arm's length, he immediately missed her closeness.

But what was he thinking? They weren't supposed to be close. Her embrace was an indulgence he couldn't allow himself. He gathered his thoughts. "I should be able to remove the stitches in five or six days. I'll watch how it heals, but now that the infection is gone it appears to be mending rapidly."

"I am indebted to you for your expert help." She looked up at him through lashes that glistened with moisture.

John felt a stab of irrational fear. He'd had enough difficulty resisting her when her face was swollen with infection and her wit muted by fever. How would he ever keep his feelings suppressed once she was completely healed and in possession of all her feminine faculties?

The princess continued. "I know you have said I owe you no debt, but in truth you must realize I owe you my life and would do anything for you. While I am here these next several weeks living off your generosity, if there is anything I can do, any service I can render, please name it. I'm afraid I suffer from a horrible sense of indebtedness, and I'd give anything to appease that sensation, however slightly."

"Your Highness." John fought off the temptation to request her embrace as full payment. The last thing he needed was to have her in his arms again. And yet, he so ached to hold her. He stepped back toward the side table where he'd left his box and fiddled with putting his things away, taking far longer than was necessary as he tried to straighten his thoughts.

He did not want or need her touch, nor would it be appropriate for him to request it.

So why did he find it so difficult not to beg to have her in his arms again?

"I have a sister." He managed to only slightly mangle the order of his words as he shoved his thoughts into proper order. "Slightly younger than your age. Elisabette. Our mother died when she was two. She's had many maids, of course, and we've courtiers to guide her. Your Highness has no doubt had the best possible imperial training in etiquette. Since you'll be with us and might enjoy female companionship, I thought perhaps you could befriend her and encourage her in the art of regal behavior."

Gisela beamed at him with such happiness that John was forced to look back down at the box he carried, though he'd already closed it and it held no interest. It was that or stare at his own pale face in the mirror before he fled in terror from the longing he felt.

"I would be most honored to make your sister's acquaintance." Gisela threw up her hands in delight.

John shuffled away before she could embrace him again. Frankish custom or not, he doubted he could endure another without confessing his feelings. "She'll lunch with us. I'll introduce you then." He fled for the door, then spun around, fearing an abrupt exit might be too rude, but not knowing what he could safely say without risking further exposure of his true emotions.

Nor did the princess seem eager for him to leave. On the contrary, she followed after him and asked, "Does the fortress have a chapel?"

"Yes. We have services there on Sunday and Wednesday mornings."

"Oh."

"Does that disappoint you?" He judged from her fallen features that it did.

"My father insists on daily worship services. Hilda

and I kept the tradition on the ship, but I'd missed praising God in a larger community."

"I pray and study the scriptures daily." John felt suddenly inadequate. "As a private discipline."

"Oh!" Her face brightened.

Realizing he ought to make an invitation for her to join him, John immediately regretted revealing his personal spiritual practices. Praying daily with Gisela would be impossible. His heart wouldn't handle it, not without increasing affection for her. And he didn't need that.

"The midweek service will be tomorrow—Wednesday." He felt as though he'd offered her a meager consolation. The woman wanted to worship God. He couldn't begrudge her that. "Perhaps I can speak to our deacon about holding services more frequently," he offered, recalling only after he'd spoken that old Bartholomew went to Sardis when he wasn't at Castlehead, and likely couldn't add anything more to his schedule.

But Princess Gisela looked pleased. "I shall pray on my own again today, and look forward to the worship service tomorrow."

John felt grateful that she was willing to accept what had to be a disappointing answer. "You're free to explore the castle and grounds with your maid, or I can provide attendants, if you prefer. I would gladly give you a tour myself, but I'm afraid I must make preparations before leaving to monitor the situation at the border."

"Yes, of course. I understand. I'm so sorry for disrupting—"

"Please don't apologize. None of this is your fault."

She nodded in understanding, though she did not appear to be convinced. "Yes, Your Majesty."

John wished there was some way for him to reassure her completely, but he couldn't think of anything—could hardly think at all, with the majority of his mental faculties intent on absorbing the radiance of her beauty. Her response goaded him. "You don't have to call me that."

"Your Majesty?"

"Your Highness, you may address me as John."

"I couldn't possibly—"

"My title is for use by subordinates. You're the daughter of the emperor."

"He's not your emperor. We're on your soil. I suppose I should bow to you as your servants do."

"No." John took a step closer to her with a stomp of finality. "I forbid you to bow to anyone in my kingdom. *I* should bow to you—protocol would dictate I do so on imperial soil."

"We are not currently in my father's empire. You are the ruler here." Her eyes glinted up at him with challenge in their blue depths.

"I've told you already—you owe me nothing. No debt of gratitude, and certainly not any deference." John wavered between taking her by the shoulders and backing toward the door again. Really, he ought to leave. Why was it so difficult for him to excuse himself from her presence? But he had to make her understand so they could avoid having the same conversation again.

"Your Majes—"

His finger covered her lips before she finished the word. Her wide eyes mirrored his shock.

He withdrew his hand quickly. "I apologize. Your lips—" He licked his own and tried to make them utter coherent words. "Forbidden."

Princess Gisela stared at him as though his touch had frozen her.

"I'm so sorry. I must go." Bowing deeply to her from the doorway, he fled.

* * *

"Your Highness?" a servant called from the doorway. "Lunch is ready. If you'll follow me?"

"One moment, please." Gisela bit the side of her finger as she paced the room.

She couldn't face him. How could she face King John? He'd bowed to her. She'd embraced him. He'd touched her lips—they burned with awareness at the contact. They burned for his contact still.

"Your Highness?" The female voice drew closer as the servant approached the bedroom through the waiting room.

Gisela couldn't put off their meeting any longer. She'd promised to meet the king's sister, to befriend the girl and teach her all about proper regal behavior. That she could do easily enough. Hilda and the maids back home were all the time reminding her of proper regal behavior, most especially whenever she did anything they felt transgressed those standards, which was often.

"Coming." She followed the woman through the hallways, thinking frantically. How was she supposed to address the king now? He'd said she ought to call him John, but that sounded impossibly *familiar*. She had to keep the formal titles prominently displayed between them at all times. They were quite nearly the only wall she could find to put up between them.

The enticing scent of finely prepared food drifted down the hallways as they neared the dining hall. Gisela felt her stomach rumble. After hardly eating at all during her illness, her appetite had returned clamoring to make up for every morsel she'd lost out on.

Lovely. She'd just turn her attention from King John and focus on eating, then. The food smelled good enough to gorge upon. There was no rule that said a proper princess shouldn't have a healthy appetite, though Hilda often chided her if she thought she'd taken too many helpings, especially of dessert. But that, Gisela suspected, was only so the maid could gobble up the leftovers as she returned the dishes to the kitchen.

Gisela didn't begrudge Hilda her interest in food. She had the woman's appetite to thank for her absence now—Hilda had excused herself an hour before to see if the cooks needed help in the kitchen. With the maid gone, Gisela had been free to pace and fret and repeat snippets of her conversation with the king to herself while watching her reflection in the mirror, in order to analyze every interaction and determine how much of a fool she'd made of herself.

Enough of a fool that she wanted to grab hold of the sides of the doorway to the dining room like a cat being dragged off to its bath and scramble away before she had to face the king again.

Unfortunately, the very regal protocol she'd promised to teach Elisabette stipulated that she not cling to doorways, yowling and trying to escape.

"Your Highness." King John appeared in the doorway just as she was longingly examining the stonework.

Startled, she straightened herself to the proper regal posture. "You can't address me like that," she refuted quietly, leaning close so others wouldn't hear. "If I'm to call you *John,* then you must address me as *Gisela.*"

"*Princess* Gisela," the king countered.

She shook her head, not trusting herself to speak and walk at the same time. King John had taken her arm to escort her in and had stolen her voice in the process.

The room was already full of strangers dressed in fine lace and silks. Either the Lydians held themselves to higher luncheon apparel standards than the people of the northern regions, or word of her arrival had spread, and King John's courtiers had dressed in their finest for her. With a sinking stomach, Gisela realized she didn't know any of them.

The king seemed to sense her apprehension and patted her arm as he led her toward the first beaming cluster of noblemen and ladies. "Don't worry, no one expects you to remember any names. They've all heard about your brush with death, and they're excited to meet you. But if you feel overwhelmed and want to leave—" he leaned close so his whispers wouldn't be overheard "—just stomp on my foot three times and we'll make our escape."

Gisela nodded, still not trusting her voice, and feeling all the more indebted by his thoughtfulness. As the courtiers turned and bowed low to greet them, Gisela couldn't help wondering how many times she'd have to stomp on John's foot if she wanted to escape from *him*. She found his presence on her arm more overwhelming than the crowds that filled the room. She was used to being surrounded by courtiers, even if the folks at home tended to be rowdier and less interested in impressing her. But the effect King John had on her was both unfamiliar and unsettling.

They made the rounds until smiling faces blurred together in her mind and she'd lost track of everyone but King John himself. To his credit, he never once let go of her arm and even thoughtfully supplied her with a light tea to drink, which was helpful since his proximity tended to make her mouth go dry.

Just as she'd begun to wonder if there would ever be any food served or if she was doomed to circle endlessly through a sea of strangers, John led her to the head of the table, where two chairs indicated she'd be seated at his side.

She'd never sat at the head of a table before. Her father's household was filled with aunts and uncles and siblings of far higher rank than she. Even when she traveled, it had always before been with older siblings who were given precedence above her. She'd feel more comfortable squeezing onto the side benches with the lesser nobility than sitting in a high-backed chair beside the king.

John must have sensed her panic, though she tried not to show it.

"Is the seating arrangement acceptable? Do you need to step out before we eat?"

"Do you intend for me to sit beside you?"

"I thought, given our earlier discussion about rank, that an equal sitting arrangement would be most practical. Or I can have your chair placed upon a raised dais, if you prefer."

She leaned close to him and turned her head so those present wouldn't witness her distress. "I've never been seated at the head of a table before. Everyone will be able to see me."

"You're very lovely to look upon."

"But I don't know your local customs. How will I know what to do? If I make a mistake it will be visible to everyone." She kept her voice to a whisper, but it inched up several panicked octaves. Having John on her arm was distracting enough, and circulating through the crowd had drained her sense of decorum. And she was absolutely starving. What if she fell ravenously on her food and made a fool of herself?

"Watch me carefully. Do what I do. If you're not sure, ask. You can always stomp my foot, you know." He looked apologetic and gestured to the place setting. "We only have one gold cup. Do you mind terribly sharing with me?"

"I've always shared a cup with someone." Gisela looked down the long table and saw that John's guests would be sharing silver cups by twos and threes. No one would expect even a king to own enough cups for so many guests to have their own. And yet, the thought of drinking from John's cup sent a shiver through her. She hoped he wouldn't notice the faint color that rose to her cheeks.

Fortunately, John was looking past her. "Ah, here comes my sister."

Gisela turned to see a dark-haired young woman approaching them, the rich brown tones of her delicately embroidered dress matching the color of her kohl-rimmed eyes. The way Elisabette's hair had been piled in delicate curls atop her head told Gisela the girl had spent far more time primping for the luncheon than she had.

Suddenly she felt backward in her simple long braid and pale green gown and wondered if she'd have anything to teach John's sophisticated little sister. Her hands were far more used to swords and horse reins than makeup brushes and curling wands, and though Hilda would have loved to pile Gisela's hair in elaborate settings, Gisela didn't have the patience for anything more than a practical braid. At least she'd had the presence of mind to clasp jewels around her neck and wrists. Still, she felt a far cry from the picture of sophisticated beauty Elisabette presented.

Gisela feared Elisabette might look down upon her for her lack of patient primping, but the girl smiled warmly as she bowed to greet them, and a moment later everyone began to find their seats.

To Gisela's relief, John had Elisabette seated beside her, and the food was quickly served. She recognized fish and cucumbers and olives, though their preparations were unfamiliar to her, and there were more foods she couldn't identify. John told her their names, but she'd heard enough names meeting people that she didn't bother trying to remember what any of the food was called for fear of confusing the two and accidentally calling a courtier by the name of an entrée at their next meeting. If she addressed a nobleman as Sir Fish, she might start another war.

Fortunately, Elisabette kept up a constant stream of questions, asking her about her wedding plans, travel experiences and the customs of her homeland, so that Gisela had to constantly stop eating to answer, which served to keep her from eating as quickly as she'd feared she might.

For the final course, broiled pears were served with a drizzle of spiced honey, and Gisela savored the dessert to the last bite. Then John stood and thanked their guests before dismissing them and turning to her. "Would you like to retire to your room to rest?"

"Is that what I'm expected to do?" she questioned, still feeling the eyes of many upon her.

"You may do as you like." He smiled warmly.

"What will you be doing?"

"I need to run drills with my men. Today is Tuesday—on Thursday I will meet my brother again at the border. There is much to be accomplished before then."

Gisela felt an instant twinge of disappointment—at the reminder that she'd sparked the situation on the borderlands and that King John would be leaving shortly. She told herself to be glad he'd be gone. At least then she wouldn't embarrass herself with him again. But at the same time, the mention of his pending journey triggered a sense of loss inside her, even though he hadn't yet left.

"I suppose I am tired."

"I'll have an attendant escort you to your room." He

dipped his head in a gesture that wasn't nearly a bow but still reminded her of the one he'd given when he'd left her room that morning.

"Thank you for all your many kindnesses."

"Thank you, Your Highness." He handed her off to the attendant who'd been hovering near before he weaved through the crowded room in the other direction.

She watched as he disappeared through the dispersing crowd, and could almost see the burden of impending war that hung on his shoulders like a mantle. She felt sorrowful that he had to bear such a burden alone—without his father's guidance, or the loving support of a queen beside him. Further, she felt guilty for whatever role she'd played in placing that burden on him. Surely there was something she could do to ease its weight. But what?

As Princess Gisela had feared, John's sister, Elisabette, was primarily interested in the very feminine and domestic pursuits that Gisela had spent most of her youth trying to avoid. And the girl wanted to quiz Gisela about her pending nuptials, which made Gisela squirm.

Gisela wanted to avoid talking about her upcoming wedding in order to prevent Bette from learning of the connection between the family into which she'd soon be married and the man who'd killed King Theodoric. Knowing how deeply John despised the man who'd killed his father, Gisela wasn't about to let that wall come up between her and Bette.

The two of them had so precious little in common anyway.

Once she'd finally convinced Bette that she truly didn't know what she'd be wearing on her wedding day, Elisabette reluctantly dropped the subject and quizzed

Gisela on what she did for entertainment in the emperor's palace.

"When we're on tours of the kingdom or in Rome, we do a lot of hunting."

"Even the women?"

"Oh, yes. Have you ever seen any of the great tapestries depicting the splendor of the hunt? The women ride alongside the men and dogs. It's great sporting fun, and I confess I've become rather handy with a bow and arrow."

"And what do you do when you're not traveling or hunting?"

"When we're in the Frankish capital of Aachen, we take a lot of baths." Gisela figured they'd have that much at least, in common, given Bette's interest in grooming activities.

But Bette only frowned. "For fun?"

"We have spas fed by hot springs in Aachen. It's relaxing."

Bette looked unconvinced. "But what do you do to enjoy yourself?"

Abandoning all hope of identifying an activity they both appreciated, Gisela admitted her favorite sport. "Fencing."

"Swordplay?" Bette's eyes lit up.

"Yes. Sometimes we organize sword-fighting tournaments."

To Gisela's surprise, Elisabette looked sincerely excited. "Do you think we could organize a fencing tournament?"

Gisela was glad to have finally found an interest she and Bette held in common. More important, if the borderlands really were in need of increased defense, a fencing tournament might be just the thing to encourage John's men to hone their skills, while identifying those who were already proficient. Acute guilt continued to plague her for the role she'd played in provoking the threat of war. If she could do something to help, perhaps that would assuage her guilt.

Perhaps John would be pleased.

"I believe we could organize a tournament in a matter of days, but before we begin, we should most certainly ask your brother's permission."

Bette frowned. "Can't we surprise him?"

"I'm afraid I've surprised him more than enough already."

"Verily, you speak the truth." Elisabette sighed. "I don't suppose *you'd* mind being the one to ask him?"

Chapter Eight

King John did not look to be in a good mood when Gisela approached him across the training field. She prayed silently that God would grant her favor with the king.

To her relief, his frown changed to a smile when he turned from instructing his men and spotted her approaching.

"Princess Gisela—" he dipped his head in deference "—you appear to be recovering quite well from your injuries."

"With many thanks to you," she acknowledged with a gracious smile. "I feel as though I'm almost my old self again."

"What brings you to the training field?"

"A request."

"Granted," he assured her without hesitation. "Whatever you desire will be done. I've instructed Eliab and Urias to carry out any request you might make."

While John stepped away to give further training orders to his men, Gisela stood still and weighed his words. His generosity humbled her. Even as a princess in the emperor's household she had never been treated with such regard, being a lesser noble in a household of many higher-ranking royals.

But she couldn't let King John's words distract her, nor did she feel she could proceed without his specific blessing—not given the scope of her project.

"Your Highness?" John appeared to be surprised that she was still waiting for him when he turned around.

Knowing he was busy and unwilling to waste any more of his time, Gisela got straight to the point. "Elisabette and I would like to host a fencing tournament among your men."

The sudden clang of swords cut off her words as the soldiers' training exercises gained momentum.

But John must have heard her, because his face registered a growing smile, and for one giddy moment Gisela hoped she'd found a way to relieve some of the burden he bore after all.

The waves of men parted and John made his way back to her side. "A tournament would provide needed incentive for the men to train. Would the emperor's daughter agree to crown the winner?"

Gisela beamed. "I would be honored."

The plans came together with surprising speed. By that evening the word had spread among John's men, not just at Castlehead, but as far as the walled city of Sardis. Nearly everyone was enthusiastic about entering the contest and lent their support making preparations. They carved out five sparring pistes in the main courtyard and another two in each of the side yards, for a total of nine. Given the number of entrants, it would take several rounds just to work through the first level of elimination, but once the less-skilled swordsmen had been eliminated, they'd move through the leaderboard quickly.

For that reason, Gisela felt no compunction scheduling the first rounds for Friday at sunrise. Even if they fought straight through with no breaks between rounds, the tournament might last until sundown. Torches had been prepared to light the center piste, if necessary, so that the champion fight could be held even if the sun set first. And though some claimed they'd watch only as long as their favored combatant remained in the running, Gisela fully expected they'd find themselves caught up in the action, and doubted many would leave before the final victor was crowned.

Indeed, she'd prepared to host a crowd. Bleachers were built and the castle cooks prepared a menu of stick-speared foods the fans could eat while watching the games. She'd had some trouble convincing King John's naysaying courtiers, Eliab and Urias, to dispatch men to dig latrines alongside the field where the spectators would be allowed to camp. Though the gentlemen had scoffed at her concerns, she'd finally won the argument when she'd told them to choose between preparing beforehand or cleaning up afterward.

They'd put a crew on the job within the hour.

Eliab's and Urias's protests aside, the majority of King John's household hastened to fulfill her every request. As the project progressed, Gisela felt a rising sense of belonging, which only intensified when they hung a board to keep records on the large wall of the castle keep and she placed her personal insignia among those of the other men on the long row of participants. She stood back and smiled as she absorbed the sight, pleased with the appearance of her personal crest among the others.

Princess Elisabette sidled up beside her as she stood looking over the row of crests that lined the board. "Who will you be cheering for?" the younger woman asked.

"Myself."

"You're fighting?"

"You're not?"

Bette emitted a shocked laugh. "Isn't the entire point of the tournament to *watch* the men parry?" The girl had already expressed disappointment that they weren't planning to invite neighboring kingdoms. Gisela couldn't imagine why the girl would want such a thing, given the threat of war looming over them.

"The *point* is to develop skills among the men, so that they'll be able to defend themselves when need arises," Gisela explained, and was relieved to see King John approaching. His appearance provided her with an excuse to change the subject.

"King John," she greeted him. "I don't see your coat of arms among the others."

He shook his head regretfully. "I must leave tomorrow to visit my brother at the border. Prince Luke is expecting me."

"Tomorrow is only Thursday. Surely you'll be back in time for the tournament on Friday. It begins at dawn, but it will take hours to work through the first level of eliminations. If you arrive by midmorning—"

"I will do my best." John cut her off. "It will depend on what I learn from Prince Luke."

His words silenced her. In spite of his protests otherwise, she still felt responsible for the situation with the Illyrians. She knew John was desperately worried, not just about the possibility of war, but about his brother's safety, as well. As she understood it, John had two brothers, but the youngest, Mark, had left for a journey by ship and was long overdue to return—a poor sign given the known activity of Saracens at sea.

As long as John refused to remarry, Luke's safety was

imperative. Luke was next in line to the throne. Gisela longed to speak with John about the situation, but it wasn't her place. He still mourned the loss of his wife. And she was going to marry Warrick.

There was no point discussing such a painful subject especially when there wasn't anything she could do to ease his sorrow.

John decided to leave Wednesday evening immediately after supper. It would give him a greater chance of finishing his business with Luke and making it back in time for the tournament. It would also keep him from seeking out Gisela's company again.

He arrived at the borderland outpost feeling like a coward who'd turned and run at the first sign of danger. His brother, Prince Luke, wanted to launch an attack and take back the village of Bern. And all John could think about was the way he'd fled from Gisela as though the woman posed some sort of threat.

Technically, he figured, she *did* pose a threat—to his heart, and his convictions. The woman was betrothed in a politically sensitive engagement. His growing feelings for her were absolutely unacceptable, which was why it was doubly alarming that, even with the threat of war looming over him, he had to tear his thoughts from her to listen to Luke.

"The population of Bern is largely unchanged from what it was four years ago. They're Christians like us. They would be loyal Lydian citizens if they could stop paying Illyrian taxes and following Illyrian laws."

John rubbed his temples and tried to follow his brother's arguments as he sat at the low wooden table of the small woodland cottage that served as an outpost for

Luke and his men. "The regiment of Illyrian soldiers stationed there might feel differently."

"They'll be easy enough to rout."

John kneaded his forehead with both hands. "I told you about the messenger the princess sent to her father."

"Charlemagne is in Rome, a world away. Assuming the messenger arrives, what does Charlemagne care what happens on the edges of his kingdom? We aren't his vassals, and neither are the Illyrians."

"Nonetheless the Illyrians must answer to him. Charlemagne has imperial agreements with Empress Irene of Constantinople."

"Which is precisely why Charlemagne is unlikely to act directly in our defense." Luke pounded his fist on the table. "Would he not first bring up the matter with the empress herself?"

"That seems unlikely. Irene has granted Charlemagne leave to enforce peace along their borders. Princess Gisela seemed to think—"

"She's not Lydian," Luke snapped. "It doesn't matter what she thinks. She's the one who got us into this mess. You know that Illyrian died—the one we shot while you were in the river? If we don't strike first, there won't be time to wait for Charlemagne, if he cares to intervene, which I doubt."

"What are you proposing, brother?" John gave up trying to argue. His brother seemed to be working up to a point, and John wished Luke would stop arguing and express what he was waiting to say. "If we take Bern back, then what? Do you believe the Illyrians will be content to limp away, licking their wounds?"

"I don't believe the Illyrians will be content to sit back, no matter what we do." Luke flexed his fingers, setting off a ripple of cracking knuckles.

John looked up and watched his brother carefully. Cracked knuckles had always been a decisive signal for Luke that something weighed heavily on his mind. John held his breath and waited for his brother's pronouncement.

"He's back."

"Who?" John asked but sensed the answer. What other name were his men so loath to speak? What other answer could Luke possibly be so hesitant to express?

What other rogue had left in his wake prayers that he might never return?

"Rab the Raider."

John let out a long breath, then stood. If Rab was back, they didn't have the luxury of waiting for Charlemagne. The Raider was violent, unpredictable...cruel. He'd led their father to believe he was willing to negotiate, then killed Theodoric in cold blood the moment the king had lowered his sword.

They couldn't afford to take any chances.

John plucked up the drab hunting cloak he'd slung over the back of a chair, which effectively hid any symbols of his identity. "I'll leave at once for Sardis and arrange for couriers to carry updates between us twice daily. I want full reports of any and all activity. Where precisely is the Raider? What is he up to?"

"He arrived last night and is staying at a house in the village. I can only assume he was called in because of the fatality. One of the villagers has informed me that the Illyrian who died was a favorite of Rab's, possibly a relative."

"Blood for blood," John muttered, hating the rules of vengeance, which never ended anything, but only cried out for more. He shook his head. "After I've made arrangements in Sardis I'll continue on to Castlehead and recruit volunteers. I will not ask any man to fight who is not willing to risk his life."

"I understand. When do you plan to return?"

"That will depend on the messages you send me. If we can, I would above all prefer to wait until Charlemagne has responded to the message from his daughter."

"I don't believe that will be possible."

"You may be right," John admitted reluctantly. "Still, you know my policy."

"You refuse to shed blood unless it is the only way to prevent greater bloodshed."

John granted his brother a wry smile, grateful Luke had been willing to learn the words, even if he spoke them derisively. "I'll have to make haste if I'm going to reach Sardis before they close the city gates for the night."

"Godspeed to you, brother."

"Luke?" John waited until his brother looked up from the map of the valley he'd been studying. "Be careful. And keep an eye out for my falcon."

With the circuit of messengers established, John left Sardis to return to Castlehead as soon as the sun rose Friday morning. Moses seemed eager to run, so John let the stallion have his head. Why not? The horse seemed eager to stretch his legs.

And John was eager to get home and learn how the Frankish princess was fairing. He told himself there was no reason why he shouldn't feel he ought to check on her. After all, she was his guest, and he'd soon need to remove the stitches above her eye. He had a duty to make sure she enjoyed her stay.

For political reasons, of course.

It wasn't as though he intended to spend any time in her company, not with the fencing tournament set to begin that morning. If he arrived in time, he'd be busy sparring in the pistes. Princess Gisela could watch the tournament from the comfort of the balcony windows, far above the noise and bustle of the crowds. If he got the chance, he'd be certain to greet her and make sure she lacked no comfort.

And then he would do his best to forget she was even there.

Moses balked at the plank bridge that spanned the salty stream which divided the Castlehead peninsula from the mainland. "It's perfectly safe," he assured the horse, urging him across. As he'd predicted, they made it to the other side without incident. It was clear the ocean waves were cutting through the ravine, washing it ever wider, and might someday make an island of his home. But that wasn't likely to occur for several more centuries, or at least not in his lifetime.

Urging Moses on, John's ears prickled at the sounds that carried on the breeze. It sounded as though the tournament was well under way. As he neared the fortress, John saw milling crowds, and men practiced sparring with wooden swords around and between a village of tents that had popped up since he'd left.

John met his guards at the gate, and was relieved to see Renwick on duty. Handing off his horse, he took Renwick to the side and quizzed him rapidly.

"Am I too late to enter?"

"Your Majesty still has time. We haven't yet worked through the first level of the contestants. The men would be honored if you would fight among them. And your skills with the sword are without peer among your men— perhaps Princess Gisela will crown *you* with the wreath of laurels at the tournament's end?"

John felt happiness ripple through him at the thought.

As Renwick had implied, John had received, as heir to the throne, unparalleled training with the sword. Few in Lydia could equal him, save for his own brothers, and they were both away.

Perhaps, if Gisela saw him fighting, her respect for him would grow. She might even pass on word of his prowess to her father. At the very least, his men would recognize his skills. He'd need their trust if he was to lead them into battle. Everything Luke had told him at the border indicated a battle was inevitable.

"Hurry, then." John nodded to Renwick. "Help me with my gear."

They paused while Renwick passed on the order to enter King John in the tournament. Then Renwick laced up the king's leather and chain mail armor. They arrived just in time for his round to start.

John lowered his mask over his face and took his stance facing his opponent. Though he scorned war and violence, there was, as the Bible said, a time for war and a time for peace.

King John was a man of peace. But if war was inevitable, he wanted his men to know that he was fully prepared to handle it. And though he didn't see her on any of the balconies or in the courtyard-facing windows, John felt confident that Princess Gisela was watching from somewhere and would see that he was a capable swordsman and a worthy leader.

Princess Gisela was grateful to finally have an off round in which to catch her breath, refresh herself and monitor how her tournament was going. If the loud cheering that echoed through the courtyard was any indication, it was a rousing success. Still, she felt a sense of duty to stay informed of all that was happening. In spite of rules to insure safety, there was always the risk of someone being accidentally decapitated.

After passing by the board listing the winners and noting her rising arms, she found Renwick, one of King John's favored messengers, watching a match on the east wing.

"How goes it, Ren?" She addressed him familiarly, having worked beside him for the past two days to prepare for the tournament.

"Splendid." The guard fairly beamed. "King John returned in time to enter."

Gisela tried to ignore the way her stomach swooped at the mention of the king's name, but it was all she could do to school her features into an impassive expression. "Which arms are his? Are they the same as the banner that hangs behind his throne?"

"A modified smaller version. The proportions are off." Renwick dismissed her question with a wave of his hand. "I don't recognize any of the men by their arms. It doesn't matter much to me. What matters is that the king is doing quite well." He pointed toward the figures battling in the piste. "He's all but won this round, and it's only just begun."

Gisela turned her attention to the masked men. She didn't have to ask which one was the king. His stature and bearing gave him away, as did his skill with the sword, which was, as Renwick had suggested, far superior to that of his opponent.

She found she couldn't tear her eyes away from him, and as the milling crowd blocked her view, she clambered up higher on the bleachers to watch the king parry. In the time he'd been gone, she'd told herself over and over again that she felt for him only respect, admiration and gratitude for all he'd done for her.

And yet, watching him, her heart pounded with emotions that felt far more like affection, attraction and awe. The man moved with grace and fought with zeal, his fierce masculinity holding her attention, making it impossible for her to look away. Every time his opponent's sword flashed near him, Gisela felt herself cringing in fear that he could be injured. Yet the skillful king didn't let the other swordsman get a point on him.

King John had skill and strength, but most thrilling of all was his ability to anticipate the way his opponent was about to strike. When Renwick had first suggested that the king would quickly dispatch his opponent, she'd wondered how an opponent who could be so easily beaten had remained in the competition so long.

But watching them spar, she realized the man who fought the king was handy enough with the sword—better than many she'd fought that day, and she'd been impressed with the overall skill of the Lydians.

No, the king's superior hand was due to his talent for staying just ahead of his opponent, blocking jabs before they came, whipping his blade with a dexterity that took her breath away.

"I told you he's good." Renwick followed her.

"Very. I think I could learn from studying him. At the very least, I'd like to get an idea of how he moves in case I end up fighting him." She didn't take her eyes off the king as she spoke, but analyzed his patterns, looking for any weakness she might be able to use against him. Of all the men she'd watched or fought that day, he showed the most potential to be able to best her.

"Are you still in the tournament, then?"

"I have a break this round, and I'm glad for it. I'm afraid I'm still weaker than I thought after fighting that fever and the infection above my eye. Without a chance to catch my breath, I might have wilted in the piste. But I'll stay in the tournament until I'm defeated."

"I'm impressed, Your Highness."

Gisela couldn't tear her gaze from King John and his sword, recalling with a pleasant shiver how it had felt to have his arms around her. "So am I, Renwick. So am I."

Gisela gulped a long drink and propped herself up with her sword to keep from fainting with exhaustion. Fighting so soon after her injury had been taxing.

"This way, Highness." Renwick tugged on her arm. "The championship round will be in the center piste. They're lighting the torches. The crowd can't wait."

"They have to wait." Dizziness overtook her as she tried to walk. She stopped and shook her head, gasping for breath after a battle she'd honestly expected to lose. If her opponent hadn't made a few costly mistakes, Gisela would have met her second elimination and been out of the running. Perhaps she'd been wrong to think she could fight so soon after her illness. "Who am I fighting?"

"I don't know yet. The other fight just started—Tertulio versus King John."

Gisela balked at her choices. Tertulio had already delivered her lone defeat of the day. She'd hate to be eliminated by a second defeat from the same man. And yet, she knew King John would dispatch her easily, especially since she was almost too weak to stand. "If they've just started, I can rest."

"But don't you want to study them while you have the chance?"

"Right, then. Lead the way." Gisela leaned on Renwick's arm as he weaved through the milling throngs of people. He found them seats on the top tier of a set of bleachers that had been facing another piste until some men had tugged it nearer the action. Gisela slumped down, her arms too weak to lift her heavy helmet and peel the leather mask from her face.

It didn't matter. No one was paying her any attention. The crowd was riveted on the battle before them. Tertulio was a giant of a man, as tall as the king but far heavier. As he had when he'd defeated Gisela, Tertulio leveraged his weight against his opponent, beating him back with his sword, his barbaric hack-and-slash method only effective because of his imposing size. The brute was graceless, especially in comparison to the king, who held Gisela's attention now as he had before, twisting her heart with concern for his safety.

Gisela whispered a prayer that King John wouldn't be injured by his opponent's aggressive tactics. Though most of his face was hidden by the protective shield of his thick leather mask, he occasionally turned at such an angle that Gisela could see the glint of his eyes. They sparkled with intensity.

If he made it past Tertulio, he'd defeat her easily. Temptation whispered to her, to withdraw her name rather than submit herself to the rigors of a battle she knew she couldn't win. She'd underestimated the skill of the Lydian swordsmen, who had spent her strength with their long-lived battles. And she'd overestimated her degree of recovery. It wouldn't be wise to fight on. She should withdraw.

But then, assuming King John vanquished his current rival, that would leave him to win by forfeit. It didn't seem right, not when such a large part of her motivation for hosting the tournament was to rally the men—to prepare them to follow their king, should the Illyrians strike.

How much more would they trust and respect their king if he won the tournament on skill alone, and not because she'd withdrawn out of weakness? It could be a great boost to their morale and their pride in their leader.

Watching King John parry, she knew he deserved their respect.

She couldn't take that from him, no matter how exhausted she felt.

Her mind made up, she determined to fight as best she could if King John went on to meet her in the final match. But if Tertulio bested him now, she'd withdraw.

John raised his sword, pumping it victoriously into the air as the crowd chanted for him.

"This way, Your Majesty." Renwick led him to the neighboring piste where the licking flames of torches cast alternating light and shadows across the faces of the waiting crowd.

John scanned their faces impatiently, hoping to see Princess Gisela. He'd spotted his little sister at a balcony above, but the Frankish princess hadn't been with her. Knowing Gisela, she'd want to be at the heart of the action.

He could only trust she was well. He hadn't realized until her absence wore at him that he'd been looking forward to their reunion with expectancy. The day was nearly over, and his longing had only grown.

"Ready, Your Majesty?" The trumpeter raised his instrument to call the start of the round.

John spun to see his opponent already in place, sword raised in a pristinely executed opening stance. The flames cast deep shadows over the figure's masked face, but John figured it didn't matter who his opponent was. All that mattered was how he fought.

"Ready."

* * *

Gisela focused on holding her stance. Helmut, her fencing instructor from Aachen, had reminded her countless times of the importance of proper form.

"You cannot control what the other man will do, but you *can* be prepared to meet him."

She'd taken the words to heart and been surprised many times before by what a difference a good stance could make even when she'd been overmatched or underprepared.

And she was both tonight. The gleam in King John's eye spoke of limitless energy. She had no such gleam in her eye. It was all she could do to keep her sword from trembling.

The trumpet blared. The round had begun. Still, Gisela stood frozen, waiting. She'd do her best to respond to any move King John made. If she sensed an opening, she might even try to strike. As much as it was up to her, she'd make it look like he earned the round, assuming she didn't faint from exhaustion before it was over.

John stared at the tip of the sword, alert for the slightest flicker of movement. He'd played this game before. Two men could stand at an impasse for many long minutes, each waiting for the other to make the first move.

He could sense the rising impatience of the crowd. They wanted to see action. Yet John welcomed a moment to collect his thoughts, which had wandered to wondering where Gisela might be, and stayed focused on her still. Was it his imagination, or did he catch a whiff of her soft rose scent over the reek of humanity that filled the air?

Surely he'd imagined it. Given the odoriferous emanations all around him, Princess Gisela would have to be quite close for him to pick up the presence of her perfume. She knew to stay well back from the action. Didn't she?

Her shoulders ached, and heat coursed through her, more than the rising heat of effort. Had her fever returned? A tremble rippled up from her legs, and fearing it would quickly work its way to her steady sword, Gisela realized she'd have to make her move.

With a flick of her wrist, she brought her sword slicing lightly in an arc below John's blade.

He blocked the move and pushed her back.

Her response was delayed a split second too long by the mind-dulling ache of fever.

She blocked him but nearly stumbled forward. The crowd gasped and roared.

Their response seemed to spur King John to action, or perhaps he'd sensed her weakness and intended to seize the moment before it slipped by. Whatever the case, his blade darted forward, seeking an opening. All he needed was to tap her leather armor to make a point. If he made five points before she did, he'd win.

Her reflexes took over, blocking each shot. Her conscience whispered to her that she ought to let him win a few easy points before exhaustion overtook her, but she'd never willingly given away points before. They had three agile-eyed judges for the final round, unlike the lone judge who'd overseen the lesser matches.

If she made it look too obvious, the judges might wonder. John might wonder. He hadn't yet looked any farther than her sword, and clearly didn't realize who she sparred with.

She preferred it that way.

Best not to make him suspicious, then. Caught up in

the action, she found her strength returning, if not in substance then in ephemeral determination. Perhaps, just to make a strong showing, she should win the first point.

Dancing backward, she replaced her right foot forward with her left, moving from a defensive to an offensive stance.

King John didn't change stance but moved in as though he'd been offered an opening.

His first point fell high on her arm.

She winced against the kiss of his blade and lowered her chin.

She could score a point before the crowd finished cheering. Or had they finished cheering? The roar in her ears only grew as John's blade sprouted mirror images on each side. There were three swords now, and three arms holding them.

Which sword was she fighting? Which man was she fighting? He seemed to have grown three heads and ten legs.

Or twelve. Or eight.

She charged at the middle man, taking the cheap thrust, only to find her opponent had evaporated. She swung back just in time to catch him on the elbow.

Her point.

The crowd roared.

Gisela gulped a breath and tried not to faint.

Stinging needles speared through John's fingers from the blow to his elbow, loosening his grip on the sword. His fingers ached and tingled. How had his opponent landed such an effective blow on that peculiarly sensitive part of his arm? There wasn't time to sort it out. He spun to face the man, hoping only to recover before he was bested again.

But the man before him staggered. Was it a strategic move, meant to distract him and land another point? For the first time, he tried to look the man in the eye, to guess what his opponent was playing at.

Torch light flickered, casting deep shadows over his adversary's masked face. John noted the very fine armor and expensive chain mail his rival wore. How very odd. It gave the man an almost feminine silhouette.

Rather than be distracted, John kept his sword up, jabbing forward. His rival seemed to be growing tired. Each block landed a fraction of a second later. Detecting a weakness, John increased the frequency of his jabs.

He landed a point on his opponent's hip, surprising the man, who emitted a sudden cry.

A decidedly feminine cry.

His earlier doubts renewed, John looked afresh at the man who faced him, whose upturned head now caught the light. Through the narrow eye slits in the armor, John caught sight of stitches.

And the blue eyes of the emperor's daughter.

Fear and fury surged through him.

"No!" He lunged his sword, point down, into the hardened courtyard soil.

The walls shook with the cries of the crowd, but John ignored them and turned away.

That was why he'd smelled roses! That was why he hadn't seen Gisela in the windows.

He started to stomp away when the crowd changed its tune to one of frightful alarm. Bits of exclamations penetrated his anger, and he spun around.

Gisela had fallen.

Chapter Nine

John pushed his way through the crowd that had surged forward on Gisela the moment she'd gone down.

"What happened?" he demanded, furious about everything. He'd fought her. She was on the ground. Everything was wrong, and she looked so pale under her mask.

"Was she injured earlier? Did someone strike her?"

"I think she fainted," Renwick answered.

John scooped her up from the ground and plowed through the parting crowd toward the great hall. He burst through the double doors with one kick and sent the heavy wooden doors swinging open. A roaring fire burned at one end, ready to host a banquet when the tournament was ended. He lowered Gisela onto the soft animal-skin rugs near the light of the leaping flames.

His fingers fumbled as he lifted off her helmet and untied her leather mask.

"Gisela? Can you hear me?" He cradled her head in one hand as he peeled away her mask to reveal a face of ill pallor.

Her chest rose and fell.

She lived. But why had she fallen?

Footsteps sounded on the stone floor behind him.

"Keep the crowds out," he barked to whatever guards might be among them. His eyes didn't leave Gisela's face.

Her cheeks felt warm. Feverish?

Knowing full well the risk he was taking, John nonetheless pressed his lips to her forehead, reading far more accurately than his sweaty palms could the degree of her fever.

Warm. Far too warm.

"What happened to Gisela?" Bette shrieked as she entered from the back way.

"You knew she was fighting? You knew I was fighting her? Why didn't you warn me?"

"Didn't you recognize her?"

"I looked only at her blade. Fetch her a drink. That might revive her."

Bette hurried over with the nearest cup from the laid table.

The liquid sloshed against Gisela's leather pants as John hastily took the cup from his sister. He scooped the princess up to almost sitting and held the cup to her lips. "Here. Drink."

Pouring mere drops between her lips, he waited for a reaction.

Nothing.

Fearful for her condition, he tipped the cup back again, pouring more this time, letting her head tilt backward as though to slosh the reviving liquid down her throat.

She sputtered and coughed, but her eyes didn't open.

Relief welled inside him along with a desperate prayer that she'd pull through. He'd saved her life once to prevent a war. But her survival had begun to mean more to him than its political repercussions. He couldn't lose her. Not now. Not after waiting two days longing to see her smile again.

"Come on, Gisela. Wake up."

* * *

She could smell his calming woodsy scent. He was near. Had she only imagined it, or had he held her again?

"Wake up, Your Highness. Please. Are you injured?"

That was King John's voice. So she hadn't imagined that he was near. And yet, he sounded so far away.

"The crowds want in. There's to be a banquet." Elisabette's voice. "I see no sign of blood."

"If she's not injured, then why did she faint?" John's hands smoothed the hair away from her face. "I'll take her to her room. Host the banquet without me."

"Won't you come down?"

"We'll see. I'll not leave the princess's side until I'm certain she'll pull through."

He cradled her against him, and Gisela sank against the hard wall of chain mail. With a flurrying activity, her memory of her duel with the king returned.

How had she stayed on her feet so long? She'd even won a point.

Then he'd recognized her. She'd seen it in his eyes the moment he did and the absolute fury that followed. He'd been so angry. But why?

Tears leaked from her eyes. She'd planned the tournament to please him. His furious reaction had snapped the last thread of determination that had kept her upright, and she'd fallen.

He lowered her onto a couch.

She gripped his arms. If he left, she might not have a chance to apologize, though she wasn't entirely sure what she was apologizing for.

He cupped her hands in his. "Your Highness, can you speak? Are you injured?"

Was she? She wasn't sure. "I've angered you." She tried to think what had done it. The king had given his blessing to the tournament. John's reaction befuddled her. His demeanor had changed so completely the moment he'd recognized her.

She reached for his face. "I apologize for whatever I've done. Is it because I fainted? You would have rather triumphed over a more worthy opponent?" The rough stubble on his cheek prickled against her hand. "Please, explain it to me. I wanted only to please you."

John felt his fury subside in waves like the ebbing tide. Gisela's soft, pleading words wore away at his hardened heart. As much as he wanted to be upset with her, he couldn't possibly.

"I fought you," he explained. "I raised my sword at you. I could have injured you."

"I'm not injured." She'd assessed her condition as she'd lain there and determined as much. "Just tired and feverish. I tried to do too much too soon after my infection. It's a horrible weakness of mine. Hilda might have warned you."

"She didn't. Nor was I warned that you'd try something so unbecoming as to pick up a sword—"

"Boden told you I fence, didn't he? That's how I hurt my eye, saving the ship from the Saracens."

"But in a tournament?"

"Much safer than fighting pirates, actually."

John tried not to smile as she looked up at him, her wide eyes begging him not to be angry. Regret squeezed his heart. Had he overreacted? "I hit you with my sword. You cried out in pain, and then I recognized you. What would you have had me do? Keep fighting?"

"Yes! You would have won. I was too tired to go much longer. If Tertulio had advanced instead of you, I'd have withdrawn."

"I should hope so!"

"Why?"

"The man was an animal. He'd have chopped you to bits."

"He only beat me by two points when I met him earlier."

"You fought Tertulio?" John couldn't keep the possessive note from his voice. "You could have been killed." He'd had his arms on her shoulders since delivering her onto the couch, and now he pulled her tighter against him as though he could shield her from the barbaric swordsman or anyone else who might have fought her.

A groan of regret escaped his lips, coupled with visions of what could have happened. "I would never knowingly raise my sword against a woman. I would never threaten violence against you in any way."

"In many corners of the world, men use violence to subdue their women."

"They are barbarians. No real man would ever threaten a woman, let alone strike her. God created man to shield and protect women, to defend and cherish them. It is not in my nature to fight a woman, least of all a princess like you. But I fear I have insulted you by ending the fight."

Gisela buried her face against his shoulder. "You were only upset because you feared for my safety?"

"I fear for it still." He clung to her, the fear of what could have happened locking his arms into place around her. He pinched his eyes shut and tried not to think about how his heart had plummeted within him when he'd turned to find her fallen in the dust.

His feelings for her were far too strong. They hadn't cooled in the slightest while he'd been at the border meeting with his brother.

* * *

Gisela held on to John's shoulders and breathed in deep breaths of his comforting scent. He'd not let her hold on to him this long, not since her fever had been at its worst a week before, and she guessed he'd tear himself away at any moment. She clung to him and prayed for time to pass slowly.

He feared for her safety. Well, of course, if she died that would entangle Lydia in an increasingly complicated political situation. But he hadn't mentioned the political situation. And he didn't hold her like a man who was thinking about politics.

He held her as she'd never been held before. She knew it would be far too easy to feel more for this man than she ought. Perhaps her feelings were already inappropriately strong, given her unavoidable pending nuptials with Warrick. But the tournament had drained away her strength, and she couldn't muster the will to pry herself away from him.

"Princess—" his arms shifted slightly around her "—have I insulted you? My reaction was quite strong. All I could think of was—" he pulled back far enough to cup her cheek with one hand "—what if I'd hurt you? I'm sorry if my words insulted you. They weren't intended to. Obviously you're perfectly capable of defending yourself. I've never known a woman like you."

"Is that a bad thing?"

King John groaned softly. He bent his head until his forehead nearly touched hers. Then he winced as though experiencing deep pain. "The only bad thing is that you're—" His words broke off and he pulled away.

"I'm what?"

He balled his gloved hands into fists, then extended his fingers before fisting them again, grasping at the empty air as though the answer lay somewhere near, if only he could seize it without it slipping away.

Gisela could see he was fighting a battle within himself. There was much she still didn't understand about the kingdom of Lydia and their relationships with their neighbors. There was much she didn't understand about King John, but she wanted so much to know him better. To ease the sorrow in his heart she'd seen in tiny glimpses. To repay, to whatever extent she could, the debt she owed him for saving her life.

King John didn't turn around. "You're promised to Warrick, son of Garren."

"Yes." She'd grown to resent the fact, but she couldn't deny it.

"Is there any chance you could peacefully annul the agreement?"

Having recently wished that there was, Gisela let out a disillusioned laugh. "Hardly. Not without incurring the wrath of my father and quite a few prominent Illyrians."

"Then my feelings don't matter."

Stunned by his words, Gisela didn't even call after the king as he fled the room.

John didn't go to the banquet. He was in no mood to face anyone, least of all his little sister or any of the courtiers who might ask him what had happened. He found Hilda hovering in the hallway outside Gisela's suite and informed her that the princess needed rest, as well as food and drink.

Then he stomped off to his own room, still chafing at all he'd said that he shouldn't have.

He flung off his leather fencing gloves. They landed on his dressing table, rattling it against the plastered stone wall. He sat and tugged off his boots.

It didn't matter that she was promised to another. Politically it mattered, yes, but that wasn't the greatest impediment between them, no matter how he'd inferred so to the princess.

He'd told himself for the past three years that he would not wed. He would not ask another woman to risk her life attempting to bear him a child. So really, it made precious little difference whether Gisela's pledge to Warrick was breakable or not.

He had no other arrangement to offer her.

His heart squeezed as he heaved his heavy chain-mail jerkin over his aching shoulders. The image of her lying prone in the dust would not leave his mind. What if she'd died there? What if he'd lost her?

"Dear Lord in heaven." John sat and clutched his head in his hands as he prayed. "I did not ask to ever find love again. Why have You sent this woman to torture my wounded heart?" He panted, yearning to understand.

There was no getting rid of Princess Gisela—not until her father sent a ship back for her, and that would still be another fortnight or two, at least. And there was no denying the intensity of what he felt for her.

And there would be no acting on those feelings.

"Dear Lord," he prayed again, "if this is some trial, I do not see how I can succeed. Grant me strength."

Gisela stared at the doorway through which John had disappeared and nearly jumped when Hilda walked in.

"The king said you needed food and drink. Shall I fetch you some, or do you need my assistance here first?"

"Food first, thank you, Hilda."

The woman left, and Gisela was alone with her troubled thoughts.

What had the good king been saying? He'd asked

about ending her agreement with Warrick. Why? For political reasons? Did it have to do with his father's death or Rab the Raider or the message she'd sent to her father at Rome?

Her heart burned inside her, denying each possibility as quickly as it occurred to her. No, she knew how it felt to be in his arms. She knew how much she'd longed to see him again and how her attention had been riveted on him once she'd found him sparring in the courtyard.

Did he feel for her anything like what she felt for him? Neither of them could act on those feelings without encroaching on the terms of her father's agreement with the Illyrians.

If she'd had the strength to move, Gisela might have gone after John to learn what he'd meant by his comments. Because even if she was right—even if he wanted her as she wanted him—that didn't begin to explain what he'd meant when he'd said that it didn't matter.

"I've brought your supper!" a feminine voice chirped from the doorway. It wasn't Hilda's voice.

"Elisabette? I thought your brother asked you to host the banquet?"

"You mean the rowdy rabble in the dining hall? They're in such a state I feared for my well-being. No one will notice my absence, and if they do, they won't care." She placed a tray of food on the side table and moved it closer to the couch where Gisela reclined. "I believe this is the last of the dessert."

"It's a large piece. Share it with me?" Gisela reached for the full cup instead and drank deeply, feeling her strength return somewhat as the fluid coursed through her. "Have you spoken with your brother?"

"Not since he carried you out of the hall." Bette picked

delicately at the honey-soaked pastry. "Have you ever seen him in such a fit?"

"No." Gisela almost laughed that Bette would ask her such a question, when the girl obviously had been familiar with the king far longer than she had. "Have you?"

"Hardly. I've seen him upset—he was livid with the Illyrians after Father's death. But when he stopped fighting you and sank his sword into the soil, I thought my heart would stop." Bette placed one hand upon her chest as though checking to be sure the organ was still going after all. "Do you know why he did it?"

"He recognized me. He said he was afraid he might have injured me."

Elisabette stuck out her tongue and blew it dismissively. "He didn't injure anyone all day. Once he knew it was you, he could have simply been more careful. *That* wasn't it at all."

Intrigued, Gisela plucked grapes from the large bunch Bette had brought her. "Then why?"

The girl grinned. "I'm not sure I should tell."

"What do you know?"

"That's just it. I don't know anything for certain, only what I've observed in the way he acts around you, the look on his face when he saw you'd fallen in the piste."

"He was wearing a mask."

Elisabette dismissed her protest with a shake of her head. "His entire body language changed. He went from being furiously upset to, to…"

"To what?" Gisela urged when the girl seemed to have trouble finding the right word.

Bette looked at the ceiling with a wistful expression. "He looked as though someone had just pulled his heart from his chest."

"You're being dramatic."

"Am I? Did you hear him in the great hall when he laid you by the fire? I know what he's said—that if anything happens to you while you're in his care, we could end up at war with the Illyrians or your father or both. But it wasn't *that* kind of fear that burned in his eyes. I know the look he gets when he's worried about war, and this was nothing like it."

Gisela's heart thumped rapidly as she waited for Bette to explain further. She had her own suspicions about what had motivated John's actions, but her suspicions were hardly objective, clouded as they were by her own very strong feelings. "What was it like, then?"

"You'll say I don't know what I'm talking about."

"I wouldn't suggest such a thing. You know your brother far better than I do."

"Not that." Bette stuck out a pouting lip and scowled at what remained of her baklava.

"What then?"

The younger woman seemed to wage a battle before she finally spoke. "I know you're older than I am, but I've recently celebrated my eighteenth birthday. Most of my friends have married already. I'm not completely naive." Something in the way she spoke suggested that she'd bottled up her secret for too long, and wanted desperately to share it with someone. Still, she held back.

"I never thought you naive." Gisela tried to encourage her.

Bette placed the rest of her baklava on the tray and nibbled at her thumb nail indecisively. "You've got to promise not to tell John what I'm about to say. It cannot leave this room."

Unsure how she could make such a promise when she hadn't yet heard Elisabette's news, nonetheless she doubted the girl would speak at all without her solemn pledge.

"My lips are sealed."

Elisabette's story spilled out quickly, as though it had been bottled up under pressure and was ready to burst. "Before my father's death, we used to travel past the mountains for festivals. We were on good terms with our Illyrian neighbors and our family got along quite well with the royal families of the neighboring kingdoms. Unbeknownst to my father or brother, I fell in love with an Illyrian prince. We pledged our hearts to one another the summer before my father's death. Since then, we've exchanged notes by courier. I still love him, and he loves me, though I haven't heard from him in many long months."

"Oh, Bette."

The girl continued. "I understand what love is—sometimes I think I understand it better than my brother. He's run from it ever since his wife died. It's been years ago, but he's never looked at another woman twice."

Gisela's heart felt as though it had been gripped in a vise. Was that the source of King John's great sorrow? She could hardly breathe waiting for Bette to finish her account.

"I shouldn't presume to speak for my brother. It's his story to tell. But you must understand that I know what I'm talking about. I know my brother, and I know love."

When the girl left off her story, Gisela finally sucked in a breath. "What are you saying?"

"He hasn't been this way since he fell in love with Dorcas. Then again, I don't think he was ever this way."

"What are you suggesting?" Gisela knew well what her heart wanted the girl to be suggesting, but at the same time, her sensible self hoped Bette would deny it.

"I think my brother has feelings for you."

"He can't."

"I know what I'm talking about."

Gisela reached across the tray and took Bette by the hand. "I know you do. I trust you do. And I fear your appraisal of the situation may be right. But you know I'm promised to an Illyrian prince."

"Yes, I know. And that's the other reason I wanted to tell you my tale. When you get to Illyria, do you think you could take a message to my prince? I haven't heard from him in weeks and weeks, and I'm very worried. Perhaps you could initiate talks between his family and mine. We long to be together, but the current political situation makes that impossible."

It took Gisela a moment to process all that Elisabette said. The girl didn't question that Gisela would soon wed an Illyrian, despite King John's supposed feelings for her. "I will try to help you in whatever way I can. What is the name of your prince?"

Bette stood and took a step toward the door, blushing at the thought of her love. She'd clearly said all she'd come to say, and now appeared ready to retreat, half embarrassed by sharing so much. "He's a prince of the Dometian tribe. Warrick, son of Garren."

Gisela stared after Bette, but there was no calling the young woman back, not when she'd scampered off in such a hurry, and Gisela couldn't find her voice anyway.

Of course, the younger princess didn't know the name of Gisela's betrothed. Gisela had purposely not told her because of the connection between Warrick's family and the man who'd killed Elisabette and John's father, King Theodoric.

Did Bette know about the connection between Warrick's family and Rab the Raider? What would she think when she found out?

Worse yet, what would she think when she learned that Gisela was pledged to marry her longtime love? Fear gripped Gisela. What if Warrick sent a message to Elisabette confessing his betrothal to Gisela? What if Bette learned she was going to lose her love to the very woman who'd promised to help her unite her to him?

"Oh, dear God in Heaven." Gisela pinched her eyes shut and prayed. "Help me, please."

John lay awake for a long time, regretting that he'd spoken aloud words best left buried. Why had he brought up Gisela's coming marriage? Why had he asked her about breaking it off? Legally and politically he knew she ought to make haste to Warrick, be married and gone from Lydia, out of his castle and out of his thoughts.

But would she really be gone from his thoughts? He hadn't managed to forget her yet. Outwardly the situation seemed so simple. She wasn't his and he had no intention of marrying. They weren't to be together. Simple.

And yet, inside his heart everything had gotten turned around backward.

He rolled from his bed and knelt at the side, his hands held tight together in prayer. "Dear Lord, *why?*" He couldn't put into words exactly what he was feeling. He didn't understand it himself. But surely God understood. Surely God knew what to do. "What am I to do?" he pleaded. "Show me what to do."

John had his eyes pinched shut when an oddly familiar fluttering sound distracted him. He quit his prayers and rose to the open window, where the moonlight cast a shadow over the figure perched there.

"Fledge." He greeted the bird before he realized his falcon wasn't alone. Another falcon landed on the windowsill beside his falcon.

His leather gloves still lay on the side table where he left them. He pulled one on and extended his arm to the bird. "Ah, Fledge, you've returned to me." He ran a hand down the bird's smooth feathers and determined that she had no injury. She was no worse off after her absence.

A sense of peace cut through his despair. Everything in his kingdom and in his heart was in upheaval, but his bird had returned to him. God was faithful. God watched over sparrows—it said so in the Holy Scriptures. Surely God watched over kings, as well.

John looked up into the starry heavens. "I don't understand," he confessed, "but if You lead me, I will follow."

Grateful for the exhaustion that helped her forget her troubles in sleep, Gisela nonetheless awoke all too cognizant of the distressing circumstances in which she'd found herself.

And Hilda was missing.

As Gisela splashed on rose water and put on a suitable gown, she thought back to the night before. If Hilda had ever returned after she'd left to fetch Gisela some food, she'd gone again while Gisela was sleeping. What had distracted the faithful maid from her usual devotion to her duties?

With her long length of braid coiled within a silken net, Gisela set off in search of Hilda or breakfast and hoped to find them both together.

A visit to the kitchen yielded no maid nor any clues to where the woman might be. However, the cook obligingly offered Gisela her choice of breakfasts, and she continued her search munching on a pastry filled with chunks of apple.

Having always been a fan of high towers and the views one could see from them, Gisela navigated through the hallways, checking her position periodically through the wide-open windows until she found the winding stairs that led to the highest tower.

She didn't expect to find Hilda there, but since she'd had her breakfast she had no more need of the maid. And she'd been so busy planning the tournament that she'd yet to fully explore the castle. The view from the tower would help her to understand the layout of King John's fortress, as well as the lay of the land. Perhaps she might even spot Hilda from that vantage point.

"Delightful," she whispered to herself, swallowing the last morsel and hoisting her skirts as she climbed the winding stone stairs.

The steps circled around and around until she was nearly dizzy. Narrow windows lit the space, but they were only wide enough to shoot arrows through, and allow a little light in. The stone walls were far too thick to permit her to see anything through the arrow slits.

Finally the winding trail ended and opened to a large room with windows all around. As her eyes adjusted to the sudden light, she saw she was not alone.

"King John."

A pair of birds startled at her voice, and John turned to her, surprise on his face.

"Shh." He extended his arm toward one of the birds, which had fluttered up to the rafters and now glared at her from his perch with an expression that was quite disapproving, for a bird.

It was a falcon. Gisela recalled that he'd lost his along the borderlands. She shrank back, not wanting to scare the birds away. "I'm sorry to interrupt," she whispered and took the first three steps down. "I'll leave you alone."

"You're welcome to stay." John held one bird on his leather glove. "You startled them. They really don't mind humans. At least, Fledge doesn't. I can't speak for this fellow." He pointed to the bird that glared at them from the rafters. John chuckled softly at the bird's antics.

Gisela couldn't help giggling as well. "I'm not entirely certain he approves of me."

"How could anyone not approve of you? No, he's just a stodgy old bird." John turned his attention back to the falcon on his glove. "I don't know why she brought him home." He smoothed the falcon's ruffled feathers.

"Fledge is a 'she'?" Gisela stepped forward cautiously.

"Yes. They have similar markings, but the females tend to be noticeably larger than the males."

"That's a bit different from humans." Gisela had arrived at his side and looked up at him, his considerable height advantage over her providing evidence in support of her words.

"Indeed. I believe the birds require that size advantage among the females to enable them to lay eggs. As for why the males are smaller, I don't know why God wanted them to be so, but I don't doubt there's a good reason."

"God does seem to know what He's doing, even when we can't understand it," Gisela agreed, reaching tentative fingers toward the bird. "May I?"

The animal dipped its head as though inviting her to stroke its feathers. Gisela couldn't suppress a delighted laugh as she ran the tips of her fingers down the bird's delicate head.

"She likes you," John murmured.

Gisela met his eyes and immediately felt a blush rising

to her cheeks. She wished she could think of something to say, but one glance at the king had addled her brain, and stolcn her voice, as well.

Chapter Ten

John held his falcon out toward the princess and tried frantically to think. She'd been ready to leave him alone in the tower. If he'd have kept silent for another few seconds, she'd have been gone. Why had he been foolish enough to invite her to stay?

Because he longed to be in her presence, that was why. Except for his reasoning faculties, which knew far better than to go anywhere near her, every facet of his being longed to be as close to her as possible.

It was as though his entire physical body had mutinied against his rational self.

It was high treason, when he got right down to it.

Perhaps he should find out why she'd climbed the tower and then quickly take his leave. At the very least, he could hope to retreat before she brought up their conversation from the night before. He rushed to fill the silence before she could fill it for him. "Are you enjoying your stay at Castlehead?"

"Very much so, thank you."

"Is there anything you lack?"

She shrugged, then laughed. "My maid has gone missing."

"Hilda?" John thought quickly, seeing an opportunity to retreat. "I shall ask my courtiers if anyone knows where she might be." He raised his arm to place Fledge back on her perch.

"It's not an urgent concern." She raised one hand, and he paused. "Since you're here, perhaps you could help me in another way."

"I am at your service."

"I climbed this tower in hopes of garnering enough of a view to understand the layout of this expansive castle of yours, as well as the surrounding landscape."

"Your Highness has chosen an excellent vantage point from which to observe." As John spoke, Fledge seemed to grow bored with him and hopped off his glove to join her new mate on the rafters. John didn't take her abandonment personally. He was quite relieved to have found the bird had returned at all, even if she'd brought along a new mate.

Gisela crossed to the nearest of eight windows, which occupied the eight walls of the roughly octagonal tower. John crossed to stand beside her and pointed out the various sights. "There is the front gate with the drawbridge, beside the gate tower. Directly across the courtyard is the large roof that covers the great hall."

"Oh. Then what is under that large peaked roof?" Gisela pointed.

"That's the chapel. Did you worship there on Wednesday?"

"Yes. The service was lovely. But an attendant escorted me from the great hall. I had no idea how I arrived there or where we were in relation to the rest of the fortress."

"We'll have Sunday worship there tomorrow morning. The bells will ring, calling everyone to come to the service, and then they'll toll three times more when the service begins."

"I'm so glad you told me. Now I'll be able to find it without an attendant. But where is my room from there?"

John crouched to meet her eye level and shuffled closer to her, his attention so focused on the architecture outside that he didn't realize how close he'd moved toward her until his shoulder brushed hers, just as he pointed. "See that window there?"

Instead of moving away from him, she leaned closer. "The arched window?"

"No, rectangle." John could smell the scent of roses rising from her, and found his thoughts consumed with her proximity.

"Oh, I see. Under that wide tower, there."

"Yes. That's the Queen's Tower. All the best rooms are situated around it. My suite is on the other side."

"So to get to chapel in the morning, I'll go down the hallway from my room." She pointed with her finger, tracing the route through the sky.

"Actually, that hallway has many confusing branches." He caught her finger and guided her hand until she pointed back to her room. "The fastest route, assuming it's not raining, is to exit there and cross the courtyard. See the double doors?"

She hesitated.

He was sure she saw it, but more than that, with all his pointing and directing, he'd gotten his arm most of the way around her shoulder and their heads quite close together. In fact, he found it nearly impossible to speak or think. Breathing wasn't terribly easy, either.

"Double doors," she repeated the words, but her attention clearly wasn't on the doors. She turned to look up at him.

He was too close. His thoughts had gone to mush right along with his knees. He hadn't planned to allow himself to be so close to her, except for when he'd removed the stitches from her eye, and for that he intended to have plenty of attendants nearby to compel him to stay in line. But they were alone now. He staggered back, disturbing the falcons.

Fledge squawked to express her annoyance before settling back next to her new mate.

"Oh, Fledge." He didn't need a bird chastising him. "I don't need a lecture from you. I could give you one of my own."

Gisela giggled, almost as though she felt relieved to have something to talk about that didn't require them to stand so close together or admit what they'd felt while doing so. "What would you lecture your falcon about? Running away from home?"

"Yes, that. And fidelity."

"Fidelity? Is that related to the running away?"

"Well, she's gone off and found herself a new mate, as you can see." John felt flustered by the new line of discussion, but he couldn't very well go back to discussing the view or he'd have his arms around her again within minutes.

"Oh, Fledge." Gisela looked up at the bird, who looked down her beak at the princess with an air of birdly disdain. "Have you been unfaithful?" She turned her attention to John. "What did she do with her other mate?"

"He died." It occurred to John that the conversation presented him with an excellent opportunity to make an important point. "But she—"

"Died?" The princess cut him off and started laughing. "That's hardly grounds for accusing her of adulterous carryings-on."

"It was only this past winter." John realized Gisela was still laughing, so he turned his accusing glare on the bird. "The two of them raised many young together, and now she's moved on as though he'd never been."

"She moved on because he's dead and she's not."

Even the bird cocked her head at him and blinked rather pointedly, as though she agreed with the princess.

John realized he was outnumbered by the two females, and on top of that, Gisela's tone was still decidedly condescending, which, as king, was something he wasn't particularly keen on. Granted, Eliab and Urias tended to treat him that way at times, but he didn't put up with it from them, either.

He'd only put up with it from the princess because her father was the emperor, and he was in no position to cross either of them. Besides, he was certain his theories were correct, if only he could make Gisela see things his way.

"Falcons are supposed to mate for life," John asserted.

"Yes." Gisela smirked at him. "For the life of one of them, not both of them. You can't expect Fledge to live out the rest of her existence alone, can you? That's not what mating for life means."

"But she's moved on. It's as though she's forgotten him."

"John—" Gisela's voice turned soft and she took a step closer to him "—if Fledge is ready to move on, that doesn't mean she didn't love her first mate. It just means she wants to move ahead with her life. She wants to hatch more young."

"But he's not there beside her anymore." John felt his jaw tighten. He wasn't winning this argument anymore. He could feel it slipping away from him, just as Dorcas had slipped away from him. He pulled in a breath.

Gisela's hand fell on his arm.

He startled away.

"I'm sorry," she apologized quickly. "Would you like me to leave?"

John looked up at Fledge and her new mate, sitting on the rafters. How long he looked at them, sitting there, he wasn't sure, but his raw emotions churned inside him, muddling his thoughts. Should Gisela stay? He couldn't say. Ought she stay? Perhaps it wasn't right for them to be alone together, with him feeling as he did toward her. But did he *want* her to stay?

There was no denying it. Finally he answered, "No. I'd rather you stay."

She didn't respond.

He turned to look.

Gisela was gone.

Hurrying toward the stairs, he looked down the long spiral but saw no sign of her. She must have tiptoed away quickly, the sound of her steps swallowed by the thick stones. He looked back at Fledge and her new mate, but they were absorbed with one another and paid no mind to him.

His sense of loss grew along with a yearning for the kind of close companionship the two birds shared with one another. Gisela had offered him that kind of companionship when she'd placed her hand on his arm.

He'd been wrong to pull away. Maybe he'd been wrong to close his heart off to her. But what did it matter? She would marry Warrick. She'd be wed by Christmastide.

The birds fluttered on the rafters above him, and Fledge looked down at him with her beady eyes almost as though she meant to give him a message.

Companionship.

Was that it? Perhaps that was why God had sent Gisela into his life—not because he was supposed to fall in love with *her*—but because he was supposed to open his heart once again to the possibility of love.

Could he do that? Could he forget the vow he'd made after Dorcas's death and move on to love another?

He stood and looked out over the sea, his thoughts troubled. Perhaps he could love another. Gisela had taught him that. But he most certainly couldn't love *her.* Loving Gisela was politically and ethically impossible.

So he could not allow himself to feel anything more for her.

John missed lunch. Gisela had heard he'd had a message from his brother about the situation in the borderlands, so it didn't surprise her when Elisabette asked her to host the meal without him, since he was in a private meeting with his advisors and couldn't be interrupted. Though Gisela suspected his absence might have also been influenced by their discussion in the tower, she did her best to be gracious and enjoy the company of the courtiers, whose names and customs she was quickly learning.

When he missed the evening meal as well, she began to get sincerely suspicious.

"Do you suppose he's avoiding me?" she asked Elisabette in a hushed voice during a lull in the meal.

The young woman smirked. "I told you he wasn't comfortable with his growing feelings for you. But he can't keep missing meals without people noticing. Tomorrow's Sunday—a holy day. He'll have to make an appearance then."

Still, Gisela spent an uneasy night contemplating her next move. With Boden dispatched to take a message to her father at Rome, she had little choice but to stay at King John's castle for as many weeks as it took to receive a reply.

She could hardly imagine going another day without talking to John. She couldn't let him avoid her for weeks on end. No, the best plan, as far as she could see, was to address the situation directly. She'd never been one to avoid important discussions—her father would never tolerate it.

Perhaps the tension between them would dissipate once they discussed what they felt. She'd observed many a romance in her father's court. Half the time, it seemed the feelings between the pair came from their uncertainties about the other's feelings. So it stood to reason that if she and John could speak openly of what they felt, the unwanted emotions would melt away and they could move on.

Even after she resolved to speak with King John, Gisela lay awake for some time listening to the surf crashing against the rocky shoreline and wondering how John would take to the discussion. He'd tended thus far to push her away. She'd have to have God's help, then, if she was to broach the subject without frightening him off.

The resolution settled in her heart and gave her peace. That was it, then. She'd rise early to pray and read the Scriptures.

Books being notoriously expensive, she herself owned only a copy of the Psalms and the Gospels, both gifts from her father, finely penned copies of the Vulgate, Jerome's fifth-century Latin translation. Her father had employed the best scholars and commissioned them with translating the Scriptures into the common tongue of the people, but the task was monumental and progress slow.

She realized she was extremely fortunate to have access to any written Scripture at all. But surely given Lydia's Christian heritage, King John would retain a larger selection of books of the Bible. He'd demonstrated familiarity with the book of Acts, so somewhere he must have a copy of it. And the chapel was the most likely place for such a treasure to be stored. The deacon had read from something during the midweek worship service. Surely something as precious and fragile as a Bible would be kept at the chapel instead of being moved between services.

Her plan was so simple, she smiled to herself. Yes, she'd simply go early to the chapel the next morning. John had indicated that Sunday morning services were held midmorning. If she rose early enough, she might have a couple of hours alone to herself to read the Scriptures before the other worshippers began to arrive.

And then, as Bette had indicated, John was sure to arrive. In keeping with their seating arrangement at table, he was bound to position himself somewhere near her. She'd just have to find a moment to speak with him privately.

And then? Maybe then she could stop thinking about him all the time and finally experience some peace.

John stared out his open window at the eastern horizon and determined that the sun was hiding somewhere just on the other side. Eventually it would have to rise.

There wasn't any chance of his falling back to sleep— not when he saw Gisela's face the moment he closed his eyes. Not when her words churned his heart to a useless froth.

Would he be happy if he wed again? Every time he began to think that he might, his conscience pricked him. How could he allow himself to be happy when Dorcas was dead?

And not just dead, but dead in childbirth. Dead from trying to bear him an heir. He'd failed Dorcas twice already—in causing the pregnancy that had killed her and in failing to save her as she fought against death trying to bring his child into the world.

If he remarried, he'd only fail her again.

His heart cried out for healing. Lighting an oil lamp, he headed for the chapel. He needed to read God's Word and absorb the teachings of Scripture. He couldn't wait for daylight. He needed God's light upon his path *now*.

Following the route John had traced from the tower, Gisela found the high-arched double wooden doors with no trouble. When she tugged on the handle the door opened easily, revealing the long lofty hall lined with arch-topped pillars and high open windows all along one wall. She'd found the chapel where she'd worshipped midweek.

Her soul sighed with relief. The good Lord knew she had many concerns pressing upon her—not the least of them Hilda's repeated absences. The maid was far older than Gisela herself and would surely scoff if she knew Gisela had been worried about her. As far as Gisela was concerned, it was a relief to be free from the woman's constant presence. Not that she disliked Hilda, but between the journey by ship and their adventures since, she was more than happy for some time away from the woman.

No doubt Hilda felt the same. As long as she returned to her duties within the next few days, Gisela would simply give her a lecture about the need to report her intended absences ahead of time.

They'd leave that at that.

Her situation with King John was far more complicated. She cared deeply about him. Not only had he saved her life, but he also made her feel things she'd never felt before. But how did the king feel about her? She'd have guessed Elisabette's analysis was right, but then there was the lecture he'd given Fledge. He was clearly still mourning his late wife.

There seemed to be no answer. But she'd often been told that God was both omniscient and omnipotent—that God knew all things and could do all things. So surely God could see a way out of her troubles and bring a better plan to pass.

The solid stone floors absorbed the sounds of her footsteps as she made her way toward the front of the chapel. Light poured through the colorful panes of stained glass that filled the last window, bringing the image of lilies almost to life. Gisela had admired the window during the midweek service. Stained-glass artistry was rare in northern Europe, though she'd seen more examples of it in Rome. She understood that artisans in the Mediterranean region had been experimenting with stained-glass techniques for centuries. Still, such designs were time consuming to produce, and only the wealthiest patrons could afford them.

Distracted again by the window, it took Gisela a moment to notice the other figure nearby. A raised dais at the head of the sanctuary was topped with an ornately engraved pulpit. Gisela spotted the open Bible on top of the reading stand at the same moment she realized she wasn't alone.

King John stood just beyond the open Bible with his back to her. Gisela suppressed a gasp, but not quickly enough.

King John spun around. His eyes widened when he

saw her. "Princess Gisela. Your Highness. You're early. Services won't begin for another two hours."

"I came to read the Bible and pray prior to the service, if I may."

"Of course you may." He must have sensed the upheaval in her soul, because he asked, "Are you well this morning?"

Since he'd addressed her, she determined it was safe to approach, and climbed the steps that led to the platform he shared with the pulpit and Bible. "I am well in body, if not in soul."

"What vexes your soul, my lady?"

"Many things. My maid has repeatedly gone missing."

"Has she made it a habit of running away?"

"Never before, but I suspect the rigors of the journey have overwhelmed her."

"Yes, she does seem a nervous sort of woman."

"I want to thank you for sending attendants to my room. With my maid gone, I made use of their help last evening in drawing a bath and preparing my hair." She patted the fresh braids, which the attendants had coiled in high heaps on either side of her head, pinning them with her jeweled clips.

"I'm glad they could be of service. You have such beautiful hair, it would be a pity not to have it properly cared for." He appeared to regret the compliment the moment he'd spoken it, and his voice faded while his cheeks flushed with color.

Gisela quickly changed the subject. "Have I interrupted your private worship time?"

"No, I'd finished my reading and my prayers. I was lost in thought."

"There are many troubling things to think about of late, Your Majesty," Gisela acknowledged.

John didn't deny it. To Gisela's relief, his expression relaxed slightly.

Gisela couldn't help wondering if Elisabette's dramatic assessment of her brother's feelings had any basis at all. She prayed silently in her heart that God would help her find a way to reach out to him so that he would share the concerns that etched worry lines across his brow. More than that, she wished there was some way to get to the root of the concerns he'd expressed over his falcon's newfound love. She pointed to the window. "The stained glass is absolutely stunning."

"Thank you. I commissioned it in memory of my late wife."

With a grateful prayer that God had led her in the right direction, Gisela took a small step closer to John and the window. "How long has she been gone?"

"It was three years this past spring. She loved lilies. I had a garden planted for her. She never saw it flower. The first buds opened the day of her funeral." He spoke with aching resignation.

Gisela's heart burned inside her. She wanted so much to speak of the feelings Elisabette had said John still clung to, but the king looked as though he wanted to flee already. Should she say anything? What if he ran?

Her heart offered a wordless prayer as she spoke. "You love her still."

John closed his eyes but didn't run.

Gisela wasn't sure what to say then, so kept silent.

When John opened his eyes again, they showed a trace of moisture. "When she died, I told myself I would always love her. That I would never forget and never love another. My brother Luke calls me a fool, but what does he know of love?"

Silence hung between them. Finally Gisela offered,

"You never know what feelings a person might carry deep inside them."

"A person has a right to keep hidden what they wish to keep hidden."

Having regretted keeping Warrick's name from Elisabette, Gisela shook her head. "Sometimes keeping secrets only makes things worse."

John moved, and Gisela was nearly certain he was going to leave. Instead he stepped closer to her. A cloud had passed over the sun, dimming the light that poured through the windows, making it more difficult for her to read his face.

But the bitterness in his words was unmistakable. "You no longer speak of my brother."

"No. Do you?"

He groaned. "You read me far too well, Princess. Am I an open book to you?"

"Hardly." She felt a wisp of a smile clinging to one corner of her mouth. "But I find you quite intriguing, and I wish to understand you better."

"What if I do not wish to be understood?"

The smile escaped, and danced across her lips in a ripple of laughter.

John grabbed her hands. "What do you mean, laughing at me? In some kingdoms it is a crime to laugh at the king." His lips bent upward, but the fire behind his eyes still burned with sorrow-filled flames.

Gisela quickly sobered. Her laughter had not been to mock him. It arose from her own embarrassment. "Pray, forgive me. I should not have laughed. How can I laugh, good King John, when you want so much to cling to your heartache?"

"You make light of my losses."

"Never. I, too, have known loss. My mother died when

I was young. I have lost siblings and beloved friends." She shook her head, not wishing to make a contest of comparing losses. "I understand the need to grieve. What I can't understand is your wish to remain grieving when God has placed opportunities for happiness before you."

"What happiness, Princess? War is coming, no matter what I do. And you—" he dropped her hands and cupped her face tenderly, tracing her cheekbones with the pads of his thumbs "—you're to be taken from me."

Gisela could barely whisper in response. "Does this vex you?"

"Far more than it should."

Her mouth had gone completely dry. She ran her tongue over her lips and tried twice to speak before she could form an audible sound. "Why?"

He pressed his lips to her forehead, then nuzzled her eyebrows. His hands slid down her back and pulled her into his embrace. "Why? Must you ask why? Must I speak the words I should be ashamed to speak aloud? You, the emperor's daughter, pledged to marry another? You, who have rescued my heart from the pit where I cast it to die?"

His lips moved down her nose with tiny, featherlight kisses, as though he warred with himself and lost each time he planted one. "You, who have captured my heart."

"And you, mine." A moan that was half joy and half defeat rose from her lips, and he silenced it with a kiss.

She melted against him, too caught up in kissing him to remember that she ought to be shocked. What would her father say?

What *would* he say?

John pulled back, cupping her face in one hand, holding her close with the other. The sorrow had been chased to the recesses of his eyes. In its place was passionate determination. "How impossible is it to break off your marriage agreement?"

She shook her head, not knowing, and not trusting her mouth to speak.

"I will pay whatever price, I will fight whatever war, if there is any hope for us to be together."

"No. If the Illyrians unite against you, they would wipe your kingdom off the earth." A horrible sinking feeling sent her knees trembling.

"How, then?"

Recent history danced through her memory, taunting her with every failed negotiation. She prayed God would give her the words to help him understand. "The Christian world is split in two. There is only one church, but two great empires and many minor kingdoms. Though my father prefers to live in Aachen, the head of his empire is Rome."

"Yes." John nodded, clearly more than acquainted with the facts. "And the head of the Eastern Empire is Constantinople. The Illyrians pay homage to Constantinople, not Rome. Yet your father wields tremendous influence among them."

Gisela offered him a taut smile. "They recognize his military might and are wise not to provoke him. My father is intent on solidifying bonds of peace between his empire and the Byzantines at Constantinople. He is especially concerned about the borderlands where the two empires meet. There have been far too many conflicts there, and they can't all be blamed on Rab the Raider."

"My brother Luke would be happy to testify if your father is in need of a detailed report."

"He doesn't like the reports he hears. What he desires is peace between our two empires. Ultimately, he would like to unite them, but some things are beyond even the great Charlemagne, and I believe he recognizes that. He tried several years ago to initiate an accord. My sister Rotrude was betrothed to marry Constantine VI."

"I remember that well. Many people in the region had high hopes that such a union would bring a greater measure of peace between the empires. Then Constantine's mother, the Empress Irene, canceled the agreement herself."

"Yes! And my father has never forgotten. He resents the loss of what he saw as being a long-term peaceful accord between our two empires."

"But Constantine VI is dead now."

"And if he'd married my sister, she might be on the throne instead of Empress Irene."

"Do you think so?"

"My father thinks so, and that's all that matters. In his mind, ending a betrothal is the worst possible offense. If he hadn't been so eager for peace, he might have declared war on Constantinople when my sister's agreement was broken."

Chapter Eleven

John listened to Gisela's account of the events in the lives of her powerful family members and felt the inkling of hope that had filled him upon kissing her recede with stomach-swirling rapidness. "So, if you tried to call off your betrothal to Warrick…"

"My father would be enraged. I wouldn't be surprised if he disowned me."

"You? But Charlemagne's reputation as a loving father is legendary!"

"I won't deny he is a loving father. But his zeal for the church is stronger yet." She took both of his hands in hers and drew close to his face, speaking in hushed tones as though she feared the truth behind her words. "My father has predicted that if Rome and Constantinople cannot be united, that someday the rifts between them will divide the church itself."

"Split the church?" John whispered, feeling the words were hardly suitable to be spoken inside the chapel. Yet he had to understand what Gisela was saying.

"Yes—split the One Holy Christian Church into East and West."

"It is not possible! You cannot split the church. That is contrary to its very nature."

"My father is not the only one who fears this possibility. He has many wise and knowledgeable advisors."

"The church cannot be split," John moaned, wishing the authority in his words could make it so. Yet, even as he spoke them, he felt a distinct chill run up his spine, and feared that the emperor and his advisors knew far too well what they were talking about.

"I have pledged my intent to see Rome and Constantinople united in whatever way they can be united, for the sake of the church. That is why I agreed to marry an Illyrian and why my father agreed to send me from my home to be wed. Such a drastic decision was not undertaken lightly. This agreement has been years in the making. I'm afraid it cannot be unmade."

John hung his head, already feeling ashamed for kissing Gisela. "What have I done, admitting feelings I can never act upon?"

But Gisela caressed his face gently. "I am glad you confessed to me how you feel. Now we can focus on the political situation around us, instead of fearing the betrayal of our affections. There are worse things than mutual affection. We must resolve to work together for peace between the empires. We must never let on to others the depth of what we feel for one another."

"Few women would see matters the way you do."

"Few men would give them an opportunity to choose. I'm grateful that you trusted me with the truth."

"You'll understand, then, if I cannot spend time in your presence as I might like?"

"I'm not sure which is more painful—being near you and unable to act on my feelings, or being away from you entirely."

John considered her question in light of the previous week's experiences. "I would rather be in your presence, but unable to touch you, than to be completely out of your sight. There is nothing that gives me more joy than to see the light of your smile." Distant sounds told him the deacon had entered the rooms beyond the nave, and might any moment walk in on them.

"I shall ask again if my courtiers know anything about your missing maid." John walked reluctantly away from her, knowing that to remain in her presence any longer was to risk kissing her again—and that was the last thing he wanted the deacon to witness upon arriving for the Sunday worship service. "I'll leave you to read the Scriptures. You should still have an hour before worshippers will begin to arrive. I will return in time for the service."

"Thank you." Gisela's voice carried after him. "For everything."

It took all of his willpower, but he somehow made it out of the chapel without turning around, scooping her up and kissing her until she forgot all about war and her obligation to marry Warrick of Illyria. Given the mighty effort his exit required, he wondered how he could possibly make it through the next several weeks.

Gisela pored over the Scriptures until worshippers began to gather and then found a place among them for the service. King John soon appeared at her side and made a formal greeting before turning to face the front of the sanctuary. Though his proximity warmed her down to her toes, Gisela kept her attention on worshipping God. When the readings and singing had ended, a bell tolled, announcing mealtime.

As the worshippers poured toward the back doors, Gisela took a moment to step forward and thank the deacon who'd conducted the service. The older man, she learned, was named Bartholomew. He spent much of his time attending to the larger Lydian population in the city of Sardis at the other end of the peninsula, traveling to Castlehead for the twice-weekly services and leaving the services in Sardis to his younger associates.

With a blessing from Bartholomew, Gisela left for lunch feeling spiritually refreshed, though she still saw no way out of her betrothal to Warrick. As she approached the dining hall, she heard King John's deep voice booming through the cavernous room as he greeted those who'd gathered for the meal.

She entered feeling embarrassed, not only because she'd arrived later than she'd meant to, but also because she wasn't sure how she could look John in the eye after the kiss and confessions they'd exchanged in the chapel earlier that morning. But when he saw her, a relieved smile crossed his face, almost as though he'd feared she'd decided not to come to lunch.

He reached for her as she took her place beside him, and he squeezed her hand.

"How was your morning?"

"A very pleasant morning. The worship service was lovely, and the king was most gracious to me when we met by chance in the chapel earlier this morning." She hadn't meant to be coy with him, but found her teasing words encouraged as he looked at her with light dancing in his eyes. She sat as he did, and the servers heaped broiled fish and roast vegetables on the plates before them. "And how was your morning?"

"I'm afraid it went quickly downhill after we parted ways."

Gisela reached for the golden cup at the same moment as King John extended his hand toward it. "After you."

"I insist." He handed it to her.

She took the cup and drank. "You are far too good to me."

"Why should I be otherwise? You are too soon to be taken from me." A melancholy note colored his words. He leaned closer and murmured, "I have resolved not to touch you. I cannot repeat my indiscretion of this morning or in any way express the affection I feel. But that cannot stop me from enjoying your presence here. There is no one I'd rather converse with, no advisor whose wisdom I hold in higher esteem."

Gisela settled the cup back into its place on the table. "I have made peace with our resolution, as well. You and I cannot be together. Nonetheless it heartens me to know that I have an ally on this side of the continent." As she finished the sentence, she raised her voice for the benefit of Elisabette, who'd just joined them. "Elisabette mentioned that the Lydians and Dometians used to meet regularly at festivals. Perhaps, if my father's peaceful interventions succeed, those traditions could be revived."

John smiled graciously. "I believe those festivals would help promote peace between the kingdoms in the region. If the way be clear, I shall do whatever I can to make them happen."

Elisabette fairly beamed at the prospect. "Oh, would you really? I always did enjoy them so."

"That is what I recall. We could include a fencing tournament such as the two of you put on here two days ago." He leaned toward his sister. "Renwick tells me you wanted to invite the Illyrians and were disappointed to be advised otherwise."

While the two siblings devised tournament plans and reminisced about the festivals they'd participated in before their father's death, Gisela sat back and tried to focus on her food, though her stomach warred against her again.

What would Elisabette say when she found out the truth—that Gisela was soon to steal her love away from her, and there was nothing either of them could do to stop it? Given the promise she'd made to the younger woman two nights before, Gisela didn't feel she could consult with John about the matter. She'd promised to tell no one and was quite certain Elisabette would place her brother's name at the top of her list of people she didn't want told.

There wasn't any way around any of it, and Gisela felt the otherwise delicious dinner turn sour in her mouth as she chewed. Elisabette would hate her.

Gisela's only hope was to avoid, for as long as possible, telling King John about his sister's secret.

With his feelings confessed and an understanding with Gisela that neither of them would act on their affections, John decided it would be safe to allow Gisela to join in the discussions with his leading advisors regarding the situation along the borderlands. Besides his desire to spend time in her pleasant company, the decision was a strategic one. The emperor's daughter was held in high esteem by his entire court. Rather than leave Eliab and Urias in charge the next time he had to be absent, John wanted his courtiers to look to her for direction. But in order for her to provide guidance, she needed to understand the complexities of their situation.

Besides that, Eliab and Urias had been pressuring him to turn his back on the borderlands—to withdraw his people from all the lands that lay beyond Sardis—and to reinforce the walls of the city. John couldn't see the sense in giving up any more of his kingdom. Gisela was on his side. Her authority as the emperor's daughter, combined with her eagerness to speak her mind, made her an invaluable ally in those discussions.

And besides that, he liked having her around. It provided great relief to him when, in the midst of high-tempered arguments, she winked at him when no one else was looking, or silenced his courtiers with a subtle retort that made him want to laugh instead of scream. Each time she did so he felt his heart inclining toward her that much more. It became more difficult for him to control those emotions, yet he decided the struggle was a small price to pay in exchange for her company.

Gisela clearly appreciated being part of the discussions. Her concern for the safety of the inhabitants of Castlehead was obvious in every word she spoke. Slightly less obvious but no less deniable was her discontent with the fortress's position at the tip of the peninsula. She pored over maps of Lydia, asking clarifying questions whenever she wasn't certain she understood the landscape represented by the drawings.

It was after the rest of the men had left them alone that she glowered that Friday morning at the parchment laid out before her. "Sardis lies at the base of the peninsula, where it joins the mainland of the continent. Millbridge lies beyond, along this road—" she traced it with her finger "—and the village of Bern in the mountains beyond." She sighed. "I know I traveled the road from Castlehead to Millbridge with you, and yet, I cannot picture it."

"Your eyes were bandaged on that ride."

"But not on the ride back."

"Still, you had limited use of your eyes, even then."

"I wish I understood the landscape better. With the sea around impassable with rocks, and only one road leading from Sardis to Castlehead, you've made your fortress easy to defend, but almost impossible to rescue or escape."

"We are indeed isolated here," John acknowledged, "but there is another path on the western ridge of the peninsula. It is narrow, far too narrow for a cart to pass. Still, it does provide an alternate route between Castlehead and Sardis. Do you desire another?"

"It seems from this map that the peninsula is so narrow, that path would lie within sight of the road."

"In places it does," John admitted.

"Then I can hardly see how it might provide an alternate route between your fortress and the city." Gisela sighed. "My father has always adamantly insisted that every major fortress needs an alternate escape route should it come under siege. I would like to explore the peninsula further. Perhaps there is some possibility I haven't considered."

"It had occurred to me," John confessed, "that I ought to visit with my men at Sardis. Gregory, the captain of the guard there, has been unable to leave his post to speak with me. I'd like to gauge his opinions personally rather than receiving them secondhand. Would you like to ride out with me?"

Gisela beamed at him. "How soon can we leave?"

"Within the hour, if we hope to return by supper time."

Gisela met King John in the stables where he had two horses saddled and ready to ride.

The broad-shouldered chestnut stallion bore a saddle emblazoned with the same royal crest John had fought under in her tournament. Though the blood-bay mare bore a saddle made for a female rider, the crest emblazoned on the saddle was the same.

Gisela ran her hand along the lustrous leather. "What a magnificent saddle!"

"Thank you." Only a hint of sadness shadowed John's eyes. "I had it commissioned for my wife as a wedding present."

"But it looks brand-new."

"She only used it a few times. I've kept it well oiled since."

Gisela caught the emotion behind his words and stepped closer, speaking softly. "You oil it yourself?"

"Yes. It gave me an opportunity to ruminate over my regrets." He appeared almost ashamed as he spoke, but once his confession had been made, his mood brightened. "In the future I shall oil it and think on the lovely ride we'll share together today."

Gisela beamed at him, and they were soon mounted and on their way.

The temperatures had begun to cool as summer gave way to fall, but the birds still sang brightly from the orchards and olive trees, and the sun warmed their shoulders. Peasants working in the vineyards looked up as they passed by and blew kisses to their king. The road was wide enough to permit them to travel side by side, and since travelers were few that day, they were able to speak without fear of being overheard.

To Gisela's delight, King John was eager to talk.

"Now that you've met several times with my council, I'd like your opinion on Eliab and Urias. I fear their lack of respect toward me will poison the attitudes of their fellow courtiers."

"Indeed," Gisela acknowledged, "Urias is especially outspoken. They must have quite a history with the crown to speak so openly."

"They were my father's closest advisors and fought

beside us at Bern the day my father died. Indeed, had Urias not pulled me injured from the battle, I may have fallen that day, as well."

"I'm glad your life was spared that day. Yet I can't help thinking Urias has been more than repaid by your extended patience." She thought to say more but wasn't sure whether her words would be welcome.

"What would your father do, given the circumstances?"

Gisela laughed. "My father would grant them both lofty but meaningless titles and put them in charge of some remote corner of his empire, where the local population would punish them daily with their whining."

John laughed with her. "I fear Lydia has no corner distant enough for them."

"Perhaps my father could provide a location for their exile," Gisela corrected herself, "or, honored position, as it should be called." She giggled. "Somewhere near Hilda's homeland might be best. Urias and Hilda seem to enjoy one another's company. It seems many of the times when she has been missing from my service, she has been in his company."

"How are matters with your maid, then?"

"I gave her a lecture. She was most contrite. Given all I've put her through on this journey, I couldn't be too stern with her. I told her that as long as she doesn't neglect her duties, she's free to spend time with Urias as she likes."

"That sounds most generous. You're not afraid she'll take advantage?"

"Perhaps she will, but seeing as my father sent her as much to keep me in line as to meet my needs, I find I breathe more freely when she's otherwise distracted. Besides, I've learned the importance of being allowed to spend time with those dear to our hearts. I may not have that freedom, but I won't deny it to them."

"You are a kind and gracious leader. When Warrick takes his father's throne, you will make him a fine queen."

John regretted his words when Gisela went silent. He studied her face and found she'd pressed her lovely lips together as though holding something back with great effort.

"I'm sorry. I shouldn't have mentioned…"

"Don't be sorry. It is always in my thoughts regardless of reminder. I thank God daily for allowing me to meet you even if we cannot be together. Your friendship means more to me." She pulled in a deep breath and shook her head. "I won't dwell on it. There's nothing to be gained. Come now, I see a bridge ahead. But surely no rivers run through this rocky peninsula?"

They neared the spot and John hastened to explain. "That is no river that runs below. The sea has cut through this finger of land. This bridge is all that joins us to the continent, and I fear the chasm widens with every storm. The bridge will need to be expanded if it is to serve for many more years."

"So Castlehead isn't on a peninsula at all. It's really an island now."

"I suppose it is." John dismounted and helped her down, securing their horses to a nearby tree as Gisela crept closer to the rocky edge of the gorge.

"It's not as steep as it looks from a distance. Shall we climb down?"

Surprised as he might have been by Gisela's desire to scramble down the rocks, John hardly blinked at her request but extended his hand to hold her steady while she picked her way down the side of the ravine.

"These rocks look similar to the bedrock at Rome. Do you suppose it is the same all the way down?"

Since she'd reached the bottom by the time she spoke, and stood next to the very edge of the lapping waves, John couldn't be sure what she meant. "All the way down, where?"

"Underground. We'd need solid rock for a sufficient depth to provide a solid barrier between the tunnel and the sea."

"You're thinking of burrowing a passageway through solid rock? All the way from Castlehead to Sardis?"

"It wouldn't do any good to only dig halfway through," she teased him. Then her expression grew serious. "The underbelly of Rome is crisscrossed with tunnels and catacombs. They precede my father's rule by hundreds of years. Still, he appreciates them and their usefulness for providing alternate routes in and beyond the city, especially in times of war. And Castlehead needs an alternate route to Sardis. What other option is there?"

"You would burrow through solid rock?"

"If this is, indeed, the same type of bedrock that we have under the streets of Rome, you'll find it's actually quite soft to dig through, and it hardens when exposed to the air. It's as though God created it expressly to be tunneled through! How can you turn your back on such a divine invitation?"

"But how?" John began, wondering if Gisela appreciated the many miles that lay between those two points, and the vast scale of the project she was proposing.

Gisela placed a hand on his arm. "My father could lend you his best overseers. They know precisely how. All you need to do is tell them where and how fast to dig."

She clapped her hands twice as though encouraging an invisible crew of workmen. Then she hoisted her skirts and started the climb up toward the horses.

John followed behind her, ready to steady her if she stumbled. She only took his hand once, and that was as she made the final steps onto the softer soil at the top of the ravine.

They continued on their way to Sardis, where John was greatly encouraged by his meeting with Gregory, who'd been running drills with his men and had a cavalry training with horses. But as they lunched in the officer's quarters, a flush-faced messenger arrived.

"Your Majesty." Martin bowed low. "I was to take this message to you at Castlehead, but since you're here—"

"You may deliver the message to me now." John nodded to Martin to proceed.

But the messenger hesitated, looking from the king to the men who lined the table with increasing consternation. "Your Majesty?"

"Is it a private message?" John guessed.

Relief filled the youth's features. "Yes, sire. I'm afraid so, sire. And important."

John excused himself from the table and pulled Martin into an empty side room. "What is it then?"

"Rab the Raider has learnt of your brother's presence in the borderlands. Rumors are swirling in Bern, and our sources tell us that Rab is hatching a plan to target your brother."

"Then Luke must withdraw to the safety of Sardis. I'll put someone else in charge. Luke is heir to the throne. His life cannot be placed in danger."

"That's just it, sire. Luke didn't send me with this message. Renwick did. He's argued with your brother. Luke fell back as far as Millbridge, but he won't budge from there. Renwick can't reason with him. You're the only one he'll listen to."

John exhaled slowly and wished Martin's words were true. Sadly, he doubted his stubborn brother would listen to reason—not even if it came as a direct command from the king.

John called Gregory and his top men into the side room to consult with him. John would have preferred to have Gisela at his right hand, but given the cramped quarters he found it quite reassuring that she stood directly across the table from him, so that he could watch her reaction as the messenger again relayed the news.

Captain Gregory growled when the youth finished. "Prince Luke's life cannot be endangered."

"He insists," Martin explained.

John hastened to clarify his brother's position. "Luke has regretted the loss of Bern since the day of my father's death. He claims that, if he'd been present, we wouldn't have lost the village."

"I've made the same claim myself." Gregory crossed his arms over his chest. "Nonetheless, neither he nor I was there. If we had been, you wouldn't have been so grievously outnumbered. But all that means nothing in the face of the current threat. If we lose the prince, we'll be more vulnerable than ever. With Prince Mark off on his journey and long overdue to return, we'd be left with only Elisabette to take the throne after you, Your Majesty. Long live you both, and all, but that's a tight spot and risk we should try to avoid."

"I agree." John felt an inner quaking at the thought of his little sister on the throne. It was nothing against her gender. Gisela would make a fine leader, but little Elisabette had never known the pressures of leadership, nor did he ever wish to have her face them. John quizzed

Martin, "Renwick's tried talking reasonably with my brother?"

"He started with reason, sire. When that didn't work, Renwick threatened to send for you himself. Your brother banished him to guard the far perimeter and said he won't look at him or listen to anything he says until tomorrow."

"Dare we remove Prince Luke from his post by force?" another of Gregory's commanders asked.

Gisela shook her head. "His safety is secure only as long as his position remains concealed. The Raider may know Luke is in the area, but if he doesn't realize already that Luke has fallen back to Millbridge, we can't risk drawing any attention to his location. I fear any party large enough to compel him to withdraw would, by its very size, give away his position."

Gregory let out a long, low whistle. "She's right. It's too risky."

Martin spoke up. "Renwick said Luke would only listen to the king."

"You can't both be out there!" Gregory threw up his arms. "If Rab the Raider comes for Luke and finds the king as well, it's the end of Lydia. Simple as that."

"I'm afraid you're right." John didn't bother to note that Luke wasn't likely to obey a direct order, even from the king. "Luke has taken this upon himself. He understands the risks as well as anyone."

John had already discussed the state of the troops with Gregory, so he knew they'd been training, but were not yet prepared to launch an offensive attack—not one they could expect to win, anyway. "How soon will your cavalry be ready to face the Raider?"

"Given the size of the army he's amassing? I wouldn't want to face them for another week at least. The longer we have to train, the better the odds of success. I'm loath to send them out now. Not unless we have no other choice."

"Our only other choice is to allow my brother to follow his own judgment and trust he understands the risks he's undertaken." John dismissed the men. "We'll leave it at that and respond as we must."

After the others filed from the room Gregory took King John to the side. "Your Majesty, I know it is not my place to advise you—"

"You're a captain of my guard. I welcome your advice."

"It's not a strictly military matter, sire, but it is one of national importance. I know you said after your wife died that you wouldn't marry another, but given Mark's long absence and Luke's reckless choices, I beg you to reconsider for the sake of the future of Lydia. You've been a good king to us, but your legacy is only as strong as your heir."

John looked into the man's earnest brown eyes. Gregory had served the kingdom well, both under his father, and even under his grandfather. The man was wise in ways John could only begin to appreciate. He understood the importance of the royal line. And he'd risked a royal reprimand to speak out for the good of Lydia.

"Thank you, Gregory. I have given much thought of late to my previous vow." John glanced through the open doorway. Gisela waited for him at the far end of the next room, watching him patiently. "And I would consider doing something about it, if I could."

Gregory's brow bunched. "If you could? You're the king."

"There are some rules even a king must follow." John decided it was past time to end the discussion and clapped the captain on the arm. "Keep me informed of every development at the border. Have your men ready to ride should the need arise but pray for peace."

"Always, Your Majesty."

Chapter Twelve

Gisela left King John to his thoughts as they traveled back to Castlehead. She knew he carried a heavy burden. The situation at the border troubled her, as well. If she'd had a solution, she'd have offered it to him, but the only hope she could see was for Lydia to hold off the Illyrians until her father responded to her message. She wished she'd told Boden to ask the emperor for an army, but that hadn't seemed necessary two weeks before.

And it was far too late to amend the message. If Boden had found favorable winds and avoided the blades of the Saracens, he'd be in port at Rome already.

"We'll be back in time for the evening meal," Gisela noted as the Lydian royal castle fell into view at the horizon.

"Yes." John sighed. "I'm sorry you've become entangled in Lydia's problems."

"Me? I arrived uninvited, and I've been nothing but a burden to you."

"A burden? Far from it!"

"This trouble stems from my arrival. If Boden had sailed us straight to the Dometians, Lydia would not be on the brink of war."

"You'd be dead," John stated flatly. "Lydia might have been granted a meager extension of peace, but without your marriage to Warrick to unite east and west, the church might someday be split and Lydia would become a battleground between two empires. Captain Gregory noted something at the end of our meeting." John fell silent, musing.

"What did he note?" Gisela prompted as they neared the castle gates.

"It was a reference to the long-term leadership of Lydia. His words gave me reason to look beyond our immediate concerns, to the future. The current situation at our borders, important as it may seem, is not nearly as critical as the long-term survival of the church."

John didn't explain further, and Gisela didn't ask him to. Their proximity to the castle made it possible for their conversation to be overheard by anyone on the wall. Besides that, John didn't seem to have quite made up his mind about whatever was troubling him. She trusted that he'd share with her any decision he made that might influence her.

John felt grateful to Gisela for choosing to chat with Elisabette over dinner, leaving him alone with his thoughts. He'd nearly made up his mind earlier and now could see no way around it. Gisela would have to be sent to Warrick now, ahead of any response from her father. The instability along the border demanded it.

With chagrin, he realized the only reason he'd allowed her to stay so long was because he wanted her near. That, and he'd trusted her insistence on staying until her father had a chance to reply to her message. In light of the feelings she'd confessed having for him, he now suspected her decision to stay in Lydia might have more to do with her interest in him personally than in any objective political goals.

It wasn't that he doubted her sincerity in maneuvering to see Rab the Raider punished. Rather, he doubted anyone as prominent as the Emperor Charlemagne would go out of his way to punish a man whose crime four years before made so little difference to the security of the Holy Roman Empire. Surely Charlemagne had far more pressing issues to attend to. If he bothered to intervene at all, it would likely only be to fetch Gisela and deliver her to Warrick himself, with only a chastisement to Lydia for their role in her delay.

John would have to send Gisela away.

She wouldn't like it. *He* didn't like it. But she was a reasonable woman who loved the church. She'd already agreed not to act on the love between them. He'd heard from her own lips that the peace of the church was far more important than her personal happiness.

And it wasn't as though there was anything to be gained by letting her remain in Lydia any longer. It only increased his affection for her and made it that much harder for him to imagine sending her away. She had to leave as soon as possible.

He would tell her tonight.

Gisela reached for the gold cup just as John's hand moved toward it.

"After you." He ceded the cup to her.

She hesitated to take it. "Your deference exceeds my worthiness."

"Hardly." The king shook his head, his disposition as morose as she had ever seen it.

She understood there was much of late to trouble him,

but his disposition still bothered her. "Would you like to discuss what has you so sullen tonight?"

"We do need to talk. They're about to serve dessert. Shall we leave now or after?"

Gisela glanced down the table. None of the courtiers appeared to require their presence, and she doubted they'd be offended if they snuck away so late in the meal. "Now."

John grabbed the recently filled glass and led her out the back door of the great hall. As they stepped past a server bearing tarts toward the hall, John handed Gisela the cup and snagged two raspberry-filled desserts. Then he led her up the stairs to the tallest tower where Fledge and her new mate had been roosting.

Beady eyes sparkled down at them through the near darkness.

"It's only me," John announced to the birds. "Take no heed."

A red glimmer of sunlight reflected off the most western strip of the sea. Save for that, night had fallen. Already the first stars appeared in the east.

Gisela shivered as the cool autumn air cut through the thin silk sleeves of her gown.

John wrapped one arm around her as he delivered one of the tarts into her hands. "Are you cold?"

"Not anymore." She thanked him for the pastry and nibbled at the corner. "You pamper me."

"Hardly. You're the emperor's daughter. Many would assume a princess is used to being pampered."

"I believe princesses are born to serve. That's how I was raised. You must know I'm not used to all this attention, sitting at the head of the table and drinking from a gold cup." She took a sip before finishing her thoughts. "In Rome as in Aachen, I am one of many princesses, and a lesser one at that. But you treat me as though…" Her words trailed off as she fought to find the words that could describe the way John made her feel.

John finished off his tart with one last bite and swallowed before speaking. "Do you feel as though I place your well-being ahead of my own?"

"Yes." She realized with a guilty pang that the king had been placing her needs above his own from the moment her ship had set anchor off the Lydian shore.

"Good. I must make a request of you. Please know that, while it may pain you, I make it for your own well-being and the continued safety of all you hold dear."

Gisela heard the heavy sorrow that John so often suppressed now rising to the forefront. She wished to ease his grief, but no matter how many times she'd made him laugh, it was always present in the depths of his heart. She'd do anything to rid him of its plague forever. "Please tell me your thoughts."

"I hardly know where to begin."

Having been curious about what Gregory had told John since the moment she'd observed them speaking together and having her curiosity further piqued by John's later reference to their conversation, Gisela asked, "What did Captain Gregory say to you after our meeting?"

Something akin to apology or regret simmered in his eyes. "That I should father an heir."

"Oh, no. Did he?" The words twisted her already-hurting heart.

John's shoulder rose behind her as he sighed. "Two weeks ago I would have told him he'd overstepped his bounds. But you've helped me to realize my allegiances lie on this side of the grave. My duties as king lie to the future, not the past."

Gisela felt her heart thumping desperately inside her.

She wished he'd get on with what he was trying to say, but at the same time, she wasn't entirely sure she wanted to hear it.

"I realized," John continued, "I've been selfish. From a purely strategic standpoint, given the current political situation—" he heaved a sigh "—and the likelihood of war…"

Gisela turned in his arms until she could just make out his features in the dying light. Deep sorrow etched its way across his furrowed brow.

"Oh, John." She reached up and traced his cheek with her palm, then laced her fingers back through his loose dark hair.

He bowed his head until his nose touched her forehead. "You oughtn't run your fingers through my hair like that."

"Isn't it proper?" She pulled her hand back.

"No, it isn't fair. I want to undo your braids and let your golden hair fly free. I want to bury my face in it and kiss each silken strand."

"I'd let you." The words leaped from her mouth almost before she realized she'd thought of them.

"Prince Warrick would never approve."

"He's not here. Does it really matter?"

"It's all that matters." John heaved a long sigh, and the light that had sparkled briefly in his eyes as she'd touched his face now dimmed to solemn darkness. "That's why I must ask you to go to him now."

"To Warrick?" A sob rose through her and nearly choked off the words. "But my father hasn't—"

"It's an excuse. We both know it's an excuse. If you go to your betrothed, there is some chance you may convince him to discipline Rab the Raider. Every minute we wait for your father, my brother's life is in danger. And not just his. All of Lydia."

Gisela's arms tightened around John's waist. His words fell like shackles, clasping her tight and stealing her freedom. A surging sob rose up through her and she pressed her face against his leather tunic to bury the sound.

"I wouldn't ask you to go," he whispered close to her ear, "but it's where you were bound before you met me. You'd have been there by now if I hadn't held you back." He caressed her back gently. "I hate to cause you pain but I can see no other route. If you stay in Lydia and the Illyrians attack, you might be accidentally killed. If I saw any other option—"

"No, I agree." She moaned softly. "You're right. The pain I feel is only that which I have brought upon myself. My decision to send Boden away without me was a hasty one and a selfish one. I see now that, in spite of the justice I claimed to seek, truly I sought to put off the time of my own leaving, to extend my time with you. If I'd have gone, I would never have known the depth of heartache I now feel. This is the penance I must pay for my selfishness."

"No, the guilt is all mine," John protested. "I could have easily called Boden back. It would have been nothing for me to send you with him. But I didn't want to send you away. I knew you weren't mine, yet I sought to keep you." His arms clasped her tighter. "I seek to keep you still. How will I ever find the strength to send you away?"

Hardly had the question left his lips than the distant sound of pounding hooves clattered toward them, and a cry came up from a watchtower. "A rider approaches!"

"Friend or foe?" another voice called out.

"Friend!" The answer carried from the rider. "Renwick, with a message for the king!"

"Martin left Renwick with Prince Luke at Millbridge this morning." John turned and pulled Gisela behind him as he leaped for the stairs.

"How did he reach us so quickly?" She trailed him as he made his rapid descent.

"If he ran at a full gallop the whole way and caught a fresh horse in Sardis, he could make the journey in under three hours." John paused at the base of the stairs before leaping down the right-hand hall. "He made just such a ride to carry the news of my father's death at Bern."

Gisela followed, wondering what message would have prompted Renwick to make such a hard ride. They reached the gate just as Renwick slid trembling from his froth-covered horse.

"Catch your breath, Renwick," King John encouraged him.

"Prince Luke, sire." Renwick sucked in gasping breaths as he spoke. "He was taken. Wounded. Along with all of Millbridge. The Illyrians, sire." He shook his head. "They outnumbered us three to one."

John felt his face quickly lose its color. He couldn't let the men and gathering courtiers see his response, or they'd become distraught, and a courtyard full of distraught courtiers would only slow him down.

He quickly quizzed Renwick for details. "Is my brother *alive?* Where have they taken them?"

"Your brother was alive when I left to carry the message. I'm sorry if I fled, Your Majesty, but if I hadn't they'd have only captured me, too, and then it might have been days before you knew."

"You made the right choice." John felt his anger with the Illyrians rising. "Was Rab the Raider among them?"

"I can only assume he was. I didn't get a close look,

I'm afraid. Prince Luke had sent me to the most distant guard." He shook his head with regret.

"I heard about that," John assured him. "I apologize for my brother's rash decision, but it may have been God's good providence that spared you to bring us word."

"They circled around by way of the bridge and struck in silence. By the time I heard the commotion there was nothing I could do."

"Did they leave many dead?"

"I cannot say. I didn't linger. The moment I saw that your brother was being carried off—" His voice broke.

"You did well to carry the news swiftly, Renwick." John clapped the guard on the shoulder. "I must gather a band and ride. If we make haste, we'll reach Millbridge before morning."

"But they aren't there anymore," Renwick protested.

Gisela took John's side. "It doesn't matter. If we've any hope of reclaiming them, they'll have to be intercepted on the road. If they reach a proper Illyrian village, worse yet, if they're taken to a fortress…" She let the implied threat in her words go unspoken.

John felt grateful that she understood his plans so readily. But he also needed to make perfectly clear that he had no intention of letting her accompany him. He thought quickly, dismissing Renwick to rest before instructing the men who'd gathered to muster the troops.

Once he'd provided the officers with their initial instructions, he took Gisela's hand, speaking quickly as he hurried back to his suite for his armor. He might have sent a servant for it, but it gave him an excuse to speak to Gisela alone. "I'd like to leave you in charge of Castlehead while I'm away."

"Why? I have no authority here, and your courtiers

know it. You'll need every sword you can get if you're going to rescue your brother."

"You understand the situation as well as anyone, and I trust your judgment. The men will recognize your authority far more than they'd respect anything my sister says. And you know I don't want to leave Eliab and Urias in charge."

"Why not?"

"You're right when you say I need every sword I can get. But I can't leave Castlehead undefended, and that's precisely where you come in. My councilmen have met with you these many days. They respect you. The men watched you fight in the tournament. Some of them even lost to you. If you have to defend my fortress, they'll recognize your authority."

"Do you really think the Illyrians would attack here?"

"They had to have a reason for taking my brother alive. If they meant to draw me out, I may be walking into a trap, or more likely, leaving Castlehead vulnerable to attack."

"But wouldn't they strike Sardis first?"

"They'll strike wherever they think they're least expected, and they'll do it at the worst possible time for us. That's here and now. I hate to burden you with the responsibility, but someone has to look after my sister and my courtiers, and you're the only one who can do it."

"Any of your ranking guards could do it. You don't want me with you because you're afraid I'll get hurt."

John couldn't deny her words. He heard the bells toll, sounding the alarm pattern that called the men to arms. John needed to be ready to address his men.

He caressed her face gently with his palm. "You read me far too well. It's much too dangerous to send you to Illyria now, not with Rab's men already on the move. And

I won't take the risk of allowing you to ride out with me. Indulge me this once, then, I beseech you. Please guard my home and my sister? With Luke taken, they are all I have left." He bent close, knowing that to kiss her was to risk falling even deeper in love, to risk encroaching on Warrick's rightful claim.

The battle within him surged as fiercely as any he'd faced with a sword. Brandishing all his willpower against the longing he felt, he brushed a chaste kiss against her cheek. The impatient clanging of the bells pulled him away.

"I must go."

"My prayers go with you."

"You'll stay?"

She nodded. "For you."

Princess Gisela forced a calm smile to her face as she entered the dining hall, where the gathered courtiers had finished their dessert while she and John were in the tower. Most of them had lingered, and now their conversation whirled with the clamoring bells and rumors carried in from the courtyard.

John hadn't given her any instructions. He must have guessed she'd know what to do. That, and there wasn't time for him to waste covering the less-urgent details. His brother's freedom—even his life—was at stake. Gisela could handle the courtiers. She'd dealt with bigger crowds in Aachen and in Rome.

She stood at the head of the table and looked down the long rows, waiting for the conversation to die down. Like a ripple of water passing across a pond, silence spread from the head of the table toward the foot, until the roar of voices had diminished enough for her to speak.

How much would John want her to divulge? Her father

had always been adamant about speaking the truth. Unless there was a specific reason why the people shouldn't know the whole truth, he'd always been determined to give it himself. Much better than letting the people find out via rumor. Not only did his approach solidify his authority, but it engendered trust.

Would the people trust her? Only if she told them the truth. They'd find out soon enough if she tried to hide any important details.

"A messenger has brought news of an Illyrian attack on Millbridge." She let the responding rumble pass while she gathered her thoughts. "The bells you hear call the men to arms. Your king rides out—" A roar of shocked murmurs silenced her.

She glanced at Bette, whose eyes had gone wide.

Gisela raised her hand, and the roar of voices eased. "King John and his men ride to recover what they can of the people who were carried off."

"Carried off?" Eliab protested loudly. "Who was taken?"

"Prince Luke." Gisela named the only person she knew with certainty. The people were getting too stirred up. She had to contain them. "Your king and his men need your prayers. If you will all join me now, let us observe a time of silent prayer while the bells toll." She sat and dipped her head.

To her relief, the stunned courtiers more or less did the same. Those who couldn't contain their chatter fled to the courtyard, where they could hear the king address his men before riding out. Elisabette reached for her hand and squeezed it.

Gisela squeezed back, grateful for a hand to hold as her heart groaned with silent prayers for the safety of John and his men.

* * *

To John's relief, the men assembled quickly. Moses had been resting since John had taken an alternate horse on his trip with Gisela that morning. The stallion looked eager to ride out. That much was a relief.

So much had changed, not just inside his heart, but also along the borders. With his brother taken, John felt a surge of gratitude for Gisela's presence. Granted, if he'd sent her to her betrothed two weeks before, she'd most likely be safe from the dangers Rab the Raider presented.

But there was no going back in time to change what they'd done, and she'd be safe enough as long as Castlehead wasn't overtaken. The fortress was the safest place in his kingdom, safer even than the walled city of Sardis. And her presence provided him a more favorable position as he rode out against the Illyrians. By leaving her in charge at Castlehead, he was able to take with him as many men as he had capable horses, emptying the stables and draining the barracks by a significant measure.

It wasn't an optimum choice, especially not with the threat of attack. But, save the possibility of a clandestine rescue operation, John couldn't see how he could get his brother and the civilians from Millbridge away from their captors, unless he could outnumber them.

With his men clear on the plan, and instructions to those staying behind to respect Princess Gisela's authority the same as they would respect his, John led his troops in a thunderous wave of hooves across the castle bridge and down the road to battle.

His heart burned with regrets as he rode. If he'd listened to Luke years before, they might have dealt with the Illyrians and retaken Bern shortly after his father's death. When Gisela had arrived injured on his shore, he could have gone for the hare's tongue without risking anything.

He could be sitting at his table in Gisela's company instead of riding out in a desperate bid to save his brother.

Luke had been right. The thought gripped John's guilty heart. Luke had understood the need to assert their military might against the Illyrians to prevent just such an attack. Whatever stupidity his brother had engaged in by not deserting his post at the border when he first received word that Rab the Raider had learned of his presence, it didn't change the fact that John's decisions had ultimately created the situation.

If war was inevitable, why hadn't he taken it on his terms, instead of letting the Illyrians provoke him? True, there would have been fatalities. But they risked fatalities today and left Castlehead vulnerable.

His fears for Gisela's safety combined with his regret that they could never be together. And why not? Because of these Illyrians—these warmongering, rift-causing Illyrians. His zealous anger burned against them with a rage fueled by the knowledge that, whatever the result of the battle, Warrick would take Gisela from him.

When they reached the end of the peninsula, John stopped to address his guards at Sardis, the walled city, the largest population center in his kingdom. He had as many men stationed there as at Castlehead.

Gregory, the captain of the Sardis Guard, had already heard Renwick's message when the man had paused there for a fresh horse.

The captain had a plan ready. "I can hold the city against any assault, even with half the men currently stationed here. I've called up the cavalry unit. They're ready to depart. I'd have sent a rider with Renwick to see him safely to you, but that would only have shorthanded us."

John cringed to think that their numbers were so small that the difference of a single rider would matter.

Gregory continued, "If Sardis is attacked, we'll go into siege mode. It will be a relief to the city to have the horses outside her walls where they can graze. Let me dispatch half of my riders to accompany you and the other half to return to Castlehead to reinforce the depleted forces there."

John appreciated Gregory's apt assessment, as well as his plan. "I cannot predict what the Illyrians are planning, but I intend to put an end to their plans today."

Gregory crossed his arms over his chest. "Put an end to Rab the Raider, Your Majesty—avenge your father's death! Put an end to Warrick and Garren and their violent rule."

"Aye." John's sympathies were roused by his captain's stirring words. "They shall inflict their violence upon our land no more!"

With a bellowing laugh, Gregory boomed, "Vanquish Rab the Raider and Warrick and Garren, Your Majesty, and my men will write songs in your honor."

"I must make haste if I'm to catch them." John realized the men had gathered thickly, and were listening to his conversation with rapt attention. He quickly dispensed instructions for half the cavalry to accompany him, and another unit to ride back up the peninsula to Castlehead to reinforce Gisela's depleted guard. He hadn't felt comfortable leaving her without adequate forces. She had the walls of the castle to protect her, but now she would have the swords and arrows of some of his finest men.

He could only pray it would be enough.

Chapter Thirteen

"Soldiers approach, Your Highness." Eliab sounded winded by the walk from the watchtower to the great hall.

Fear shot through her. "Illyrians?"

"Lydians, my lady."

"King John can't have completed his mission so soon."

"They appear to be a regiment dispatched from Sardis, possibly to reinforce our depleted ranks."

Gisela felt rising frustration with the courtier. Why hadn't he told her as much in the first breath? He'd purposely tried to alarm her. John had warned her that the man didn't appreciate having anyone younger than himself in authority. No doubt it rankled Eliab doubly to play messenger to a woman.

Rather than depend on such an unreliable source for information, Gisela rose. "I'll meet them at the front gate, then."

"Are you sure that's wise?"

"Which way do they approach?"

"Toward the front gate, my lady."

"Then it would hardly do to head toward the back gate. Although you may take that route if you wish, Eliab." She nodded at him with a straight face and lifted her skirts to make haste to the front gates.

She found Elisabette already there, along with Renwick, who was supposed to have been resting after his frantic ride to warn them. He looked disheveled but obviously wasn't about to sleep through the arrival of soldiers.

Not knowing any of the approaching men personally, Gisela climbed the gate tower to address the men stationed there. "Do you recognize the men by their faces and not their uniforms? I wouldn't put it past the Illyrians to try a ruse."

"Aye, that's my brother. I'd recognize his ugly mug in my sleep." The guard pointed to one of the men, who'd come to a stop before the raised bridge. "And I trained with half the infantrymen in the front row. Should we let them in?"

"Lower the bridge."

As the guard moved to heave the beam, Gisela hurried back down to the courtyard to receive the men. Though she'd met some of the soldiers in Sardis that day, and many had likely attended the fencing tournament, she didn't know how many would recognize the authority John had given her over the castle. Knowing Eliab's penchant for usurping power, she felt it best to assert herself before the courtier opened his mouth.

"What news do you bring from King John?" she asked the commander at their head.

"He and the cavalry are trying to intercept the Illyrians. King John rides like a man with a fire under his feet. He'll avenge the death of his father with the death of their princes."

Elisabette's mouth fell open. "My brother is a man of peace. He doesn't kill for vengeance."

Gisela immediately recognized the source of Elisabette's fear. Unless the girl wanted to give away her own secret, Gisela would need to quiet her quickly. "The commander speaks figuratively, Elisabette. He means only that King John will return in triumph and restore your brother Luke to Lydia." Surely Bette would recognize that her brother's safety was more important than the rowdy claims of the warriors.

But the commander only laughed at Gisela's retort. "Captain Gregory challenged the king to end the violent rule of Rab the Raider and the Illyrian princes. Our king is a valiant fighter! I've no doubt he will end their rule and their lives."

"No!" Elisabette shouted. She spun around and ran for the stables.

"Elisabette!" Much as Gisela wanted to establish her authority over the incoming soldiers, there was nothing for it but to leave them to Eliab while she chased after John's little sister.

Fortunately the stables were empty of horses in the wake of the cavalry's departure, so Elisabette couldn't do anything rash such as ride off after her brother—which Gisela feared was precisely what Bette wanted to do. "Elisabette!" She caught her by her shoulders and tried to calm her down.

But the young woman spun around and faced her with tears streaming down her cheeks. "Why? Why would he attack Warrick?"

"Warrick's family was commissioned with the responsibility of restraining Rab the Raider, the man who killed your father. They haven't restrained him at all. Elisabette, please understand—your brother Luke has been taken prisoner."

"Warrick would never allow harm to befall my brother. He esteems me too highly."

"That may well be, but is King John aware of that?" Gisela gripped Elisabette's shoulders, propping her up as she drooped with distress.

"No. My brother knows nothing of my love for Warrick, nor of his love for me. Someone's got to warn him not to hurt Warrick. Send a rider."

Gisela closed her eyes and tried to think. They were short enough on men, and shorter still on horses. "We cannot spare the few horses we have. What if we need to send an important message later?"

"What could be more important than this?"

"Our lives, Elisabette. If Warrick is among those who mounted the attack at Millbridge, then you must know that he has chosen to take on the inherent risks."

But Elisabette's sobs only grew stronger. "He can't die! He can't!"

With Elisabette's shouting replaced by muffled sobs, Gisela heard a commotion in one of the empty stable stalls. Realizing with horror that their conversation might have been overheard, Gisela patted Bette's shoulders. "I don't think we're alone," she whispered.

The young woman looked up at her with round eyes.

"Shh." Gisela tiptoed down the central path, searching the dark empty stalls to see what had caused the noises she'd heard. She recognized two figures whispering in a dark corner. "Hilda! Urias! What are you doing? The Illyrians have attacked and taken Millbridge, and yet you're in here."

Neither of the pair answered. Had they been spying on her? "Go find Eliab," Gisela told Urias. "*Try* to keep him out of trouble." She wasn't sure what good her instructions would do. The two men were as likely to help one another into mischief as keep each other out of it.

"Your Highness." Hilda bowed.

Gisela took her by the elbow and led her down the stable toward where Elisabette remained. At least the girl hadn't run off to stop the king. Not yet, anyway.

"Hilda, I must entreat you with an important mission."

"Anything, Your Highness," the maid promised contritely.

"Elisabette is in need of your watchful care. As you can tell, she is in some distress."

"Yes, I heard—" Hilda began.

Seeing there was no reason to disguise any of the situation from Hilda—not if she was already privy to every word Bette and Gisela had spoken in the stable—Gisela spoke frankly. "She's of a mind to take a horse and run into trouble. I can't blame her for her distress, but neither can I risk having her take off on an expedition that would be dangerous for her and Lydia's soldiers, as well as the king."

"Yes, Your Highness."

"I appreciate your diligence, Hilda. Now I must attend to the men before they try to make plans without me."

"Between the tracks and scattered debris, it's obvious they headed toward Bern."

John listened solemnly to the report. The men had ridden half the night to reach Millbridge, which had been in shambles. There had been no sign of life about the place. Only blood spilled on the ground, and that was an ominous sign indeed.

"Have the men rest here. They haven't slept all night. I'll take a scouting party toward Bern. The village was Lydian until four years ago. No doubt the citizens of Millbridge, few as they are, have friends and relatives who'll watch over them in Bern. I can only assume they were taken to ensure their silence. My brother was undoubtedly the true target. If we can free him, the rest of the people should be safe."

"But, sire, what if your attempts to free him are met by an attack? The men are worried that we may be walking into a trap."

John considered the man's words. If he located his brother before the full light of day, he might have some chance of freeing him before the Illyrians would think he'd have had time to hear of the attack and respond. They weren't likely to know that Renwick had alerted him to their activities. He wished to take advantage of the time Renwick had bought him with his valiant ride.

But at the same time, he didn't want his men to get close enough to Bern that the Illyrians would realize he'd arrived so quickly. But he needed them close enough to ride to his aid if it came to battle. That was, after all, the reason he'd brought so many horsemen.

For an instant, John missed Fledge, his falcon. But the last time he'd brought her to the area she'd gone missing for days. He had only his wits and his men and the weapons they'd carried. Somehow, it would have to be enough.

Reluctant as he was to waste the time it took to make them, John quickly laid out plans to have his men positioned in stages behind him. They needed to be close enough to hasten to his defense should the Illyrians notice him, but not so close that they'd draw that notice themselves. To that end, he stationed three small parties at intervals behind him, each with a pyre and dry tinder wood.

If they needed reinforcement, they'd light their fires. The men at Millbridge would be watching. The moment they saw smoke, they were to hasten to his aid. What happened then would be any man's guess. John suspected the Illyrians outnumbered them still. Worse yet, he didn't want to engage a battle too close to the village of Bern itself for fear of injuring his people. Though he needed his men to be ready to fight, King John preferred to accomplish his mission without them—without shedding any blood, if possible.

He wouldn't run from battle, but he would pray for peace.

Eliab and Urias wanted to send the cavalry after John.

Gisela couldn't see the sense in it. "Your king ordered these men to defend Castlehead. Why would you attempt to defy his orders?"

"Our king does not appreciate the demands of war. If you want to see King John alive again, send the men to defend him."

Rather than let the courtiers imply that they knew better than their king, Gisela sent them from the council chambers. "See to Hilda," Gisela instructed Urias, "insure that her charge is still in her care."

It took Gisela the better part of the next hour to convince the rest of the men assembled that, other than doubling the guard, the most important thing they could do to help John was to let the men get their rest. They'd been up half the night already.

She was in the midst of directing the men to eat a meal in the great hall before taking shifts to sleep, when Hilda burst into the room, her face white.

"What is it? Where's Bette?"

"Urias said he'd watch her for me while I went to see about victuals. When I came back, she was gone."

"Gone? Gone where? Are any horses missing?" Gisela quickly put a guard in charge of seeing to the meal while she hurried after Hilda across the courtyard.

"Urias let her take a horse," Hilda confessed, just as they found the man conferring with Eliab in the courtyard.

"Urias!"

He spun around to face her, his expression of regret far too smug to be sincere. "Yes, Your Highness?"

"You let Princess Elisabette take a horse?"

"She ordered me, Your Highness. She *is* of rank."

"And she was in your charge!" Gisela could have lectured him on order and rank half the night, but her concern for Elisabette exceeded even her fury with Urias. She crossed to the gate tower. "Did Elisabette pass through here?"

"Yes, Your Highness. She ordered me to lower the bridge."

"How long has she been gone?"

The tower guard exchanged a look with Urias, who looked at Hilda. Gisela glared at them all. She hadn't personally seen Elisabette in two hours. If the girl had that much head start, she could have already reached Sardis. She could be over halfway to Millbridge.

Gisela realized quickly that there was nothing more to be gained by quizzing those in the courtyard. She hurried to the stables, thinking quickly. *Someone* would have to go after Elisabette. Someone who wouldn't be intimidated if the girl tried to pull rank on them.

Someone who understood about Elisabette's love for Warrick, who knew enough of her motives to think like a woman whose love was endangered, who could look for her and, if she evaded them first, could formulate a secondary plan without wasting a day riding back to Castlehead for orders.

There was no one else for it. King John was already at his wits' end with concern for his heirs. With Luke in danger and Mark long overdue to return, Elisabette's well-being was more important than ever. She might be all King John had left.

Gisela found the stable master overseeing the care of the horses that had arrived with the cavalry.

"Your Highness? What can I—"

She didn't have time to let him finish his question. "I need your best horse."

"Best for battle or sprinting or—"

"For a fast trip to Millbridge."

The stable master shook his head. "I gave that horse to Princess Elisabette over an hour ago."

"So I heard." Gisela took a deep breath of the horse-scented air and tried not to let her emotions get the best of her. "Then give me your next best horse."

The low hut was guarded by two Illyrian soldiers, red feathers extending upward from their helmets into the predawn sky. There were no windows through which to see what lay inside, but given the location of the building on the far side of the village, as removed as possible from the Lydian border, John figured it was the most likely place where they'd imprison his brother, assuming Luke still lived.

The only other reason John could imagine the hut being so heavily guarded was if Rab the Raider lay sleeping inside—and they needed to find him as well.

"I see no sign of the Raider," Sacha whispered.

John looked at the four men he'd chosen to accompany him: Sacha, Farris, Dan and Vasil. They were young and brave and bright, but most important, none of them had families of their own. The mission was simply too dangerous. John didn't wish to make any widows that morning.

"It seems quiet," Dan agreed. "You don't suppose Rab

and his men have moved on with your brother, do you? What if that hut is a trap filled with soldiers?"

John appreciated the man's astute grasp of strategy. "The Raider should not be expecting us so soon. He emptied Millbridge so that none would warn us. He wouldn't have bothered to do that if he'd known Renwick had already fled."

The men nodded solemnly.

"We'll have no way of knowing whether Luke lies in that hut until we take it. If we wait until the sun rises, we'll have no chance of succeeding." John didn't have to note that they had little chance of success as it was. They'd come on foot, save for one horse meant to carry Luke if he was badly wounded. Though it meant slowing their possible retreat, horses were simply too large and noisy. Their secondary party held extra horses, should John and his men need them.

Vasil spoke up. "Your Highness should wait here while we take the hut."

John hated to send the men in without him, but he understood the wisdom of Vasil's plan. As king, John had a duty to stay alive, even if it meant hiding in the bushes while other men risked their lives for his brother.

"The guards haven't budged from the front door of the hut," Farris observed. "The roof is low and made of straw." His eyes twinkled mischievously.

Vasil's eyes brightened. "We could remove part of the roof."

"It will be too dark to see inside."

"If it is a trap and many men hide inside, we may flee before we are spotted. If it is a lone figure, or few, we may be able to take them."

John liked the inventiveness of the plan, but certain

aspects concerned him. "If my brother is too injured to climb out, how will you escape?"

"Through the front door." Vasil shrugged. "But we will only fight the guards if we have no other choice."

It seemed as good a plan as any John might contrive, even if he had all morning to plot. And they didn't have much time. Already the sickly gray-green of dawn smeared the eastern mountains with its light. If they waited until roosters began to crow, the village would awaken and they'd lose the advantage they'd ridden through the night to obtain.

"Go silently," John commissioned them. "My prayers go with you."

Gisela was grateful that the guard on duty at the Sardis gate recognized her. "Has a horse and rider passed this way?"

"An hour ago. The rider did not stop. He rode like a woman."

Gisela might have laughed at the man's confused description, had his words not confirmed her worst fears. "Which road did she take?"

"Toward Millbridge. I can only assume it was a messenger."

"Of sorts. Thank you for the information." She pointed her horse down the same road.

Her body ached for want of sleep and from a second long journey within the span of a day. When Eliab and Urias had realized what she was planning, they'd tried to send a guard with her. Perhaps it had been a reflexive protest, but she'd refused. Furthermore, she'd purposely left Castlehead under military command rather than put Eliab and Urias in charge.

Gisela felt her horse tiring and she rubbed the animal's

neck, encouraging the gelding onward. With any luck, Elisabette's mount would be tiring, too. Gisela could only pray it would. She'd have little hope of overtaking her otherwise, not with the considerable lead she'd gotten.

John had Dan double back to report the plan to their reinforcements, while the other three men crept toward the low-roofed hut. By the time Dan caught up to them again, John had watched them quietly pluck enough straw free from the roof to create a space big enough to climb easily through.

Vasil leaned his head inside, then turned back toward where John hid in the bushes and gestured with his fingers upright from his forehead.

A crown.

The smile on Vasil's face confirmed it. They'd found Luke.

With the feathered plumes at the front of the hut still unmoving and the misty gray of morning creeping higher in the east, John's men wasted no time. Dan bent his knee for his fellows to use as a step up, and Farris and Sacha vaulted the wall.

John watched the red tips of plumage dance on the other side of the hut. The men had turned their heads. Hopefully they were only conversing, perhaps questioning each other about hearing a noise. As long as they didn't disappear inside the hut, John had hope.

He waited a tense moment. Farris and Sacha would have to evaluate Luke's condition. With any luck, freeing him would be a simple matter of cutting any bonds that held him before leaping back out through the roof.

The longer they took, the greater their chances of being caught, and the likelier that Luke was too badly injured to be easily moved.

While three red plumes stood still near the door, the other three bobbed away.

With rising fear, John realized one of the guards had decided to circle around the hut. John tried to gesture to Dan and Vasil to dive inside the hut as well, but their backs were to him. The dome of the roof blocked their sight of the bobbing plumes, which were already nearing the corner of the hut.

John thought quickly. His men still outnumbered the guards. As long as no alarm was sounded, they had a chance of making their escape without provoking a battle. And though it was difficult to tell for certain, John estimated that Bern held at least as many soldiers as he'd brought to Millbridge. Whatever Garren's and Warrick's relationship to Rab the Raider, they'd granted him uniformed Illyrian war scouts.

It hardly counted as disciplining the man.

John fitted an arrow to his bow and pointed it at the corner of the hut. He was at the far limit of his range, but if he could weaken the man, even if his shot missed but gave Dan and Vasil a split-second's warning, perhaps they could dispatch with the Illyrian quietly.

The clang of sword on sword would only draw the other guard, if not awaken the entire village. He'd do whatever he could to avoid that.

Just as the Illyrian came into view, John let his arrow fly. He watched the man's face as the Illyrian spotted Dan and Vasil.

The soldier opened his mouth to cry out.

John's arrow struck him in the leg.

Instead of a shout, he let out a groan of pain.

Three red plumes left the front door and came toward the back at a run, just as Dan grabbed his sword and leaped toward the soldier who gripped his injured leg.

Dan slammed the hilt of his sword against the man's helmet, and the figure sank silently to the ground.

John fitted another arrow as the second set of plumes reached the corner of the hut.

Where were Luke and Sacha and Farris? Vasil was head and shoulders inside the hut as John let fly a second arrow, pulling back harder and erring higher than the first shot he'd taken.

It struck leather armor, sticking to the guard's shoulder for just a moment before the man pulled it out with a roar.

Dan silenced him with his sword, but the cry had already been raised.

Vasil leaped away from the hole they'd made in the roof.

Where were Sacha and Ferris? Where was Luke?

Three more figures rounded the hut. John had an arrow fitted before he realized his men had escaped with Luke through the briefly unguarded front door.

Sacha and Ferris had Luke propped between them. The prince sagged as he ran.

John pulled the horse closer. He met his brother just as Illyrians emerged from their dwellings, rubbing their eyes before crying out.

"Can you ride, brother?" John helped Luke onto the horse. "Can you make it to Millbridge?"

"That way?" Luke pointed. He looked feverish. Disoriented.

John would have to see to his injuries soon, but he'd have to get him to safety first.

At least Luke had pointed in the right direction. "Fly." John gave the horse's rump a swat.

"Run, Highness!" Vasil practically shoved him after his brother.

John wasn't about to let his men die defending him.

The Illyrians were still organizing, only a few had taken after them on foot. The rest were mounting horses.

He wasn't sure how far they could get before they were overtaken, but the closer they got to the rest of their party, the less likely they were to be slaughtered. And it wasn't as though the Illyrians would stop after killing the four of them. They'd follow Luke's horse and cut down his men all the way back to Millbridge.

John screamed at the men in his raiding party. "Retreat!"

Gisela tore down the road toward Millbridge. She hadn't traveled any farther than Sardis since she'd ridden blind with King John, but the trampled hoof prints left by King John's cavalry made the way unmistakable as the pink glow of morning lit the way. She prayed Elisabette's prints were among them. If the girl had wandered from the path in the darkness, Gisela feared she might never find her.

As it was, she'd owed John too many apologies. He was right, of course. If she'd gone straight to Warrick instead of sending Boden on his mission that day, Luke would not have been taken and Elisabette would not have run off. It had been pure selfishness on her part that had caused her to stay, whatever virtuous claims she'd made to excuse it.

Innocent Lydians might die because of her decision.

Guilt and fear goaded her onward as exhaustion threatened to pull her from her horse. She practiced her apology to John, but no matter how lofty her words or how generous her promises of future compensation, nothing she could think of erased the truth.

Elisabette was in danger. And it was Gisela's fault.

* * *

"Where is she?"

"Where is who, Luke?" King John inspected the gash on his brother's side and marveled at the fine stitches that held him together. This was no brute patch job. Whoever had tended to Prince Luke in the night had known what they were doing.

John was impressed.

Luke was delirious. "A vision of beauty. She bent over me in the firelight. Her hair was as pale as the moon's light."

"I don't believe I've ever seen hair that color." John sat back from his examination, satisfied that he could do no more for his brother.

"I must find her." Luke moved as though he wanted to sit up.

"You must rest." John left instructions for the guards, then he left the private room at the Millbridge Inn and went in search of Dan and Vasil. He'd spoken with Farris and Sacha since their return, but his men had been so scattered over the course of their retreat—some no doubt hoping to lead their pursuers away from the injured prince—that John still had a dozen men unaccounted for.

It was likely any number of those were lying in the forest, their bodies too close to Bern for John to risk sending men to bring them back. The villagers might be able to help them. John couldn't risk any more lives.

As it was, the only thing that had likely saved them was the absence of Rab the Raider. In his delirium, Luke hadn't been able to tell John of Rab's whereabouts or if he'd even been with the party that had raided Millbridge the day before.

It worried King John. Rab the Raider had been in the area recently—that much they knew from several informants. Why was he absent from Bern that morning? What mission could possibly be more important than guarding the prince they'd stolen? Were Sardis and Castlehead safe? As soon as he could round them up, John hoped to dispatch units back to the city and his fortress. But the men were exhausted, scattered and wounded. Reorganizing would take time.

"A rider approaches from the Sardis road, sire!"

John ran toward the shout. News? Good or bad? It seemed far too soon for a message from Castlehead or Sardis, unless Rab had attacked shortly after John and his men had left. His heart clenched with concern for his loved ones. He leaped up the brow of a hill and spotted the approaching horseman.

It was no man.

Gisela's golden hair streamed loose behind her as she urged her horse toward him.

He ran to meet her.

"Your Majesty!" She slid from her horse and dropped immediately into a deep bow. "I must apologize. The fault is all mine."

John pulled her up by her shoulders, and since her shaking legs seemed unable to hold her upright after her arduous ride, he propped her against him.

"She insisted on going. I left Hilda to watch her. Urias gave her a horse."

"What? Who? What are you talking about?"

"Elisabette. Isn't she here?" Gisela straightened and looked around. "She had to have reached you before me. She had an hour's head start."

"An hour ago my men and I were fighting for our lives throughout these woods. Many are still missing. Are you telling me Elisabette rode into this?"

"She should have reached you by now." Gisela bit her

hand as though to hold back a sob and looked frantically around her as though the younger princess might be somewhere in their midst, unnoticed.

Given Gisela's obvious distress, John felt inclined to pull her more tightly into his embrace. Her hair had come loose and hung in thick waves to the backs of her knees. But his men, exhausted as they were, were already gathering around, watching and listening.

John couldn't embrace Gisela, not this close to the Illyrian border. Instead, he held her at arm's length. Warrick and Garren could all too easily hear of it. He focused on the unthinkable message Gisela had brought him. "Where did you last see Elisabette?"

"Castlehead. But Hilda reported that Urias had given her a horse, and the watchman at Sardis saw her ride past, headed this way."

"Whatever would compel my sister to ride toward battle?"

Gisela bowed her head. "She feared for the safety—"

A sound like a guttural growl carried from the road behind Gisela.

John looked past her to where a man flanked by soldiers had stepped from the thick cover of the woods onto the middle of the road.

His crooked nose was unmistakable. That face had haunted John's nightmares since the day the man had killed John's father.

Rab the Raider stood with his blade tucked under Elisabette's throat.

The Raider shouted something fierce and angry. John's grasp of the Illyrian language, which varied by innumerable dialects according to region and tribe, wasn't perfect. Rab the Raider's use of it was dreadful, and his anger only seemed to make it worse. In spite of his lack of eloquence, certain aspects of his announcement carried clearly. He was angry. He wanted something. And if he didn't get what he wanted, he was going to kill Elisabette.

Chapter Fourteen

Gisela thought quickly. Since the moment she'd heard Elisabette had fled, Gisela had feared Rab the Raider might somehow capture her.

The barbarian's Illyrian was awful. Gisela had been studying the language in preparation for her marriage to Warrick, and she quickly recognized that Rab's leadership skills lay not in diplomacy but in his blade. If the rumors were to be believed, Rab the Raider was only half Illyrian, born of a Frankish mother and raised near Aachen. It wasn't until Charlemagne had broken his nose and sent him into exile that Rab had traveled south, and he had yet to adopt much more of the local language than the basest curses.

Nor did he likely speak Latin, the official language of the Roman Empire. If he had, he'd have used it already, since John and most of his nobles were fluent in the tongue. Undoubtedly the Raider had no more aptitude for foreign languages than she had for playing the lyre. She had no choice but to address him in the tongue of the Frankish lowlands where he'd been raised.

Gisela stepped past her horse toward Rab and his men. The blade crept closer to Elisabette's slender neck. The kohl that rimmed Bette's eyes had been smeared over the course of her flight, and now her fear-filled eyes looked that much wider.

Raising her open palms slowly in a gesture of innocence, Gisela addressed Rab in their common native tongue. "Please, don't hurt the girl."

Rab's eyes widened at the sound of a language he had likely not heard since he'd left the Holy Roman Empire six years before. "Who are you?"

Figuring she'd have more to gain than lose by identifying herself, she admitted, "I am Princess Gisela, daughter of Charlemagne."

Rab's blade twitched, and Elisabette let out a tiny gasp.

"I have heard you were soon to be traveling this way. Your father broke my nose and banished me from my homeland."

"And my father can help you gain what you seek. Don't hurt the girl. Tell me what you want."

"I want equal standing in my father's household."

His request made sense. Of course, rumors had long swirled that Rab's father was an Illyrian nobleman of some sort, who'd fathered him while on a campaign in the north. Rab's violent incursions were more than the natural overflow of his aggressive temperament. He was trying to get his father's attention.

"Who is your father?"

"King Garren of the Dometians."

The name was unmistakable. Elisabette straightened. She couldn't have understood their conversation to this point, but she clearly recognized the name.

So Rab was Warrick's illegitimate older brother, then. The Raider had taken Bern and given it to his father as an offering, looking for acceptance.

But no one seemed to know that Rab was King Garren's son.

The king obviously had yet to accept him.

Gisela chose her words carefully. "My father has business with King Garren. He can bring your request—"

"It's an order! Not a request!"

"Yes." Gisela watched the blade press tighter against Elisabette's skin. The girl had already recoiled as far as she could against the half brother of her beloved. If Rab pressed his blade any closer, she'd be cut.

Gisela tried to soothe him with her words. "Yes, you are right to make this request. Every son has a right to be recognized by his father. Given Garren's previous reluctance, my father can compel him to do that which he, by rights, ought to have done already."

As she spoke, Gisela crept slowly closer, studying the Raider's face. Had his nose not been so crooked, he'd have borne clear resemblance to his father. She didn't question his claim. "My father will see it done. Now please, hand over the girl."

"I will keep her as a guarantee until your father does as you have said."

Gisela closed her eyes and thought. She couldn't let Rab take Elisabette. She couldn't imagine the girl would be properly treated. More likely she'd be horribly abused. But at the same time, how was she going to get Elisabette away from the Raider?

There was too much distance between them for her to attempt the use of force, besides the fact that Rab was surrounded by half a dozen armed men, each of them wielding a steady blade. The risk to Elisabette was simply too great. And Gisela feared that if she let Rab walk away with the girl, they would never see her again.

The simple fact was, exhausted though they were,

John's men outnumbered Rab's. If she was going to get Elisabette back, this was her chance.

She'd have to try to make a trade. But who would the Raider take in exchange for a princess? Gisela had seen no sign of Prince Luke. The only other person of rank was King John himself, and she couldn't offer him. He was the only one holding Lydia together. There would be no rescue mission without him to lead it.

That left only one person. Gisela lifted her head and looked Rab the Raider in the eyes. "My father does not value this girl. He values me. If you wish to compel him to see through your requests, trade her for me."

John listened with an anguished heart as Gisela argued with his father's murderer. The guttural sounds they exchanged were unfamiliar to him, but he could gather some meaning from the tones they used. As near as he could tell, Gisela was making inroads toward his sister's release. As long as John thought the Frankish princess had a chance of talking the Raider into letting Elisabette go, he wouldn't interrupt them.

But at the same time, he glanced warily around at his men who'd gathered near just before the Raider's appearance, and who had been slowly creeping to more advantageous positions while Rab spoke with Gisela.

His men had fought hard already. For the most part, they hadn't slept all night. Some of them were wounded. But they were armed, and from the glances they gave him, he knew they lacked only his signal to pounce on Rab and his men.

John watched the Raider carefully and waited for an opening.

To his horror, Gisela stepped toward the man.

Rab barked at her, and she undid the scabbard from her belt, and laid her sword upon the road.

No! John wanted to scream. Gisela was offering herself in exchange for his sister. No doubt the headstrong woman thought herself strong enough to endure whatever they might do to her. Truly, she was stronger than Elisabette, and far better with a sword. But her sword now lay in the road. She would be defenseless against the merciless barbarians.

He couldn't let her sacrifice herself.

And yet, unarmed as she now was, and closer to his enemies than his men, if John made any move, she'd likely be killed, and his sister as well.

The Raider's men tensed around him, alert to any move John or his men might try to make.

But what move could they make? None that wouldn't endanger the princess further.

Gisela spoke to Rab, her tone instructive.

The man's blade moved away from Elisabette's throat.

His arm relaxed from around her.

John watched without blinking. What if the murderer tried to take them both? What if he ran them through and fled? John had watched Rab at work before. Four years before at Bern, King Theodoric had no more than lowered his sword when Rab had slaughtered him.

John couldn't take that risk with the princesses.

"Take me." He stepped forward.

Gisela turned to look at him, and Rab's blade rose again toward Elisabette's throat.

John could only hope that, however poor the barbarian's skills at speaking it, Rab understood the Illyrian words with which John pleaded. "Take me. Let them go."

The Raider said something harsh to Gisela.

"You're of no value to him," she explained.

"No value? Then why did he take my brother?"

Gisela didn't translate, but spoke to John in Latin. "Don't do this. Lydia needs you on the throne."

"What does he want?" John asked quickly, hoping to understand enough to help him plan strategically.

"His father is King Garren. He is Warrick's elder half brother. He wants the king to acknowledge him as his son and heir."

John absorbed the news, and quickly explained his fears. "You cannot trust him. He killed my father by first convincing him to lower his sword."

"He would gain nothing by killing me," Gisela insisted. "He has no reason to let you live. You cannot take my place."

"You cannot go with him."

Rab the Raider interrupted them with more angry, guttural words.

Gisela spoke to him in soothing tones.

To John's horror, Rab began to smile. He looked greedily from John to Gisela and back again before barking out a demand.

"What did he say?" John asked when the woods fell silent.

"He wants us both."

John let out a slow breath. If he was with Gisela, he could protect her. "Would he let Elisabette go free?"

Gisela spoke to the barbarian, who grunted his response.

"Yes," Gisela translated, "but he grows wary. He fears he has been kept talking too long. He fears a trap."

"If only I had some way of laying one," John muttered in Latin, then addressed the Raider in Illyrian. "I agree. You may have us both. Hand over my sister."

The Raider barked.

Gisela translated. "Put down your sword."

John approached slowly, his eyes never leaving his enemy. He addressed him in clear Illyrian. "Lower your blade. Let the girl go free."

"Put down your sword," Gisela repeated again as the Raider grew more anxious.

John fingered the clasp that held his scabbard. He'd been inching closer. A good leap would bring him within range to use his weapon on the man. His men would know little of the words that had been exchanged thus far, but they knew him well enough to pounce on any opening he gave them—but he had to get the women clear.

"I will put down my sword when you lower your blade."

The Raider only tightened his grip. Elisabette's eyes widened.

"Know that if you hurt her, you will die here in this road." John used the words common to every Illyrian dialect. The barbarian had to have understood. John watched him weigh his choices.

Another guttural utterance. Gisela translated it. "He will put down his blade as you take off your sword."

"Fair enough." John watched the glint of metal move away from against his sister's neck. He unbuckled his scabbard. With one hand on the hilt, he lowered his sheathed weapon toward the ground.

Rab lowered his hands and allowed Elisabette to take a step away from him.

With a flick of his wrist, John freed his sword from its scabbard. In the same motion he leaped forward and swung his blade between his sister and the Raider, effectively cutting Elisabette off from her captor.

Rab raised a cry. Immediately Illyrians leaped from the woods, their swords raised.

Just as quickly, John's men leaped to meet them. John heaved his sword at the Raider's chest while pushing Elisabette toward Gisela with his other arm.

Rab leaped back, and John's thrust glanced off his chain mail.

In the time it took John to look back to be certain his sister and Gisela were safely out of harm's way, Rab shuffled back, and John's men pounced to fill the gap between them. With shouts and the clang of blade on blade, they fought the Illyrians back until they fled down the road.

The weary men did not give chase very far.

John didn't blame them. He buckled his scabbard back into place and resheathed his sword, knowing well he might have to draw it again at any moment. Then he quickly pulled his trembling little sister into his arms, and met Gisela's eyes over her head. He'd have loved to hold her just as tightly, but he'd taken enough risks that day.

"Thank you," he whispered, a thousand times more weary now that his fear began to ebb away. They stumbled toward the inn, where John's men quickly met up with them. "The princesses must be escorted back to the safety of Castlehead."

"I'm too tired to move," Elisabette protested.

"Then rest here. We'll post a heavy guard. Luke is in no condition to be moved, either." John eyed his sister. "How many men did the Raider have with him?"

"Dozens," Elisabette answered. "I stumbled upon them looking for you."

John still didn't understand why she'd come looking for him, but he was far too exhausted to delve into the matter. "He won't attack again, not without reinforcements. We must rest."

With Luke lying wounded in one private room of the Millbridge Inn, John assigned the other to the princesses.

He lingered to speak with Gisela as Elisabette flopped wearily onto a mattress.

John pulled Gisela into his embrace and ran his fingers back over her golden hair. "I would not have let you sacrifice yourself."

"The Raider is the half brother of my betrothed. Would I have been any worse off with him than I would have been had I reached Garren's household by now?"

John closed his eyes and breathed in the gentle scent of roses that clung to her in spite of the ardors of the morning. Her words pierced through the lies he'd been telling himself. He'd thought she would be safe in the castle of his neighboring king. But having been faced with the prospect of losing her to her fiancé's half brother, he questioned whether his presumption was correct.

Would she have been better off if she'd gone on to her betrothed weeks before?

He could no longer answer that question with any certainty. "I don't know how I can ever let you go." Her hair surrounded them both like a golden cloak as he pulled her tighter against him, feeling the reassurance of her presence close to him—for now.

"I need to rest," Gisela admitted. "We both do. It's been a long night, and I expect the day will hold unpleasant surprises. We'd best not meet them so exhausted."

"You are right. I must go."

John pulled himself away and found a mattress beside his brother's bed, and collapsed into sleep without even removing his sword.

That afternoon, the women were sent under heavy guard toward Sardis. John remained at his brother's side, praying for his recovery. Luke's injury appeared to be healing without infection and his delirium had ended, but he was still too weak to travel.

And he spoke of alarming news.

"The rumor in Bern is that our father's death was not an accident."

"Rab the Raider ran him through with his sword," John admitted. "I saw it with my own eyes, but wasn't quick enough to prevent it."

"Father was betrayed to the Raider."

"Somehow Rab was told of our pending visit," John admitted with a sigh. "It was no secret. It was an annual tradition."

But Luke's insistence only grew stronger. "The villagers claim that our father was thrust into the confrontation with Rab, that he could have escaped much sooner, but instead was compelled to a deathtrap disguised as a negotiating table."

"What do you mean?" John had only been observing his father from a distance that day. He'd been there to learn the art of wise ruling, not to participate in it. He hadn't been privy to his father's discussions.

"Father knew better than to confront a man with such a violent reputation. He had no reason to negotiate with Rab. Urias told him to do it."

"Urias pulled me from battle that day." John shook his head. "He saved my life."

"He pulled you out of there before you could overthrow Rab again. The villagers of Bern speak of the zeal with which you fought that day. Urias didn't save your life. He stole the village out from under you and gave it to our father's murderer."

John listened to the words with regret. He'd long trusted the man, if only on the grounds that his father had trusted him. Had that trust led to his father's murder? "Why would he do that?"

"I don't know, but it fits, doesn't it?"

"Gisela said something about Urias—he sent Elisabette on the crazy journey that got her caught this morning by Rab the Raider." John realized the implications aloud. "And now I've sent the women back to Urias, not knowing that he cannot be trusted."

"Go to them," Luke insisted. "Leave me here under guard. I'll return to Sardis once I am well enough to travel. You cannot leave the women to face Urias alone. They don't know the evil treachery he's capable of."

Reluctant as John was to leave his injured brother's side, he knew Luke spoke the truth. "You must come as soon as you are able. I fear we've only upset Rab further. Those Illyrian soldiers do not follow him by accident. His father has granted them to him. King Garren uses his son's desire for approval to compel Rab to do his dirty work, then Garren reaps the benefits. If Rab returns asking for more soldiers, King Garren may well send his entire army."

"Especially if Rab reports that we're withholding Warrick's rightful betrothed."

John cringed. "You're precisely right. And yet, how can I give her up to his household, knowing of it what I do now?"

"You can never give her up." Luke's words held no accusation. Instead, he spoke with respect and a note of authority, as if he'd defend John's right to have the princess to himself.

Surprised, John met his brother's eyes. "What do you mean?"

A smile bent Luke's weary face. "You were willing to hand yourself over to our father's murderer in order to save the emperor's daughter. You love her more than you care for yourself. How could you ever hand her over to another?"

John realized his brother was unaware of the greater political situation Gisela had explained to him. And there wasn't nearly time for John to explain the threat to the Christian church. "Nonetheless, I may have no choice but to give her up."

"You would die before you would see that happen."

John hung his head and measured his words. When he spoke, his voice held raw emotion. "All the more reason why you must recover, brother. If I die, you will be king in my stead." He shook off his somber tone. "Now I must hurry if I am to catch up to the women in time to be of any help to them. Rest well and stay safe. It is your duty as a prince of Lydia."

To John's relief, he and the small band who returned with him reached Castlehead shortly after Gisela and Elisabette. Not only had Urias not had time to act, he wasn't even around.

"Urias took offense that Gisela put Castlehead under military command," Eliab explained as he met King John at the gate. "He left with Hilda. I haven't heard from him. I can't say where he went."

"The members of his extended family are all in Sardis, aren't they?" John figured the courtier would likely stay with them.

"On his father's side, yes. They're all noblemen of standing for many generations back. But his mother's extended family all hail from the countryside." Eliab took John's horse by the reins and led the animal toward the stable.

John's ears perked up. "Where? Along the peninsula or on the mainland?"

"Beyond the mainland. Somewhere near the Mursia River, I believe."

"Beyond the Illyrian border?"

"I suppose so, since the Mursia runs through Illyrian land." Eliab shrugged. "Well, if he's gone that far there's no sending for him."

"Yes." John dismissed the courtier to see his horse to a stable hand. He hadn't realized Urias had family inside the Illyrian border. It seemed Urias had kept that detail from him deliberately.

Gisela heard the watchman announce the king's arrival, but she couldn't leave her chamber just yet. Elisabette had sent her attendants. Gisela had soaked in a hot bath, and the women were still braiding up her damp hair. The moment they were finished, she hurried to dress and then scrambled off in the direction of the king's chambers.

"I'm sorry, he cannot see you now. He's still dressing after his bath." The chamberlain began to shut the door of the outer receiving room.

"Is that Princess Gisela?" John's voice carried through from the cavernous rooms beyond.

"Yes!" Gisela answered, earning herself a scowl from the chamberlain, who hadn't been so quick to answer. "Shall I come back later?"

Sounds of a scuffle were nearly drowned out as John called to her, "No, please stay. I'll be right there."

"Your Majesty!" The chamberlain rushed off to provide whatever sort of help he was supposed to be providing.

"Just a moment!" the king called, then muttered, "Really, it's faster if I do it myself." He called out again, "Please come in, Gisela. There's a waiting room—" His words gave way to a muffled argument about shirts.

Gisela stepped into the waiting room. She was eager to see John but feared her intrusion had inconvenienced him. "I can come back later if—"

"Please stay." John skidded into the room on bare feet, pulling a habergeon over his undershirt as he entered.

The chamberlain chased him with a comb. "Sire, I must insist. You are unpresentable. I must comb your hair."

John took the comb. "I can handle my grooming from here. Thank you, you're dismissed."

The chamberlain looked relieved to leave, though he cast John's bare feet a pointedly disapproving look as he left.

The king hurriedly plowed the comb through his dark hair. "Are you offended by my unpresentability?"

"Far from it." She looked up at him, wanting so much to be in his arms, yet mindful of her betrothal to Warrick. A shudder rippled through her as she recalled how close she'd come to losing John to Rab the Raider that morning. It was enough to know they'd both survived—that she could be in his presence, if not in his embrace.

"Are you all right?" He finished combing.

"I feared I might lose you. When Rab asked you to put down your sword—" she suppressed another shudder, hugging herself tightly "—isn't that just what he did before killing your father?"

"It's true. I was nearly certain he would try the same with me."

"You were too quick for him."

"I would hardly attribute our success to my skill. Your

words made all the difference. If you hadn't been there..."
He shook his head. "You were right, Gisela, and I was
wrong to say you were wrong."

She laughed at him. "Whatever are you mumbling
about?"

"You were right to send Boden for your father. You
were right not to go to your betrothed." He reached for
her, then lowered his arms as though doing so required
great effort. "I tremble at the thought that you might have
been in his castle tonight instead of mine."

"Nonetheless, Warrick is to be my husband," Gisela
reminded him with regret. "You know the reasons why
our arrangement cannot be ended. In light of the circumstances that were revealed to us this morning, it is
all the more necessary that Rome have a representative
in Illyria."

"I agree that your father should have an emissary in
Illyria. But given the violence that has been visited upon
us, I am convinced that presence must be military in nature." He took half a step closer to her. If he reached out
his arms he could touch her, but he kept his hands at his
sides. "I cannot give you up to them. You are far too precious to me, and they are far too violent."

"But what would you do, John?" She looked at him
imploringly. "Any intervention from my father is at best
weeks away. Garren's men have already made significant incursions into Lydia. The longer we wait, the
greater the risk to your land and your people. Something must be done now, and we are the only ones who
can do it."

"You are right," John admitted softly. "The risks are
great. I cannot let you face them."

He was interrupted by the chamberlain at the door.
"The Princess Elisabette, sire."

* * *

John turned to see his sister looking meekly past the chamberlain. "Yes, come in."

The chamberlain shuffled away with a disdainful sigh in the direction of John's bare feet.

Elisabette bowed as she approached him. "I understand that my actions endangered many lives. For that I am sorry."

"You're sorry that your actions endangered lives," John parsed, "but not sorry for the actions themselves." He knew his sister well. "Pray tell me what was so important that you felt you had no choice but to risk your life and the safety of the kingdom for it?"

"John," Gisela whispered with a note of caution in her voice. "Perhaps it would be best—"

But Elisabette was already answering. "The men announced that you were going to exact your vengeance on my love!"

"Your love? Elisabette, you're, you're—" he sputtered, wanting to remind her that she was only a child, not nearly old enough to have a love, let alone race on horseback through the night to save him. Whatever could his sister be talking about?

"John!" A note of pleading caution had entered Gisela's voice.

It occurred to him that Elisabette was nearly as old as Gisela. She wasn't a child any longer. Could she be in love? His thoughts swirled even as Gisela tugged on his arm. "Who is this love of yours?"

Elisabette blinked up at him with stars in her eyes. "Prince Warrick, son of Garren. We pledged our love to one another years ago."

"Warrick?" John recalled Captain Gregory encouraging him to exact vengeance against their enemy.

At the same time, his sister's declaration made little sense. "But he's to marry Gisela."

Chapter Fifteen

The instant the words left his mouth, Gisela stopped tugging on his arm, and King John realized why she'd been trying to quiet him.

Elisabette looked at her rival with betrayal and anger warring across her face. "You! *Warrick* is your prince? You knew of my love for him, yet you sent my brother to defeat him?"

John tried to keep Gisela behind him, fearing that his little sister might fly at the princess like an angry cat and tear her apart with her fingernails. "Elisabette, no! She did not send me!"

But even as he tried to keep Gisela guarded, the Frankish princess seemed intent on facing his sister. "Elisabette, listen! Rab the Raider is Warrick's half brother! He held his blade to your throat this very morning. How can you say you love Warrick still?"

"Warrick despises the Raider!" Elisabette defended her love with zeal. "He has apologized a thousand times over to me for any connection to the man who killed our father. Yet you would punish him for a crime that was not his? He cannot help who his brother is!"

John had to shout to be heard above his sister. "Listen! Gisela will not marry him. I will not let that happen!"

"Because you will kill him!" Elisabette shouted.

"No!" John thought quickly. "If Warrick has apologized for his half brother's crimes, then he may be our only ally in his father's household. I will not kill him, not if he can negotiate peace between our kingdoms."

"You will not kill him?" Elisabette latched onto the words. "Promise me you will let him live!"

"If he can negotiate peace—"

"Whether he can or not, promise me you will not kill my love."

John closed his eyes for a moment. Could he make such a promise? Did he have a choice? "I promise. I will not kill him."

The fury finally left Elisabette's eyes. She turned to Gisela. "Will you promise not to marry him?"

"I do not love him. I have never loved him, and I never meant to mislead you." Gisela seemed to choose her words carefully, knowing full well the delicate political nature of the agreement. "When you confessed to me that you loved my betrothed, I did not know how to admit to you that I am promised to him." Gisela stepped slowly out from behind John.

"Let us make a trade then," Elisabette proposed. "Warrick loves me. He would take me over you."

John wanted to hope that his sister's plan could be fulfilled, but he knew of the many entanglements that could so easily bring them all down. "We can *try,* Elisabette, but the situation is politically complicated. Warrick agreed to the marriage contract with Gisela through her father."

"No," Elisabette choked out, "he would never do such

a thing. He loves *me*. He would never agree to marry another."

"When did you last hear from him?" John asked.

"Not for months. He sent me a message—"

"Do you still have it?"

"I have them all."

"May I see them?"

Elisabette blushed furiously. "They are private in nature."

"Please?" John pleaded. He didn't want to invade his sister's privacy, but given that Urias had long been deceiving him, John feared another deception. Were Warrick's feelings for Elisabette sincere? Or was he simply leading her on to learn what he could about Lydia? While John didn't want to think that any man would hurt his little sister, such a deception certainly seemed possible, given that Warrick had agreed to the engagement with Gisela. Why else would he agree to marry another if he sincerely loved Elisabette?

John implored, "I need to understand everything I can about this situation. Warrick's messages may give a clue to the situation in his father's household. We need to know what's going on if we expect to defend Lydia."

Gisela placed a gentle hand on Elisabette's shoulder. "I want only your happiness, Elisabette. Prove to us that he has no intention of attacking Lydia. Can you help us?"

Elisabette watched them both warily, but finally relented. "I'll get you the messages." She took a few steps toward the door, then turned. "You mustn't tease me about the contents. Warrick's words were meant only for me."

John blushed to think what he might soon be reading. "I would never tease you about love, Elisabette. It is far too precious."

* * *

Gisela read the notes over John's shoulder. Elisabette had been too embarrassed to stay, and Gisela understood why.

"Warrick's feelings for your sister seem emphatically sincere," she noted.

"I shudder to think this went on without my knowledge." John moved on to the next note. "Just as I shudder to think he would feel this way toward my sister and still allow himself to become betrothed to you."

Finally he laid down the pile of parchment and sighed. "There is nothing here to hint of military maneuvers. The most recent message was sent five months ago and only speaks of how he pines for her. There's a faint insinuation that he intends for them to someday marry, but he may well have been lying. You say your agreement with Warrick was years in the making?"

"I was first told of it over two years ago and understood that my father had mulled the invitation for some time before asking whether I would entertain the offer."

"The Illyrians initiated the contract, then?"

"Indeed."

"But Warrick's messages to my sister date back long before my father's death. Why would Warrick agree to marry you if he was so enamored with my sister?" John spun around on his bench and leaned back against the table.

"I met Warrick only twice. We never spoke privately. He seemed…detached, but not disinterested. He certainly didn't act as though he was being compelled against his will."

"Yet he did not behave as though he was amorous for you?"

Blushing, Gisela confessed, "You have behaved more

amorously toward me whilst trying *not* to, than he did when we were closest."

"I wonder…"

"What?"

"Urias is missing. Luke heard rumors in Bern that Urias betrayed my father at the battle of Bern—that I'd have kept the village four years ago if Urias hadn't pulled me away when he did."

"I thought you claimed he saved your life?"

"*He* claimed he saved my life," John corrected. "My injury wasn't fatal. I could have kept fighting, but he insisted we were outnumbered, then blamed my father for not falling back more quickly in the first place. Regrettably, I've believed him these long years."

"Urias gave Elisabette a horse and sent her toward the battle."

"You'd noted that. And I've just learned he has relatives across the Illyrian border."

"So he's been siding with them all this time?"

"I fear so. But if Warrick has been sending messages to Bette, I can't help wondering if Urias received his instructions in a similar manner."

Gisela nearly leaped off the bench. "Do you suppose he might have left any notes behind in his haste to flee?"

John rose after her. "We must search diligently. The man has deceived me long enough. It is time I learned the truth."

If there was truth to be found anywhere in the castle, John did not find it in Urias's room. But it wasn't for lack of looking. To his frustration, not even Eliab was of much help.

"You know, I never trusted Urias. I only tried to get along with him out of respect for your late father," Eliab confessed with such regret on his face that John begrudgingly believed him.

John spent the next three days reorganizing his men and exchanging messages with Luke, while he prayed for clarity and God's help.

On Tuesday, Hilda arrived alone, hungry and exhausted and quite worse off for wear. Given the woman's affection for Urias, John immediately feared a trap. But Hilda handed him a pouch full of parchment as Gisela led the maid to the kitchen.

John pored over the notes with Gisela while the cooks saw to Hilda's appetite.

The notes were out of order, but each one hinted at some element of a conspiracy between Urias and the Illyrians. John pressed Hilda to tell how she'd come by them.

"Urias and I left for his homeland. He told me he wanted to present me to his family. I thought it odd, him leaving the castle at this time, but he spoke of marriage. I was such a fool!" Hilda wept onto her plate a few moments more before Gisela coaxed her into saying more.

"He kept that pouch close every moment. It made me curious. So when he went to the river to bathe and left it behind, of course I looked in the pouch. When he returned and caught me looking, he accused me of spying on him!" Hilda choked up.

Gisela handed her a cup.

She drank and sputtered the rest of her tale. "He said 'twas true! He never loved me, only made me think he did to gain access to Her Highness." Hilda pouted sadly as she looked to her mistress. "I'm sorry, Your Highness. I never suspected he was insincere."

"All is forgiven, Hilda. I'm sorry you've had such a

horrible experience. You did well to bring us the messages. How did you ever get the notes away from him?"

"He drew his sword as though to kill me. I had no choice but to knock him in the head with a rock and run him through with his own sword." She sobbed into her hands.

"You left him dead?" John confirmed, knowing the importance of being sure.

"Certainly."

John and Gisela left Hilda to the comfort of her lunch and carried the messages to the privacy of the rookery to examine them further. Fledge and her new mate peered over his shoulders as though eager to help.

"You're not an Illyrian spy, are you?" John directed his question at the new bird with a wry smile, as though newly wary of everyone he'd ever trusted.

The bird only cocked his head and looked at him as though he was insulted by the king's suggestion.

"Fine, then, you can stay." John spread out a note where a bright sunbeam splashed against the wide ledge of the tower parapets.

Gisela didn't understand all the Illyrian words, so he did his best to translate for her. Unfortunately, unlike the notes between Warrick and Elisabette, the messages weren't dated. John had some difficulty discerning whether the events portrayed therein were long past or pending.

But one thing was perfectly clear: Urias had long been plotting against the Lydian crown, first under the rule of John's father, King Theodoric, and for the past few years, right up to the moment Hilda had run him through. "All of Lydia owes Hilda a debt of gratitude."

"The poor thing." Gisela shook her head sadly. "She's heartbroken."

It wasn't until they'd read through all the messages that John and Gisela were able to piece together the full picture.

"It seems Garren has long coveted the Lydian coastline, and has even gone so far as to call us fools for not making better use of it. He would build docks and wharfs and create a commercial metropolis."

"Is that even possible given the rocky shoreline?"

"It would be a risky endeavor, and an expensive one. I've never thought it desirable, given that it would expose Lydia to all manner of traffic and end our peaceful existence. I would rather rule a little-known nation in peace than a polestar of wealth where crime and greed run rampant." He shook his head. "Garren is a fool."

"On many levels," Gisela agreed. "But he is certainly cunning. When Rab arrived from the north and claimed to be his son, Garren shrewdly hatched a scheme that would procure the Lydian coastline for him, or rid him of an unwanted son, or both. By commissioning Rab to take Lydia in exchange for recognition as his own son, Garren placed himself in a most advantageous spot."

"Of course. If Rab failed, Garren could claim no connection to him. If Rab succeeded, Garren got what he wanted, and at little cost to himself." John hated to think that his neighbors had been plotting against him for so long. "That's why Illyrian soldiers have been answering to Rab. Garren sent them to do his bidding."

"No doubt, if questioned, he would deny the connection and claim the men were rebels banding together to give him a bad name."

"That is precisely what he has claimed, though he occupies Bern." John rubbed his temples as the depth of Urias's betrayals sank in. "Urias conspired with them at his mother's urging. She wanted a place in Garren's court. Urias was promised to be regent of this area once the Illyrians gained control."

"None of the messages give any indication that Urias or even Garren realized that Warrick was in love with your sister."

John relished the insight her words provided. "They may not have known. I gather from Warrick's messages that he was no more eager to confess his love to his family than Elisabette was to confess it to me."

"Still—" Gisela shivered uneasily "—it doesn't explain what their intentions were with me. I wonder…" She shuffled through the bits of parchment until she found the pieces she was looking for. "When do you suppose this message came? It suggests there is a greater plan, one more certain to unseat you from your throne."

"But how would they have used you to gain control of Lydia? They couldn't have known you would land here first. Your captain was under orders to take you directly to Warrick. He'd have done so, had the Saracens not attacked you first."

"The Illyrians could not have predicted that. Have there ever been dealings between the Saracens and the Illyrians?"

"The Illyrians fear the Saracens as much as we do. The pirates are far too foreign for even the Illyrians to plot with them."

"And yet, Warrick gave Elisabette no indication that he intended to marry anyone but her. So why did he agree to have me sent to him? What was he planning to do?" Gisela shivered.

"Whatever it was, it can't have been good."

John mulled over the question for the next two days. Even through the Sunday morning worship service he didn't gain any clarity, though the time spent with Gisela further solidified his determination not to give her up. But how could he keep her?

His attempts to rebuild the army were hampered by the distance between Castlehead and Millbridge. To John's relief, on Wednesday morning the old deacon Bartholomew arrived for the midweek worship service with the news that Luke had just arrived safely in Sardis. John consulted with Gisela after the service while he made preparations to meet with his brother.

"I regret to ask you the favor of taking charge of Castlehead in my absence, especially in these trying times."

Gisela only laughed at his concern. "You know I'm quite capable of leaving the castle under military command if I feel I must ride after you." She looked at him longingly and her expression sobered. "You know I would do anything for you. I'm honored that you leave your fortress to me."

"You have proven yourself a most capable leader." He gazed at her, memorizing her every feature to tide him over until he would see her again. "I esteem your judgment above all others."

John left her reluctantly. He rode with a band of men in hopes of hearing better news from his brother. With Urias dead, they could hope to avoid further betrayals. With any luck, the Illyrians would be disinclined to make a move without their inside man.

Or they might have grown more desperate, and be willing to try anything. John supposed he'd know the answer all too soon.

Gisela divided her time between prayers for John's safety, and overseeing the falcon tower. There Fledge's new mate peered at her curiously, as though wondering what she'd done with the other falcon. Fledge was nowhere to be seen.

Elisabette had taken to her room, and Hilda had taken over her post keeping track of her, which was easy enough since the girl rarely emerged, even to eat. The troops kept up steady drills in the courtyard and outlying fields. They kept busy making arrows and sharpening their swords, and patching any holes in their armor.

Bartholomew arrived Sunday morning with a surprise in a wooden cage. "Do you recognize this creature?" He held up the falcon for her to see.

Fledge glared at the deacon through the bars.

"Yes, I do! Where ever did you find her?"

"She surprised King John yesterday. Flew right up to him as he stood on a high open tower. The king asked me to deliver her back to you."

Gisela thanked the deacon for returning the bird, and carried Fledge back to her mate, who almost looked relieved, if a bird could wear such an expression.

Worship had a somber tone, and afterward Gisela quizzed Bartholomew for news of John and Luke, since messages between them had been few and brief.

"His Majesty longs to return to Castlehead, but Prince Luke fears for the safety of Sardis," Bartholomew informed her with an apologetic shake of his head. "His scouts report that the Illyrians are drawing near the city pulling three catapults, each as tall as six men."

Gisela pinched her eyes shut as Bartholomew delivered the news. Her father had catapults and trebuchets among his war machines. She'd watched them in action in practice drills, the missiles they flung pounding the earth with a force like thunder. The memory of it rumbled through her bones ominously. If three of the deadly machines bombarded Sardis, the city's strong stone walls would fall, crushing those they'd been built to protect.

"King John and Prince Luke hope to mount an offensive against the Illyrians before they reach the city, but from the reports the scouts have brought, the Lydian forces are vastly outnumbered. To ride out might be suicide."

"To stay in the city might be the same." Gisela wished there had been time to build an escape tunnel, so that the people of Sardis could travel safely to Castlehead. But then, the Illyrians would simply drag their war machines on down the peninsula.

Gisela gripped the old deacon's weathered hands. "Catapults are mighty, but they're not unstoppable. They're built of wood, with ropes to fling the missiles. The best defense is to shoot at them with flaming arrows, or better yet pelt them with burning coals from the small catapults mounted on the Sardis walls. If you can catch them on fire they'll have to stop shooting long enough to get the fire out."

"Would they really catch on fire and burn, do you suppose?" Bartholomew questioned.

"I've never seen it done, but my father always said it might be possible. The only other hope would be to get a runner behind the enemy to set them ablaze by hand. The fire would be more likely to catch, but there's little chance that runner would return alive."

"Dear God, help us." The old deacon shook his head.

"You're welcome to stay in Castlehead." Gisela was reluctant to let Bartholomew leave Castlehead after the Sunday services.

A surprisingly fierce look sprang to Bartholomew's eyes when she suggested that he stay. "If I let the fear of the Illyrians stop me from doing the Lord's work, they might as well kill me. I intend to ride my circuit until I die."

An ominous feeling rose inside her as Gisela watched him go. Would the old deacon die doing the Lord's work? She prayed it wouldn't come to that, and yet his words echoed through her mind, boding ill warnings. The air itself seemed ripe with expectation, and a crisp fall wind blew in from the sea, pushing distant thunderclouds toward them.

Gisela didn't like the look of the clouds as she studied them from Fledge's tower, where she'd climbed to get a better look. They teemed with angry power, surging and billowing, changing constantly, now hiding, now revealing ships in their midst.

She squinted at what appeared to be sails riding ahead of the clouds that loomed just west of them. Had the Illyrians decided to strike by sea? They weren't known for their seafaring ways, having very little decent coastline to sail from. It was for that very reason she suspected King Garren was so intent on obtaining the lands of Lydia—he wanted ports to sail from, but had little idea just how poor a port might be off the rocky shore.

Once Gisela was certain the shapes she saw were not just shifting clouds, but ships—three of them, in fact—she lifted her skirts and hurried to the gates.

The watchmen there had been studying the approaching sails, as well. The brisk winds pushed the ships rapidly closer, so that in the time it took for Gisela to reach the other tower, already she could make out some detail on the sails.

"They are my father's ships." She nearly cried with relief when she recognized them. It had been nearly five weeks since Boden had left with the message for her father. If he'd made good time, her father could have sent ships in response to his message, which would even now be pushing toward them ahead of the strong winds.

Gisela ran for the wharf, reaching the end of it just as the first smattering of rain hit the wooden planks. The first ship had let down a boat, and the rowers pulled mightily to stay ahead of the sheet of wind-driven rain that pursued them.

"Father!" Gisela called, waving happily when she recognized for certain the great man who stood at the prow.

He grinned back at her, and leaped with a great stride for the dock as the boat slid alongside it. "Gisela!" He scooped her up into a great hug. "We've got to get in out of the rain."

"Hurry to the castle!" She ran alongside him, jealous of his longer legs that propelled him forward ahead of her, in spite of his age and stout size. As they neared the gate she darted ahead and waved the men in behind them before darting under the roofline that overhung the walls rimming the courtyard, leading them to the great hall where a fire still burned from the noon meal.

She sent the servants to fetch food and drink, then turned to her father, who clasped her by the shoulders.

"Gisela." He beamed. "You look as well as I have ever seen you. And where is this King John to whom, my men tell me, I owe a debt for saving your life?"

"Oh, Father, I hardly know where to begin." She launched quickly into the story of all that had happened from the moment she'd arrived in Lydia up until that very day. As she spoke, the servants carried in a lunch.

The emperor ate, but his eyes hardly left his daughter's face. Partway through her tale, Gisela sent men to fetch the maps of Lydia she'd been studying with King John, so that her father could better understand the details of what she explained.

"John says the Illyrians have long caused trouble, but I know my arrival was the spark that lit the fire of war. This good Christian kingdom may well pay the ultimate price for their kindness to me."

Charlemagne scowled. "I should have killed Rab the Raider instead of unleashing him on unsuspecting lands."

"You were only trying to be merciful," Gisela consoled him.

"He didn't appreciate my mercy, or he wouldn't be so intent on ending innocent lives." Charlemagne glowered. "And what of this King John that you've spoken of so well and so highly with nearly every sentence from your lips?"

Gisela felt herself blushing furiously. She'd thought she'd gotten through the story without giving away any of her feelings for the young king, but obviously her father knew her well enough to listen between the lines. "He saved my life. He's a good king, and I fear…" She bit her hand, chastising herself for showing weakness in front of her father.

Thankfully, Martin rushed into the great hall at that moment. "Old Bartholomew approaches through the rain, Your Highness."

"Bring him in, by all means. The poor dear must have turned around to escape the storm." But even as she spoke, Gisela couldn't help but wonder. The afternoon had turned to evening while she'd been explaining the events of the past several weeks to her father. Even traveling slowly, Bartholomew should have arrived at Sardis long before.

She'd no more than expressed her concern to her father when the old deacon was shuffled in, dripping and coughing. She had him brought near the fire and sent a servant to fetch him a mug of hot spiced wine.

"Please." He coughed and sputtered, raising his hands

to ward off their attempts to help him. "Listen. As I approached the city of Sardis, I saw the catapults and the Illyrian army."

"They approach the city?"

"No." A fit of coughing took him, and Gisela had to wait long painful seconds before he explained. "They're fighting. They've got Sardis surrounded. The city is under siege."

Chapter Sixteen

As night fell, John remained in a tower with his brother. A storm had moved in, darkening the day, dousing all hope that their flaming arrows might catch the catapults on fire, and finally, blocking out all light from the moon and stars with thick clouds.

Even the wind blew so fiercely that John could no longer hear the sounds of battle.

"I believe they've given up the fight for the night," Luke observed as he peered through the narrow arrow-slit window.

"I pray they have." John felt the ache of battle in his every limb. His throat was sore from shouting, his arms weak from pulling back his bow and his legs trembled from the many times he'd rushed from one tower to another to monitor the press of battle. "If they make many more direct hits against our walls, they'll bring them down completely."

"The men are trying to patch the breach on the west end, but the rain is complicating their efforts."

"Fortunately the cliffs beneath the city are high at that point. If the Illyrians want to make use of the hole they've made, they'll have to do a great deal of climbing first."

"They may well do it."

John agreed. "They've come at us with their full army. This is no mere raid they can blame on rebels."

"They have no intention of answering to anyone afterward. I doubt they intend to leave any of our men alive."

John groaned at the thought. If he truly loved her, Warrick might spare Elisabette to be his bride. But what would happen to Gisela? John still hadn't figured out why the Illyrians had requested a match in the first place, so he couldn't begin to guess what they'd do with her now. "I suppose even Warrick himself is down there somewhere."

"All the better to rush in and take the crown," Luke pronounced with disdain.

"We can't let it come to that." John rose determinedly and peered through the arrowslit into the thick darkness. Nothing but wind and pounding rain greeted him, but he knew that somewhere, far too close and yet not near enough to see, lay a vast army and munitions of death.

"How are we ever going to stop them? I've worn myself out today making no inroads against them, and I'm still not recovered from their last attack against me." Luke held one hand to his side, which had healed thanks to the stitches of the mysterious pale-haired woman, though Luke reported that he still felt aching pain in the spot.

"We could mount an offensive," John suggested.

"'Twould be suicide."

"If we had a second team to come at them from behind—"

"We don't."

"If we'd built the tunnels Gisela suggested—"

"We haven't." Luke's sigh was almost a laugh. "And there isn't time."

"How do you know?"

"How long do you think we have?" Luke answered his own question. "Not nearly long enough."

John slumped against the wall and slid down until he sat beside his brother on the floor. He thought for several long minutes before asking, "What do you suppose they'll do with us?"

"With you, the king, and I, the prince?" Luke made a musing face. "Assuming we survive the battle, they'll find the most miserable way to kill us and then leave our bodies somewhere awful as a warning to their enemies."

John pondered a moment longer. "I'd rather ride out and meet the battle, even if it means certain death."

Luke fiddled with an arrow, pointing all the barbs of the feather until they spread out in perfect symmetry. Finally he asked, "At dawn?"

"No, the rising sun would blind our eyes."

"At sunset, then?"

"If we live that long."

Luke stood and offered John his hand. "I'll ride out beside you," he promised, pulling his brother to standing, "if we live that long."

Torches lit the great hall as Gisela spread out the maps. Her father and his ranking men stood along one side of the long table. John's remaining military men faced them from the other side.

"How many fighting men came with you?" she asked her father.

"Thirty-five on my ship, thirty-seven on each of the two others."

"That's over a hundred men." She turned to Renwick, the highest-ranking of the men John had left behind. "And we have five dozen more?"

"Three score, Your Highness," Renwick calculated, "sixty men and twenty horses."

Gisela scowled at the maps. "It's the lack of cavalry that would hurt us most. A man can ride to Sardis in an hour at a full gallop. Walking might take him all day."

Emperor Charlemagne ran his fingers along the outline of the coast. "I brought three ships. What's to stop us from coming by sea?"

"You noted the rocks when you came in?"

"Are they as thick all along the coast?"

"Thicker. Only fishing boats can make it through."

The emperor made a thoughtful sound in his throat. He looked at Renwick. "How many fishing boats are there in the area?"

"Oh, dozens, sire. Many along the peninsula make their living on the sea. But a man would have to knock on every door for miles to round them up."

Charlemagne chuckled. "If you round them up, I'll fill them." He turned to Gisela to explain, "The Illyrians might take notice of a ship. Fishing boats may approach with greater stealth."

While Renwick rushed off to dispatch men to commandeer all the fishing boats they could, Charlemagne crossed his arms over his chest and addressed Gisela. "Now, how are we going to get a message to King John to let him know when we'll be arriving? I'd like him to mount an offensive from the city at my signal."

Gisela wished they had a tunnel to send a messenger through. Nor did she expect a messenger could get past the Illyrian siege to deliver a note. "We'll just have to hope they see what we're up to and respond."

"It would be more effective if we could coordinate an attack."

"I'm sorry, Father. The only way we could get a message to them at this point would be to fly it to them through the air." She intended the words to express the futility of his request, but the moment she spoke them, a thought occurred to her. She snapped her fingers. "We could fly it through the air!"

Her father eyed her skeptically, but when she explained that Fledge had found King John in Sardis once before, Charlemagne chuckled happily. "The Illyrians won't try to stop a bird. Do you really think this creature can find your king?"

"She's faithful to him. I've had to keep her caged to prevent her from flying back home. The greater trick will be getting her to carry a message without trying to tear it off."

As they formulated their plans, Gisela penned the message in tiny script on a scrap of parchment, thankful that nearly all Illyrians were illiterate. Just as rare as those who could read or write were Illyrians who could speak a word of Latin. Even if the note was intercepted, no one would be able to translate it.

Sometime after midnight the rain tapered off. Gisela sent a servant to fetch the falcon. She tied the message securely to her leg, while a guard held the animal to keep Fledge from biting. Then she told the bird to find King John, and had her set free through the window.

"Do you suppose that will work?" Charlemagne asked, as the falcon disappeared into the dark night.

"If it doesn't we're no worse off than we would be otherwise. And if it does—" she grinned up at her father and felt her hope returning "—it may tip the battle back in Lydia's favor."

John awoke to the sound of fighting. His entire body ached, but he leaped to his feet and rushed to throw open the shutters to the room where he'd spent the night. The murky glow of dawn tinted the eastern sky. Below him, past the walls of the city on the plain near the rocky coast, John could just make out the outline of the three hulking catapults waiting like giant beasts to unleash their destruction.

Now that the rain had ended, John and his men might finally have a shot at setting one of the massive death machines ablaze. If they were quick, they might even get the job done before the catapults inflicted much more damage.

John pulled his head in from the window just as something hurtled toward him through the air. He caught sight of it out of the corner of his eye and was about to pull the shutters closed when he recognized the falcon.

"Fledge! Have you been stalking me?" he accused. "I am not your usual prey."

John slipped on a leather glove before extending his arm toward the bird. The raptor alighted on his arm but pranced somewhat uneasily.

"Why are you fidgeting? Oh, you've got something on your leg." John felt a curious smile spread across his lips. The bit of parchment had to have been intentionally tied there, and he only knew one woman cunning enough to do such a thing.

His heart warmed at the thought of his beloved. If he lived to see her again, he would never let her go.

At her father's insistence, Gisela relented to staying at the rear of the cavalry unit as they made their way down the peninsula toward Sardis. The boats had rowed out before dawn, each weighed down with as many men as the varied craft could carry. She'd told her father about the catapults, so many of the men carried kettles filled with burning coals.

They walked to save the horses' strength for battle, besides which many of the men had no mount, so if they intended to arrive together they all had to travel on foot. With any luck, they'd be within sight of Sardis by the time her father and his men mounted their surprise attack from the rear.

And if John received his message in time, he'd be watching for Charlemagne's signal, a wide swath of crimson fabric to be unfurled the moment Charlemagne wanted John's men to charge. If John could keep the Illyrians' attention from the "fishermen" scrambling up the rocky shore, the buckets of coal might stand a chance of reaching the catapults.

She could only pray John and his men were still well enough to mount the attack.

John braced himself against the battlements as the catapults thundered their missiles against the city walls. The men were ready. Every horse in the city was mounted to ride out. His best archers manned the walls to keep the encroaching Illyrians at bay, while a second wave of footmen prepared to follow the cavalry out the front gate and across the bridge the moment John gave the signal to have it lowered.

The boats had been weaving through the rocky waters for almost an hour. John had watched the men, disguised by cloaks to look more like fishermen than soldiers, as they clambered up the cliffs toward the Illyrians, who were too consumed with bombarding the city to recognize the threat that crept stealthily up behind them.

Had John not known of the plan, he might have feared the Illyrians themselves were up to mischief, if he'd paid the fishing boats any heed at all. As it was, he felt a wild hope clamoring inside him. Was the Emperor Charlemagne himself really among the figures creeping to the aid of his beleaguered city?

As the men rose to their feet, one figure stood taller than the rest. His broad shoulders made him easy to pick out. While the others crept closer to the catapults at the rear of the Illyrian ranks, carrying buckets John doubted held fish, this lone man stood still and reached inside his cloak.

The wind caught the red cloth, billowing it wide. It rippled in the wind three times before the figure let it go. It blew back toward the sea and the man charged forward.

John looked to the guard at the next tower and lowered his arm, signaling him to raise the portcullis and lower the bridge.

While the heavy counterweights ratcheted loudly in obedience to his order, John leaped down the steps and found his stallion, Moses, waiting beside his brother's horse. He met his brother's eyes for one silent moment, knowing they would fight to the death if necessary to protect their loved ones and their kingdom.

Then the front horses broke free, pounding across the heavy planks, as the Illyrians surged to meet them.

The roar of battle rose up everywhere around him. John didn't have to nudge Moses to move. The stallion lunged forward the moment the animal in front of him led the way. John held his sword ready and prayed that God would be with them.

As Gisela had promised her father, she let the men take the lead as they reached Sardis. It wasn't as though she could have gotten to battle, anyway, with the wall of clashing swords in front of her and the rocky sea on either side.

Her horse pranced anxiously, dancing first forward and then back. Worried that the animal would waste its strength in nervous dancing, Gisela took cover in the nearest olive grove, where she could watch what was happening and determine where her sword might be most useful.

Smoke rose from the rear of the Illyrian ranks, belching black and ugly through the morning sky. Had her father's men caught a catapult on fire? It was the only thing she knew of that could create so much smoke, but she could see little past the ridges of rocks and the sea of fighting soldiers.

She watched the men make their way down the drawbridge toward the Illyrian front. For several tense moments she feared the red-plumed soldiers would prevent John's men from advancing, but a grave push from the city broke through in a wave of hooves and swords, and the men poured out of Sardis.

Gisela searched for John among them, but the fighting was too thick. Instead she turned her attention toward her advancing men. They'd made some headway toward Sardis, even as the Illyrians who besieged the city turned to fight them off.

Hoping to ride forward with them, she nudged her horse forward, almost reaching the men who marched at the rear when the clatter of hooves behind her caught her attention.

A score of Illyrian riders had forded the shallows and now crept up the rocky bank toward the peninsula. For a moment, Gisela feared they were about to pounce on the Lydian soldiers from behind.

Then, with an even more sickening fear, she saw they weren't interested in her soldiers at all.

They pointed their horses down the road to Castlehead at a full gallop.

The Illyrians had obviously guessed that Lydia had spent its forces riding to the aid of Sardis. Castlehead now lay virtually unguarded, save by Elisabette, Hilda and the fresh-faced youths Gisela had deemed too inexperienced to march out with her.

If the twenty cavalrymen ahead of her reached Castlehead, they could easily breach its defenses. Even if Sardis was saved, Castlehead might fall.

Gisela called to the men in front of her, but saw with a sinking heart that all those on horseback were far too engaged in the battle ahead to hear her or break away. The infantrymen nearest her looked where she pointed, and though realization dawned on their faces, there was little they could do on foot, not chasing after horses.

Gisela had no choice. She shouted to the foot soldiers to send the next available riders after her, then turned her horse and went after the Illyrians alone.

John recognized the royal insignia on the sword that clashed with his.

"Prince Warrick." He spat the man's name back at its bearer.

"King John." Warrick wielded his weapon with cunning and skill.

A question had burned inside John for days. Since he and Warrick could both die at any moment in the heat of battle, John saw no reason to put off asking it. "Why did you agree to marry Gisela, daughter of Charlemagne, if you're in love with my sister, Elisabette?"

Warrick snarled at him as he blocked every jab of his sword. "I never intended to marry Gisela. If Charlemagne had been paying attention, he'd have realized my father's contract was for Gisela to marry his eldest son. And if Charlemagne assumed otherwise, why should my father feel compelled to correct him?"

"Rab the Raider?" John's surprise was so great that his sword faltered.

Warrick slashed forward, pushing him past the men who raged by the city, nearer the road that led down the peninsula. "None other. If Charlemagne assumed the contract was with me, it can't be helped."

"But Charlemagne would never agree to give his daughter to a landless raider. He'd destroy Rab and take Gisela back!"

"Rab does not intend to be landless. He'll sit on your throne and rule your kingdom and defend his right to have her with the swords of your people."

Fury surged through John that Gisela might be forced to marry the awful brute who'd killed his father. He spurred Moses forward and lunged at Warrick. His horse pushed Warrick's horse back against the stone wall that rimmed the road. Warrick leaned back over the wall, holding tight to his reins with his free hand. His eyes widened when he looked down the far side, to the deep gorge that encircled the city of Sardis.

John held his sword to Warrick's throat. "If I push you back, your bones will be broken against the rocks and you'll die in slow agony."

"The sword then." Warrick closed his eyes. "Kill me quickly."

"Sire! King John!" Voices called out to him over the throng, and John turned just long enough to see footmen pointing down the road to Castlehead. Gisela made for the narrow path at high speed. And up ahead, beyond her, twenty horsemen galloped down the wide road.

In an instant, John realized that Gisela intended to stop them—alone, if none could help her.

John leaped away from Warrick. "I promised my sister I would not kill you." He did not wait to see how Warrick took the news, but pushed forward through the charging horses that blocked the road. Surging forward, he used his sword to clear the way, knocking aside Illyrians, while his own men, once they saw his fierce charge forward, scrambled to clear the way for him.

He'd nearly made it through the thick of it when a stallion black as midnight blocked his way.

Even past the scrap of leather mask that shielded the man's face, John could see that his nose was broken.

"Rab the Raider." John raised his sword and lunged at the man who'd plotted to take Gisela from him. "You killed my father."

"Today you will join him in death," Rab sneered, wielding his sword with brutish thrusts.

John blocked his blows, but the Raider had an advantageous position high on the side of the road. Hemmed in as they were on all sides by the flashing swords of fighting men, there was little John could do but back down the road.

He was more concerned about reaching Gisela than ending Rab's life, at the moment. But he couldn't escape the relentless blows, though Moses pranced farther back with every stroke of Rab's sword. Too soon, John felt the press of cold stone against his leg, and looked down to see the very rocks upon which he'd threatened to leave Warrick dying.

Rab raised his sword.

John lunged desperately forward, hoping somehow to block him, when a scream turned both their heads.

Prince Warrick charged toward him with his sword raised.

There would be no blocking them both.

Gisela let her horse have its head. She had to reach the plank bridge that separated the island of Castlehead from the rest of the peninsula. If she arrived in time, she'd have a chance to knock the loose planks free, down into the steep ravine, preventing the cavalry from advancing en masse. They'd have to make their way down and back up the rocky sides of the gorge—tricky enough for a man on foot, quite nearly impossible on horseback, not without snapping the poor animals' legs. Even if they made it up the other side, they'd be scattered and tired, and much easier to pick off one by one.

But she had to reach the plank bridge before them for the strategy to work. They had the advantage of the wide road that led straight to the bridge. She'd be going out of her way by taking the narrow path on the far side of the peninsula, but it was the only way she'd have a shot at passing them. She could only hope their horses were tired, and slower due to their heavier riders.

Glancing back, she tried to determine if any of Lydia's horsemen had made it through to help her. She wasn't even sure if she could budge a single plank of the bridge herself, let alone send them all toppling into the ravine before the Illyrians made it across. She urged her horse onward and prayed that somehow, she'd make it ahead of them. Somehow, she would stop them.

* * *

"You held my love at sword point!" Warrick screamed as he attacked.

For one disoriented instant, John wondered what the younger prince was referring to.

Then Warrick's blade knocked Rab the Raider back, and John realized precisely what was happening.

Warrick was ridding himself of an unwanted rival.

John didn't waste a second to see how their battle ended, but pushed off the wall with a mighty kick, turning Moses toward the road that led to Castlehead.

The Illyrian cavalry had gotten far too generous a head start. Gisela was up there, alone.

"Ride with me!" John shouted to the mounted Lydians nearest him. He pointed with his sword and charged forward, trusting that those who could follow him would.

There was no time to go around by the narrow path Gisela had taken. The alternate route would only be advantageous if he hoped to pass the Illyrians. It would be difficult enough for him to catch up with them riding by the straight route.

Moses charged forward eagerly, his hooves licking up the ground beneath them as he stretched out, flying as though he understood John's desperate need to catch up to those who would take his castle and harm his family.

With the wind whipping in his eyes, John glanced back to see a handful of riders pounding down the road after them. He recognized a few of his Lydian men, and at the rear, bloodstained sword gripped tightly in his hand, Warrick charged after them all.

John could only imagine he'd dispensed with his unwanted rival and now came to seek his revenge against Lydia. There was no point engaging him now, not if it meant leaving Gisela alone to face the Illyrians. Still, it would not do to let Warrick catch up to him.

"Fly, Moses, fly!" John urged the stallion to greater speeds as the haunches of the Illyrian cavalry came into view ahead of them.

They rode as men saving their strength for battle, and not with desperate speed.

There was some chance John might catch up to them, had the plank bridge across the ravine not already come into view. It was just wide enough to accommodate the widest merchant carts. Two horses could ride abreast, but they'd have to take care not to miss a step. The sides had no railing to keep them from falling.

"Your Majesty," a voice panted from just behind him.

John turned to see his men, including Tertulio, the great ox of a man who'd nearly eliminated him from the fencing tournament.

"The bridge!" John directed them. "We've got to topple it!"

He could see Gisela had already dismounted and heaved at the massive timbers.

John and his men blew through the midst of the Illyrian cavalry, scattering them to the sides. "On your horse!" John shouted to Gisela as he approached. "Defend the far side!" If she could cross with her mount before the beams fell, she'd have the advantage over any men who might make it up the far side.

"Ride with me!" she urged him, leaping on her horse.

Tertulio leaped from his stead and lifted a beam, heaving it down. "Cross quickly, sire."

John didn't hesitate, but rode after Gisela as his men scrambled to topple the bridge while defending it from the Illyrians who'd already reached them.

Tertulio sent three more of the dozen or so beams

tumbling down into the ravine before the first Illyrian riders pushed past him. There wasn't enough left of the bridge for them to cross in any formation but single file, and they slowed their steps to prevent an accident. Still, six mounted men took to the bridge while the Lydians struggled to stop them.

John heard Warrick shouting something at his men, but the pounding of hooves against hollow wood drowned out the meaning of his words.

"Stay behind me." John maneuvered his way in front of Gisela, glancing at her only briefly and wishing he could take her in his arms again. He'd have to cut down the approaching soldiers before he could do that. "Be prepared to ride ahead to Castlehead if they get past me."

"They will not get past us." Gisela drew her sword, but obligingly stayed off to his right, just behind him.

The Illyrians leaped from the bridge with their swords drawn. John hastily unhorsed the first rider with a swipe of his sword and sent him sprawling back over the lip of the ravine. The next man proved to be a better fighter, pushing John back and making room for his comrades to come across.

John fought to see as sweat poured under his helmet, filling his eyes, transforming the bright flash of swords into a dazzling blur. The pounding of hooves was replaced by the clang of swords as Gisela fought alongside him.

Timbers boomed and cracked as they fell into the ravine, but John saw another horseman make his way across.

Warrick.

"Stand down!" the Illyrian prince commanded his men with drawn sword.

When the blade before him no longer flew, John

peeled back his helmet and swiped the sweat from his eyes, unsure precisely what Warrick was up to, but unlikely to discern anything without the clear use of his eyes. He turned to Gisela, whose horse had pranced backward under the press of swords.

She gripped her leg where a bloody gash rent her skirts, staining them deep crimson.

"No!" he screamed and leaped from Moses's back. Even from a distance he could see the wound was deep. He hurried to her side and tore the slashed fabric from her skirts, quickly using it to bind her injury and stem the flow of blood. Warrick rode on toward Castlehead with four men behind him.

John let them go. He doubted Warrick would do anything to hurt Elisabette. Whatever happened, John could address it later. He couldn't lose the woman he loved.

Gisela held tight to John's chest as he rode with her toward Castlehead.

"What of the battle for Sardis?" She could feel her thoughts swimming from the loss of blood, and hoped by speaking to keep from slipping out of consciousness.

"I believe Rab the Raider is dead, killed by his half brother Warrick. From what I could see of it, your father disabled the catapults and overwhelmed the Illyrians with his surprise attack. Once the remaining Illyrians realize Rab is dead and Warrick has fled, they'll likely surrender."

"They won't chase us all the way to Castlehead?"

"If they do, Tertulio will knock out the rest of the beams of the bridge."

She sagged against him and felt her strength waning.

"Gisela?" He touched her face, obviously aware that

her strength was leaving her. "Gisela, my love, don't leave me."

"I shan't leave," she whispered. "But I must rest."

The weary horse beneath them gathered speed. Gisela felt it, but let her fingers loosen their grip on King John's arms. She lacked the strength to hold on any longer. And she trusted John would keep her safe. He would not let her fall.

"Is she going to live?"

John turned at the sound of the heavy accent. The Emperor Charlemagne approached him.

John immediately dropped to bow before him. "She is strong. I've stopped the bleeding, and she roused enough to drink earlier. She should recover."

Charlemagne crossed the room to where John knelt by Gisela's side, supervising her every breath as if by the force of his will alone he could compel her to continue breathing.

The emperor placed a hand on his daughter's forehead. "She is strong," he agreed, then turned to John, who'd risen from his bow just high enough to keep watch over Gisela. "King John, accompany me to Constantinople. We must present Warrick and Garren to Empress Irene for punishment. I understand their crimes are many. I'll need you to testify to their extent."

John reluctantly stood. "I'll do as you command. But my kingdom—"

"Your brother Luke is holding Sardis, not that the remaining Illyrians are likely to give him any trouble now. As for this fortress of yours, a man arrived by ship with many men in time to reinforce my advance at the Illyrians' rear. He claims to be your brother Mark. He fought valiantly. Can we leave Castlehead in his care?"

John felt a surge of relief that his brother had finally returned. He smiled. "I believe we can."

Charlemagne continued, "As for you, I've been told repeatedly, first by Boden and his men, and since then many times by my daughter and her maid, that I owe you a debt for my daughter's life. Name your price."

John swallowed. He owed the emperor for saving his kingdom. The man was powerful, and protective of his family. He might destroy John and take his kingdom from him for daring to request a treasure beyond what he deserved.

And yet, John knew he would not be able to live with himself if he did not ask. "Your Majesty? I would ask for your daughter Gisela's hand in marriage."

Chapter Seventeen

Christmastide, Castlehead, Lydia

"A ship approaches, Your Highness. Her sail is spread with the Carolingian cross." Renwick stood in the doorway of Gisela's chamber to deliver his message.

"They've returned?" Gisela rose and hurried after him, hope rising inside her. King John had been gone with her father for many long months. She knew of the dangerous nature of their mission, and the many threats that lay between Lydia and Constantinople.

Boats approached from the anchored ship by the time Gisela reached the wharf. She searched the faces of the men aboard, quickly finding the two that rose higher than the others. King John's face glowed with health. So did her father's.

She dropped to a low bow as they stepped onto the dock.

"Gisela." Charlemagne extended his arms.

Gisela flew to her father's embrace, holding him tight and thanking God for his safe return. But even as she did so, she looked past him to King John.

He had been away so long. She knew the political situation was complicated. The men might have made any number of promises for the sake of peace with the Byzantines. Did he still care for her as he had once claimed? Did their feelings even matter, given the complexities of the relations between the empires?

"How was your journey?" she asked her father.

"Long," he said with laughter in his eyes, "but fruitful. We have strengthened the allegiances between our empires, and forged agreements to ensure the safety of Lydia."

"Praise the Lord." Gisela fought to keep her eyes on her father as he spoke, but found it nearly impossible not to look at John. His eyes twinkled. Did he long to hold her as she longed to be held by him? She wet her lips and tried to think clearly. "Where do matters stand with the Illyrians?"

The emperor began to walk down the wharf toward the castle. He held her arm and pulled her alongside him, explaining as they went. "Garren and his son Warrick have been chastised. They have repented of their actions against Lydia. Their apologies were sincere."

Gisela felt cold dread fill her. If the men survived, the agreements between them might stand. "Do they remain in power?"

"In light of their activities with Rab the Raider, Garren has stepped down as king and Warrick has taken his place. To secure peace in the region, we've negotiated a marriage alliance."

Gisela pinched her eyes shut and gripped her father's arm. She couldn't bring her feet to carry her forward another step. "A marriage between..." Her voice failed her.

"Between Warrick," Charlemagne began, "and the Princess of Lydia, King John's sister, Elisabette."

Gisela sagged with relief and let out a yelping sigh.

Her father laughed. "Are you encouraged by this news?"

"It is wonderful news, Father."

"The purpose of your journey was to marry Warrick. And yet, he never intended to have you." Charlemagne looked down into his daughter's eyes. "I have negotiated a different marriage contract for you, but I must know whether the match pleases you before the final plans can be made. If you could choose your own husband, who would you wed?"

Gisela felt her mouth drop open. She looked behind her and found that King John had followed them down the wharf.

Charlemagne extended one hand toward King John, but kept his focus on Gisela's face. "He must be a worthy man."

Finding her voice, Gisela asked, "Would you consider King John a worthy man?"

"There is no man more worthy."

Hardly had her father spoken than John fell to his knees before them both. He looked up at Gisela with tears sparkling in his eyes. "Would you have me?"

Gisela struggled to speak past her joy. "Yes." She reached for his hand and pulled him to his feet, then looked to her father for his blessing.

Charlemagne threw back his head and laughed a great billowing laugh toward the sky. "Do as you desire. You have my blessing."

Before the emperor finished his statement, John wrapped his arms around Gisela and found her lips with his. She kissed him eagerly, then pulled away just long enough to ask her father, "How soon may we be wed?"

Charlemagne gestured to the crates of goods that were being unloaded from the boats. "We've brought the finest silks for your dress, and spices for the feast." He turned to Renwick, who still stood near. "Have your messengers deliver the invitation throughout the kingdom. King John is to wed Princess Gisela three days hence."

Three days hence

Gisela stood by the window while three maids and their needles held on to the long train of her white gown, working feverishly at an elaborate embroidery along the edge of the train. The courtyard was filled with those who would not fit inside the chapel.

"We've finished this layer of embroidery, Your Highness," the head seamstress announced. "Would you like us to do another?"

"I don't believe there will be time." Gisela looked at Bette.

The girl hopped up. "The veil." She nodded to Hilda, then examined Gisela's face. "You look as lovely as any bride ever has."

A steward arrived at her door. "The Emperor Charlemagne," he announced.

Gisela flew to meet her father, who took her arm and led her down the hall.

Outside the chapel, Emperor Charlemagne paused and lowered the veil over her face. The lutes and horns ceased their festal notes and sounded her arrival. Gisela trusted her father to guide her forward. As she made her way on her father's arm through the crowded hall, Gisela focused on breathing as King John had taught her when he'd stitched up her eye. Still, she feared she might faint from happiness.

"Emperor Charlemagne, if it is your intent to see this woman married, please present her to the groom."

Gisela watched John's hands take her veil by the edges and lift it up past her face.

She beamed at the sight of the man she loved.

Deacon Bartholomew proceeded with the service. When he reached the Scripture, Gisela listened with respect, all the while gazing at King John, still hardly able to believe he stood before her. Finally the old deacon pronounced them married, and John pulled her back into his arms, kissing her soundly as a cheer went up from those assembled, the noise nearly shaking the stone walls.

Finally the people quieted their cheers while her father turned to face them. Charlemagne announced blessings and gifts from the Holy Roman Empire.

"Lydia now holds all the lands between this coast and the Mursia River," he declared, and a shout rose up from those assembled. He extended his hand toward King John, presenting him with a marvelous jewel-encrusted scepter. "A token of my esteem for your kingdom."

John accepted it with thanks, but his eyes hardly left Gisela's face, and she rose up on her tiptoes to kiss him again, as the emperor announced, "Hail to King John of Lydia and his queen. Long may you reign."

* * * * *

Dear Reader,

Charlemagne was King of the Franks from 768 A.D., and was crowned the first Holy Roman Emperor in the year 800. Many of the historical events noted in this book are real; for example, Charlemagne's daughter Rotrude was engaged to Constantine VI, until his mother, Irene (Empress Irene at the time of our story), broke off their engagement. The Illyrians, who were ruled by various tribal kings, dominated the area where our story takes place. However, the Kingdom of Lydia is a fictional nation inspired by Lydia in Acts 16 in the Bible. Warrick and Garren are fictional characters, as is King John himself. History records that Charlemagne had a daughter named Gisela, but no details survive of the events of her life. It is unlikely that her experiences were precisely as I have recorded them; nonetheless I've taken care to make my story as historically accurate as possible without obscuring the romance of the tale.

If you would like to learn more about Charlemagne, one resource I heartily recommend is *Two Lives of Charlemagne* by Einhard and Notker the Stammerer. If you are interested in more stories about the Kingdom of Lydia, look for my Reclaiming the Crown series by Love Inspired Suspense, and the forthcoming books in the Protecting the Crown series, which include more suspense tales set in Lydia, as well as the romance between John's brother Prince Luke and the mysterious woman with hair pale as moonlight. Visit my website, www.rachellemccalla.com, for the most up-to-date listings of the books in my series.

God's blessings on your journey,
Rachelle

Questions for Discussion

1. When Charlemagne's ship is spotted off the Lydian shore, King John goes to meet it instead of taking refuge in the castle as his courtiers suggest. Similarly, Princess Gisela was supposed to be hiding below when she saved her ship from Saracens. What do these details tell you about their personalities? Do you agree with the choices they made? Why or why not?

2. Princess Gisela felt much more at ease talking to King John before she saw how handsome he was. In what ways do the appearances of others influence your reactions to them? Is it easier to get to know someone before you know what they look like (for example, talking on the phone or chatting online)? How are your in-person interactions different? Should physical appearance influence how we act toward others? Why or why not?

3. Hilda and others assume King John has a "gift" for healing, though he insists his skills lie in the knowledge he's been taught. Gisela likens his abilities to her sister's aptitude for music, noting that the "gift" is a combination of God-given talents combined with training. How would you define King John's gift of healing? Do you feel God has given you gifts in certain areas? Have you sought additional study within your area of giftedness?

4. When John's first wife died, the king feared that his "gift" for healing had evaporated, even though his

knowledge of herbs and remedies remained. How would you explain his failure to heal her? How do you react when your God-given talents seem to putter out?

5. Emperor Charlemagne was a godly man who supported the work of the church and gave generously to charity. As noted in the book, Charlemagne attended worship services on a daily basis. Unlike many other rulers in his time period and before, Charlemagne did not ask his subjects to revere him as a god. How do you feel about the historical figure Charlemagne? How might history have played out differently had he not been ruler of Europe?

6. Gisela sends Boden to Rome with a message for her father, refusing to marry Warrick until Rab the Raider is disciplined for murdering King John's father. Later she regrets this decision and confesses she was acting selfishly by extending her visit to Lydia. Later still, she realizes her choice saved her from a more horrible fate. Was her decision right, wrong or both? Is there any benefit to passing judgment on the rightness or wrongness of her actions? Do your choices in life sometimes fall within that blurry void between good and bad? Can we ever really know the full impact of our decisions? Is it wise to judge others or ourselves? Discuss.

7. King John refuses to fence against Gisela when he recognizes her in the tournament. How do you feel about his decision?

8. When Gisela learns that Elisabette is in love with Warrick, Gisela chooses not to reveal that she's engaged to the same man. How do you feel about her decision, given the circumstances?

9. As King John comes to terms with the reality of his feelings for Gisela, he reasons that his every faculty has mutinied against his rational self—a treasonous act, given that he is king. Do you ever find yourself behaving in a manner that is in conflict with what you think you ought to be doing? How do you reconcile the two? Where does God fit into the picture?

10. King John resolved never to love another after the death of his wife. He explains his motivation at various points as he wrestles with the love he feels for Gisela. How do you feel about his decision? Have you ever felt similarly? Are you glad he ultimately decided to fall for Gisela?

11. Rab the Raider's father refused to officially recognize him as his son, instead sending him on dangerous raids to prove his worth. At the same time, however, he benefited from Rab's exploits. How do you feel about the decisions he made? How do they contrast with your beliefs about right and wrong? Where did the trouble begin—and how could these men have peacefully ended it?

12. Even as King John and his brother Luke are facing death while under siege at Sardis, they resolve to ride out together to face their enemies. Have you ever felt as though you were riding out, with little hope for

success? Has God ever led you in a direction that felt like a futile mission, only to reward your efforts?

13. As Gisela and the watchmen study the approaching storm clouds, they see Charlemagne's ships riding ahead of the storm, coming to their rescue. Has God ever sent storm clouds to save you? Do the dark clouds in your life have a silver lining, or do you fear the storm?

14. What do you think of King John's leadership skills? What about his love for his people? Do you think he is a good king?

15. How do you feel about Princess Gisela? Is she, as John notes, a godly woman? Do you think she will make a good queen of Lydia? Will they live happily ever after? Why or why not?

COMING NEXT MONTH
from Love Inspired® Historical
AVAILABLE JANUARY 2, 2013

THE COWBOY'S SURPRISE BRIDE
Cowboys of Eden Valley
Linda Ford
Traveling to Canada to escape a dreaded marriage, Linette Edwards eagerly accepts Eddie Gardiner's written proposal. Eddie planned for a well-bred bride, and Linette is not who he expected...can they make a home together before spring?

COLORADO COURTSHIP
Cheryl St.John & Debra Ullrick
In these two heartwarming stories, two women find love in unlikely places. Violet needs a fresh start away from scandal, and Sunny wants a chance to prove herself. Will they both find the courage to trust their hearts?

BEAUTY IN DISGUISE
Mary Moore
Lady Kathryn conceals her beauty since Society will never overlook her scandalous first Season. Lord Dalton begins to fall for the mysterious young woman until he learns of her deception. Can both find hope of forgiveness?

THE MARSHAL MEETS HIS MATCH
Clari Dees
In a world of marriage-minded females, Meri McIsaac is steadfastly single. She's happiest riding horses on her ranch. At least until the town's new marshal startles her and causes her to fall—literally—at his feet.

Look for these and other Love Inspired books wherever books are sold, including most bookstores, supermarkets, discount stores and drugstores.

LIHCNM1212

REQUEST YOUR FREE BOOKS!

2 FREE INSPIRATIONAL NOVELS
PLUS 2
FREE
MYSTERY GIFTS

Love Inspired
HISTORICAL
INSPIRATIONAL HISTORICAL ROMANCE

YES! Please send me 2 FREE Love Inspired® Historical novels and my 2 FREE mystery gifts (gifts are worth about $10). After receiving them, if I don't wish to receive any more books, I can return the shipping statement marked "cancel". If I don't cancel, I will receive 4 brand-new novels every month and be billed just $4.49 per book in the U.S. or $4.99 per book in Canada. That's a saving of at least 22% off the cover price. It's quite a bargain! Shipping and handling is just 50¢ per book in the U.S. and 75¢ per book in Canada.* I understand that accepting the 2 free books and gifts places me under no obligation to buy anything. I can always return a shipment and cancel at any time. Even if I never buy another book, the two free books and gifts are mine to keep forever.

102/302 IDN FEHF

Name _____ (PLEASE PRINT) _____

Address _____ Apt. # _____

City _____ State/Prov. _____ Zip/Postal Code _____

Signature (if under 18, a parent or guardian must sign) _____

Mail to the **Reader Service:**
IN U.S.A.: P.O. Box 1867, Buffalo, NY 14240-1867
IN CANADA: P.O. Box 609, Fort Erie, Ontario L2A 5X3

Not valid for current subscribers to Love Inspired Historical books.

Want to try two free books from another series?
Call 1-800-873-8635 or visit www.ReaderService.com.

* Terms and prices subject to change without notice. Prices do not include applicable taxes. Sales tax applicable in N.Y. Canadian residents will be charged applicable taxes. Offer not valid in Quebec. This offer is limited to one order per household. All orders subject to credit approval. Credit or debit balances in a customer's account(s) may be offset by any other outstanding balance owed by or to the customer. Please allow 4 to 6 weeks for delivery. Offer available while quantities last.

Your Privacy—The Reader Service is committed to protecting your privacy. Our Privacy Policy is available online at www.ReaderService.com or upon request from the Reader Service.

We make a portion of our mailing list available to reputable third parties that offer products we believe may interest you. If you prefer that we not exchange your name with third parties, or if you wish to clarify or modify your communication preferences, please visit us at www.ReaderService.com/consumerschoice or write to us at Reader Service Preference Service, P.O. Box 9062, Buffalo, NY 14269. Include your complete name and address.

LIH11B

*Brave police officers tackle crime with the help of their
canine partners in* TEXAS K-9 UNIT, *an exciting
new series from Love Inspired® Suspense.*

Read on for a preview of the first book,
TRACKING JUSTICE by Shirlee McCoy.

Police detective Austin Black glanced at his dashboard
clock as he raced up Oak Drive. Two in the morning. Not a
good time to get a call about a missing child.

Then again, there was never a good time for that; never
a good time to look in the worried eyes of a parent or to
follow a scent trail and know that it might lead to a joyful
reunion or a sorrowful goodbye.

If it led anywhere.

Sometimes trails went cold, scents were lost and the
missing were never found. Austin wanted to bring them all
home safe. Hopefully, this time, he would.

He pulled into the driveway of a small house.

Justice whined. A three-year-old bloodhound, he was
trained in search and rescue and knew when it was time
to work.

Austin jumped out of the vehicle when a woman darted
out the front door. "You called about a missing child?"

"Yes. My son. I heard Brady call for me, and when I
walked into his room, he was gone." She ran back up the
porch stairs.

Austin jogged in after her. She waved from a doorway.
"This is my son's room."

Austin followed her into the room. "How old is your son, Ms....?"

"Billows. Eva. He's seven."

"Did you argue?"

"We didn't argue about anything, Officer..."

"Detective Austin Black. I'm with Sagebrush Police Department's Special Operation K-9 Unit."

"You have a search dog with you?" Her face brightened. "I can give you something of his. A shirt or—"

"Hold on. I need to get a little more information first."

"How about you start out there?" She gestured to the window.

"Was it open when you came in the room?"

"Yes. It looks like someone carried Brady out the window. But I don't know how anyone could have gotten into his room when all the doors and windows were locked."

"You're sure?"

"Of course." She frowned. "I always double-check. I have ever since..."

"What?"

"Nothing that matters. I just need to find my son."

Hiding something?

"Everything matters when a child is missing, Eva."

To see Justice the bloodhound in action, pick up
TRACKING JUSTICE by Shirlee McCoy.
Available January 2013 from Love Inspired® Suspense.